NOBILITY

NOBILITY

THE SUPERNATURAL TALE

OF A DREAM WORLD

THAT CONQUERS HUMAN REALITY

NATHANAEL WHITE

NOBILITY

by Nathanael White

Printed in the United States of America

Copyright © 2011 by Nathanael White

ISBN: 978-0-9836936-0-4

All rights reserved.

This book or parts thereof may not be reproduced in any form, stored in a retrieval system, or transmitted in any form by any means – electronic, mechanical, photocopy, recording, or otherwise – without prior written permission of the author, except as provided by United States of America copyright law.

Published in association with Megaphone Publications,
www.megaphonepublications.com

This book is dedicated:

To my father and mother, on whose shoulders I stand, that your legacy may be honored in my life,

And,

To my children and their children unto generations I will never see, that you may have a heritage of what was important to me and an inheritance from my gift.

Special thanks to:

Amy White, for being the most incredible wife,
David Sluka, for teaching me so much and opening many doors,
Rhonda Kalal, for opening windows for me to write,
B.J. Schultz, for telling me I needed to write a fiction book
when I said I couldn't,
Jamey VanGelder, for leading me into a kingly foundation,
and Dad and Mom, for your immeasurable lifetime of help,

This book would not exist without you.

To the countless others whose encouragement spoke this book into being, and to my very special volunteer editorial team, thank you.

Cover design by Steve Fryer, www.stevefryer.com. Thank you
for giving me a work of art.

CONTENTS

Prologue 7

Chapter One: The Battle 9

Chapter Two: You Want Me To Do What? 11

Chapter Three: Rebellion 31

Chapter Four: A Mysterious Find 57

Chapter Five: Picking Apples And Hunting Boar 91

Chapter Six: The Seer 115

Chapter Seven: Job On The Rocks 133

Chapter Eight: The Encounter 159

Chapter Nine: A Difficult Choice 169

Chapter Ten: A Slice Of Pie 193

Chapter Eleven: Finding Perspective 213

Chapter Twelve: A Changed Man 241

Chapter Thirteen: The Conquest Begins 261

Epilogue 289

PROLOGUE

It was my birthday, and I had just turned 13. This is the infamous birthday that officially begins the "awkward years" – the years of wanting to be an adult and yet not having the experience to be accepted as one, the years of longing for approval, the years of trying to figure out who you are and what it means to grow up.

I experienced these remote unsettled emotions, these unasked questions yet to be answered, as every teenager does.

That was before October 10 a few years ago. I remember it because of my dream. Who could forget what I dreamed that night? I had never thought much about my dreams before then. I thought they were only shadows of real life mixing together in mysteries not worth deciphering.

As a child I always pretended to be a knight or a king or some other mighty warrior, noble and brave, leading my men to glorious victory. I was caught up in great stories and whole campaigns worthy of song.

Oh, my imagination was vivid! Yet not even in the height of my days of make believe did I dream like this. No matter how engulfed in my imaginings I might have been, I never once crossed into believing they were real. But this dream, I tell you that this dream was more real than waking life.

Chapter One

THE BATTLE

"DUCK, LAD!" a voice called out and I obeyed instinctively, no idea what was happening. As I bent low I saw the bright gleam of steel sweep right over my head. In shock I realized it was a sword, and it was already red with blood.

The man wielding the sword was a large man with a strong build. He tumbled past me, looking at me with bewilderment in his wild eyes. Without slowing his pace, he refocused and charged after a bigger target, but the man he attacked rode upon a horse. My assailant was no match. The horseman slashed once and the warrior fell, his head severed cleanly from his shoulders.

"Get on my horse!" the victor shouted. I recognized his voice as the one that first spoke to me, but had no ability to obey this command as I had the one before. I had just witnessed a man being cut down not three feet away from me and had nearly lost my own head as well.

Completely overwhelmed, I was confused about how one moment I was peacefully going to sleep in my bedroom and the very next thing I saw was this! The whole scene opened itself to me in a matter of seconds, lived out as though it happened in slow motion, and the sound and action of the battlefield crashed over me.

I heard the cries of men not far from me and turned in horror to realize that horses were charging all around me and the men on foot, like the one who had nearly taken off my head, were being driven before them. Those who were not trampled were soon hacked down by the sword. Blood poured out everywhere on the field.

Nausea washed over me and my head began to swim as I stood there, unable to move. I swooned and would have fallen underneath the charging horses if it hadn't been for the one horseman. He skillfully maneuvered his horse to me and swept me up in front of him just in time. Consciousness failed me, and as blackness swallowed me up I heard his seemingly distant voice shouting again.

Chapter Two
YOU WANT ME TO DO WHAT?

My dad woke me up early, more excited than I was about it being my birthday. He had never been this excited for my birthday before, but today he insisted that he was going to take me out to breakfast.

"You ready?" he asked, poking his head through my door.

He was obviously in more of a hurry for my birthday to start than I was. I groaned some amazingly alert response into my pillow like, "Unngh..." and rolled over to go back to sleep.

My efforts were about as effective as shooing a hungry mosquito. "C'mon," he said, "today's a special day!"

"I know, Dad," I moaned without opening my eyes, "It's my birthday."

"Of course it's your birthday, but this one's extra special."

I don't know what's so special about it, I thought. *Of course I like having birthdays, but I have friends who are already 13 and there didn't seem to be anything special about when it happened to them.*

Whether I liked it or not, my dad obviously had something in his mind. There wasn't anything else to do about it, so I got up, showered, dressed, and went downstairs to go with him.

My family gave me their usual birthday greetings – An enthusiastic "Happy Birthday!" from my little sister, Amy. She raced all seven years of herself up to me and gave me a big hug. Her pink polar fleece jammies passed some static to my blue jeans before she ran off to finish her breakfast.

My brother Steve was next, saying, "Yeah, Happy Birthday," with his mouth full of cereal. He was 10, and we had always been pretty close. Mom and Dad taught us that brothers come before friends, so I tried to be nice to him even when I didn't feel like it. Of course, this just happened to most often be when he was reminding me of his "rightful" spot on my priority list.

My mom was last, her voice calling from the kitchen, "Happy Birthday, hon! How'd you sleep?"

"Short," I replied.

"Yeah, your dad said you were a little slow getting up this morning," she called over her shoulder as she pressed together two halves of a peanut butter and jelly sandwich. It was a Thursday morning, and my siblings still had to go to school. We always took our lunches to school with us, and Mom was usually the one who made them.

"I guess I was expecting to get to sleep in when you said I didn't have to go to school and that Dad was taking the whole day off. I figured breakfast didn't have to be early if both Dad and I are staying home."

Mom replied with an unsympathetic, "Oohhh," and turned to hide a suspicious smile behind the refrigerator door.

Leaning against the counter, I noticed that my dad was not around and asked, "Where is Dad anyway?"

"He's out in the garage loading up the car," Mom replied in a playful tone.

"Loading up the car? With what?" I asked, curiosity beginning to grow.

"Oh, you'll see," my mom said, no longer hiding her smile.

Just then my dad came through the door, bits of chill fall air riding in his wake. "Hey, there you are! You ready?" he asked.

"Sure," I replied, a little guarded, "but what are we doing?"

"Going out for breakfast," he said, eyes bright with a teasing expression that meant he obviously had more planned than he was telling me.

I could clearly see that I had been duped. My parents certainly had more in mind for my birthday than they had let on until now. A mix of excitement and mystery quickly stirred inside me. I was sure that whatever my parents had planned would be good, but their excitement was just over the top. I wondered, *What on earth could possibly make them act like this?*

I lost myself for a moment trying to figure out what might be going on while Mom and Dad kissed each other goodbye for the day.

"We'll see you later, Gorgeous," Dad said, grabbing his keys off the counter.

"Don't forget to call when you're on your way, John, so I can have dinner ready when you two get home," she said.

"Will do, Connie," Dad said, giving Mom one last peck on the cheek.

I came back to reality with a start. Dad was already halfway out the door and calling back, "Let's go!" Still half lost in my thoughts, I tripped a little as I tried to catch up, throwing on a hoodie on my way out the door.

"Bye, Mom!" I yelled as the door closed behind me. I made my way around to the passenger door, scanning the back seat for any clues of what my parents were planning and, finding nothing, resigned myself to the front seat. Since my questions in the house had gone nowhere I did not bother asking any more, instead choosing to let my dad bring up whatever he had in mind whenever he was ready. The result of this, of course, was that my dad was as equally successful in driving me crazy as he was in driving me to the restaurant, because he didn't say anything helpful whatsoever the whole way there.

Breakfast reminded me of times when I was younger and my parents would take each of us kids out on "dates," just one of us and one of them. As when I was young, it was nice to have my dad all to myself for a bit, but it was weird at the same time. It was unusual for Dad to keep something from me, especially something as simple as where we were going or what we were going to do when we got there.

Knowing that there was more to this day than just breakfast with Dad, I tried to find out what that more would be.

"So what are we doing after breakfast?" I asked.

"You'll see," he responded.

I decided to try a less direct approach, "What time do you think we'll be home?"

"It depends," he said while gazing around the room.

"Depends on what?" I asked.

He looked back at me and said with that same teasing smile, "On when we get done."

Our food came just then and I gave up my interrogation, turning to conversation about school and my friends instead.

"Liz just got braces," I said, chomping on a mouthful of thick sausage. "She said it hurt so bad that she couldn't eat anything but applesauce and oatmeal for the first three days."

"Really?" Dad asked. "I had braces once, too, but it was so long ago I don't really remember it."

"Do you think I'll ever have to have them?" I asked, a little worried.

"Well, most people do get them these days, it seems, but I don't know," Dad answered. "Your mom and I were going to ask the dentist what he thinks the next time you have an appointment."

"Oh good," I muttered sarcastically, thinking of eating oatmeal and applesauce for three days straight and not liking the thought much.

"Hey," Dad interjected, "Not to change the subject, but I haven't heard you talk about Austin in a while. How's his dad doing? Has he found a job yet?"

"No," I replied, "He doesn't have a job yet. It's been over a year now. He said his dad's thinking of just getting a part time job somewhere, anywhere he can."

"That's a smart way to go," Dad said. "As hard as it is to work a job that doesn't make the money you need and isn't something you want to do, sometimes you just have to do it. How is Austin doing with all of that?"

"Well, he doesn't talk about it very much anymore," I answered. "I think it's really hard for him. He doesn't seem as happy as he used. He's pretty quiet about everything now, even with me."

Dad picked up on my sadness and said, "Michael, I'm sorry that he's not quite the same friend that he's always been for you. I'm sure he still wants to be the same Austin that he's always been since you guys became friends in first grade, but right now is about as difficult a time for his family as they can go through. Things probably aren't very happy inside his home right now, and I'm sure that is what's making him change at school. But with so much instability in his home, he needs you and his other friends to stick with him now more than ever."

"I just wish there was something more I could do to help them," I said.

"Well, there may be some practical things we could do for them," Dad said, "like help them to pay for groceries or that sort of thing if they need it every now and then. Really, though, don't underestimate how powerful your friendship with Austin is, and not just for him, but for his parents, too. It would be a lot harder for them to go through a difficult time if Austin didn't have you as a good friend to help him through it."

"Yeah, I suppose you're right," I admitted, thinking about how I would have to try harder to cheer up Austin.

Conversation drifted on to a number of other subjects, but as the food on our plates gradually disappeared I grew more excited, thinking of all the things Dad and I might be doing together.

Maybe he's going to take me shopping for my birthday present and I'll get to pick whatever I want. Or maybe we'll go watch a movie, or go to a game, or... The list went on and on in my head, and I struggled to keep track of which one I thought was most likely.

When we both finished and the bill was paid, we finally returned to the car. Getting in, I thought, *Ok, here it is, the moment of truth. Dad has to tell me what we're going to do now.*

"So I suppose you're wondering where we're headed," Dad said while buckling his seatbelt.

Finally.

"Um...well, yeah, I have kinda been asking you what's going on," I answered a little sarcastically.

"Well, I thought it would be nice to take a short road trip together," he said, turning to look at me with a loving smile.

I looked back at him a little doubtful, knowing that he surely had more planned than just a short road trip, but was along for the ride literally and figuratively. It took little time before we were on unfamiliar roads, winding our way over miles of empty pavement interrupted by only a few small towns.

We drove on for about an hour, south southeast to a town called Red Wing, a historic city on the Minnesota/Wisconsin border framed in the bluffs of the Mississippi River. I had no idea where we were, but the scenery was gorgeous.

High rock outcroppings and dense forests line the winding road, offering occasional glimpses of the mighty river. The highway makes its way into town, past old buildings now being used for more modern things – like the big railway station that's now a coffee shop – and past old buildings still being used for their old purposes – like the fancy hotel down near the river.

Meandering our way through downtown, we turned onto a street that followed the river, passed a marina, and drove out onto a little peninsula where there was a park.

"We're here!" my dad announced.

I perked up from my casual sightseeing to take a more detailed look at where we were.

"Nice place," I said as I stepped out of the car, continuing to look all around.

"Yeah, isn't it great?" my dad replied, joining me outside the car. "Hey, come look at these."

He wandered off a few steps and pointed to several houses right on the river itself. These odd structures were definitely not houseboats. No, what I saw were literal garages suspended in the water, each sharing the walls of those next to it so there was no space in between. It reminded me of pictures I've seen of row houses in San Francisco, only these sat right on the surface of the water.

"You can't find a more protected place to store your boat, eh?" Dad said, explaining why in the world you'd build a garage on the water. *Suppose it beats an ordinary dock*, I thought, and kept looking at the little boat village while my dad headed back to the car.

I heard the trunk open, followed shortly by the sound of it closing and his steady footsteps coming back to me. He handed me a cold bottle of Mountain Dew – my favorite drink in the world at the time – and I noticed that he had a bottle of flavored sparkling water for himself and a game tucked under his arm: Risk.

"We're going to play a game?" I asked, laughing incredulously.

"Yup!" he said, "Just you and me."

"And we had to come all the way down here to play it?"

"Of course not, but are you complaining?" he said, gesturing to the forested bluffs.

It's true he had a point. The trees had all changed into their fall clothes, brilliant red, yellow, and orange each one of them. Rock bluffs protruded out from among the trees, providing a rugged contrast to the smooth shape and gentle rise of the wooded slopes. The wide river flowing calmly through it all reflected the colors and shapes on its banks. It really was a breathtaking scene, made complete by the bright sunshine and crisp fall-scented air.

"Besides," my dad said, "I know how much you love the outdoors."

He had me there for sure. It seemed like he'd somehow tailor made the day just for me.

"Thanks, Dad," I said, "This really is a lot of fun for me."

"I'm glad," he said, putting his free arm around me and pulling me close.

"Is this the end of the mystery?" I asked, leaning into him, "Or are you still planning some other surprise for me?

"Well, it is your birthday," he answered, "I wouldn't count out mysteries being a part of it until the day is done."

We stood there for a moment, just enjoying all the nature around us. After a few quiet moments, Dad interrupted the silence. "Are you ready to play the game?" he asked in a challenging sort of way.

"Yeah, let's go," I challenged back, "I'll take you down!"

"Uh huh, I bet," he replied sarcastically, "I'm gonna school you."

"We'll see," I said with a smile as we walked over to a picnic table and set up the game.

Now, if you don't know about the game of Risk, it is simply a game of world domination. As big a task as it sounds, the game can take several hours to play, especially with only two people. I knew that I had a full day of competition with my dad ahead of me, and I loved it.

Conversation was sparse for the beginning part of the game, except for playful jabs at one another, each declaring victory before a single piece was laid. We were familiar with this routine; we had done it many times before. But for whatever reason, it felt as though there were more to this game than usual.

We put ourselves to it, scheming against one another, trying to position ourselves as quickly as possible to take the first whole continent we could, for once you hold a whole continent your armies begin to grow much more rapidly and you hold a distinct advantage.

It used to be that my dad could beat me with one hand tied behind his back, so to speak, but I had become a pretty even match for him by this point in my life. And so it stood all morning, each of us trading blows with the other, seemingly deadlocked with neither one of us making much progress.

The sun was now high in the southern sky and our stomachs were starting to growl.

"My strategy's going to suffer if I don't eat something soon," Dad said. "How about breaking for lunch?"

"I don't know, Dad, if you're strategy's about to go down the tubes, maybe I should try to hold out a little longer," I said with a smile.

"Well, you go on playing by yourself, then, if you can. I'm going to get some lunch for us out of the car." And with that he got up from the table and left me to ponder the game board before me.

Man, I thought, *I'm going to be in trouble soon if I can't loosen Dad's grip on Asia.* As the biggest continent, full possession of Asia is rewarded with a large number of reinforcements at each turn, and my dad held almost full control of it. I bent myself over the board, analyzing my troop locations. *The trick is in how to take Asia without losing what I already have.*

Dad returned before I discovered anything helpful. Setting our strategies for the game aside for the moment, we each grabbed our lunch, slid over to the empty part of the table, and began to eat. Dad leaned back with his bite of turkey sandwich, breathing in deep the warming air, and took the scenery in afresh. He broke the brief silence saying, "Have you ever thought what it would be like if this game were happening for real?"

"What do you mean?" I asked.

"Well, you know, what if the whole world was ruled by people who all wanted more to rule? What if all the powerful nations of the world fought continually with each other like this until one of them completely destroyed every other nation and dominated the whole world?"

"Um…I guess I never really thought about it," I replied, wondering why Dad was asking me these questions. "I mean, I know there already are a lot of wars going on and a lot of people fighting. But it's not like the game, though, right? It's not like everyone wants to kill everyone else until they get the whole planet for themselves and there's only one winner, right?"

"No, you're right," Dad answered back, "There are a lot of wars going on and a lot of people fighting, but not everyone wants to conquer the world. There are a lot of reasons that people fight, and a lot of ways they fight, too.

"Many people fight wars because someone hurt them or their people, and they believe that the only response they can give is to fight back until those people can't hurt them anymore. Other people fight because they disagree so much about various ideas. Honestly, there aren't very many nations I can think of that have fought to conquer the world who have actually come anywhere close."

I nodded my head with a mouthful of ham and Swiss, confused enough about Dad's odd comments that I had to force myself to look natural.

Dad continued, "The nation of Babylon once ruled much of the known civilized world, but a country called Persia conquered them. Persia once stretched all the way from India to Ethiopia, ruling over 127 different nations, but they were conquered by Greece, and then Rome conquered Greece. Rome ruled the Western world and the Middle East for the better part of 400 years, and longer depending on how you look at it.

"Even with as big as Rome became and as long as it remained powerful, we've learned now that China and Mongolia were massive empires during that time, too, battling with each other for supremacy in Asia."

"Wow, so there're a lot of nations who have tried to conquer the whole world, huh?" I asked, clumsily shifting gears mentally. I hadn't expected a history lesson on a day off from school.

"There really are many that have tried," Dad said, "And even quite a few in more modern history, too, but it's interesting to note that none of them ever succeeded."

"Really? Why not?" I asked, trying to stay in the conversation while crunching a potato chip.

"Well, for one, the world's a big place," Dad gestured with an apple slice, "And there're a whole lot of people in it. It seems that the conquering nation could only defeat so many enemies before they were stretched too thin to keep going. They couldn't maintain victories already won and expand territory through new victories at the same time. As you might imagine, a conquered people doesn't typically like to stay conquered."

"Yeah, I'll bet," I said, sure that I would feel the same.

"There's only one nation I know of that, for the most part, successfully integrated each nation into itself so they became contributing citizens instead of conquered rebels, though that doesn't really say it quite right. When Rome conquered a nation, they had a specific type of general that would come in after the army with enough men to enforce the victory, and his job was to bring the culture of Rome to the defeated nation. That way, they would start thinking and acting like Romans, eventually thinking of themselves as Romans instead of whatever they were before. That's the only reason I believe that Rome was able to keep its empire for so long."

"Huh," I said, not really sure what to make of what my dad was saying or why he was saying it.

Dad crunched his apple slice and said, "The important thing to take from all this is knowing that in order to conquer the world, you have to give the people you conquer a new identity, and you have to do it in such a way that they become glad you conquered them."

"Why are you telling me this, Dad?" I asked uncomfortably, "Do you want me to conquer the world or something?"

"In a way, yes, I do want you to conquer the world. In a way it's what you were born for, but not like this," he said, gesturing to the game board. "The reason they can make a game out of conquering the world like this, by dominating all the other people, is because it can't be done. It's fun because you can do something in the game you could never do in real life."

This was obviously not the response I expected him to give me. I lost interest in my food, swallowing hard on the bite in my mouth. "I don't get it, Dad. You're sounding really weird and not making much sense. You want me to conquer the world?"

"Well, yes I do. But remember what I said, 'Not like this.'" he answered slowly, again gesturing to our game. "You were born for a very important reason. You have something special inside of you that no one else has, Michael, and your mother and I are going to begin trying to help you find whatever that is and use it. The whole world is waiting for you."

I looked hard at my dad, trying to see if he might be somehow pulling my leg, making a ridiculous joke for some reason. But, no, he looked genuine. His eyes were bright and steady, looking right at me in a mix of love and pride. He had a gentle smile spreading into his I-have-the-day-off scruff, but it wasn't his joking smile. I didn't understand everything I saw in his face, but I understood enough to know he meant what he said.

Putting down the last few bites of my sandwich I asked, "Is this the real reason why you were so excited this morning?"

"In part," he answered. "This is only the beginning, and I'm definitely excited about it, but what I'm really excited for is what's coming."

"And what's that?" I asked.

"To be honest, Michael, I don't really know. Your mom and I feel that there is something important about your thirteenth birthday. Because of that, we're doing some special things that we don't normally do, like letting you take the day off of school. But no one did for either of us what we are beginning to do for you, so we don't know exactly what it looks like in the end. Really, I think it depends on the person; it will look differently for you than it will for your brother and sister when they get to your age. We'll have to see when we get there."

I nodded slowly, my mind stirring with the small bit of understanding my dad had given me. Something on the inside of me fought against what he had said – I think it was my mind that just didn't understand it – but something else inside me came alive at his words.

Not knowing how to respond, I sat quietly for a moment, feeling the weight of an immense yet undefined expectation looming over me.

Dad saw the strained look on my face and tried to comfort me, "Michael, this won't happen all at once; we'll take it one step at a time. And I will help you, too. You don't have to carry the burden alone."

I looked up at him, surprised at how well he had read me, but trying not to let on.

"At the same time," he said, "I realize that part of what it means to be your age is that you want to carry things on your own. You want to figure it out for yourself, and to some extent you need to. But don't worry, it's just one of the many transitions you'll have in life. And your mom and I will be there for you so you don't have to carry all the weight of it by yourself."

I nodded slowly, feeling a little relief from how well Dad sensed what was going on inside me without me having to say anything. It seemed like he actually had better words to describe how I felt than I did.

Dad reached across the table and gave my shoulder a comforting rub. He said, "You know, you're almost done with your lunch. Why don't we get going with that game again so we can be home in time for dinner?"

"Yeah," I said, trying to shove my thoughts aside, "Let's do that."

Dad gathered the trash from the table, took it to the nearest garbage can, and returned to his spot by the game board.

I stuffed the rest of my sandwich into my mouth and slid my chips and pop over with me to my side of the game.

It didn't take long before my competitive nature took over again and I was back in "game mode," pressing the attack and trying to find some weakness in my dad's defenses that I could exploit. Scanning the board again, I thought I found my best option – make him fight on multiple fronts.

You see, while my dad had control of almost all of Asia – and the promise of virtually endless reinforcements that came with it – he had not done much to take ground on the surrounding continents, leaving them all to me. This meant that I'd had no more than skirmishes in the process of taking Europe, North America, and Africa.

Now I was receiving plenty of new men each turn to replenish what I lost in battles, and my dad received very little because he only had Australia and South America, and what little he got he had to commit to Asia lest I take that and quickly defeat him.

Really it was just a matter of time. He did not advance quickly enough early on and was paying for it now. He couldn't manage his men within the large continent as quickly as I could capitalize on my advantage and before long I'd taken the Prize. The rest of the game was just a mop up operation.

"Good job," he said as we put the game away. "It looks like I taught you well."

"Yeah," I said with a bit of a gloating smile, "maybe a little too well. That was the easiest I've ever beaten you."

My dad was quiet for a second and then said, "You'd be surprised. In a way, it's actually more of a joy for me to lose to you than to win just for that very reason – that I've taught you 'too well.' A father's job is to do everything he can to make his children better than himself. I'm proud of you for how well you've learned."

Dad's abrupt serious tone brought the weight of our lunchtime conversation rushing back on me. I was glad for the drive back home to give me a chance to process it before seeing the rest of my family.

What in the world was Dad talking about? He wants me to conquer the world? The whole world is waiting for me? Seriously? And all this is somehow because I just turned 13; that's why he's talking to me like this. I really don't get it.

I poured over anything I could remember him ever telling me that might somehow help it all make sense, but nothing helped. By the time we got home I was just as confused as when we left the park.

We got home as the sun was setting in the early evening and walked into the house to find the usual activities of that time of day going on without us.

Mom was the first one to give us a greeting as we walked in the door, standing right where we'd left her that morning. "Hey!" she said, "How was your day?"

"Good," I said as Dad walked past me to hang up his jacket.

"Good? That doesn't tell me very much," she said proddingly.

"Well, it was definitely a fun day. I won the game with Dad and it was great to have the time with him…"

"But…" my mom said, continuing my thought for me.

"Do you know what Dad was talking about today?"

She smiled at me and said, "I know some of what he wanted to do with you today, but I'll have to talk to him before I'll know what exactly how your conversation went. I wouldn't worry too much about it. I'm sure he'll explain more soon."

"But he was saying some really weird things, Mom."

"Well, maybe I'll be able to explain it better to you after I talk to him. For now, though, why don't you start setting the table; dinner's almost ready," she said, handing me a stack of plates.

I realized that I wasn't going to get any answers that night, at least not until I had a chance to talk privately with my parents again. I tried not to think about it, which only made me think of it more until I suddenly remembered. *Hey, it's my birthday. I wonder what presents I'm going to get!*

The thought of presents quickly drove away my questions and put me in the mood to celebrate again.

Soon we all sat down to a feast, and what a wonderful feast it was! Mom always makes our favorite meals on our birthdays, which meant that I enjoyed a heaping plate of spaghetti with extra buttery garlic bread on the side.

Dessert was by request, too, so after dinner we had our choice of cherry or pumpkin pie – or both in my case. Odd, I know, but I always liked those pies better than cake (and candles work just as well in pumpkin pie as they do in cake).

I opened presents after dinner, receiving a couple of movies and some gift cards for buying music online. My semi-subconscious appraisal of the gifts told me that my hoard's value was a little on the light side. I was about to politely say my thank-you's anyway, figuring the day's trip accounted for the difference, when my dad spoke up.

"We'll get you the rest of your gift when we get a chance to go shopping with you," he said.

I looked at him, a little confused. "The rest of my gift? Do I get to pick out whatever I want since you're waiting for me to go with you?"

"To an extent, yes, but your mom and I are going to pick out the general type of things you can choose from, and then you can pick what you like best," he explained.

"Oh, well that's cool. When do you think we can go?" I asked.

"We'll find some time, don't worry, maybe tomorrow after dinner or this weekend," he said.

"Tomorrow night, then," I replied excitedly and my parents laughed. "What types of things do I get to pick from?"

"That would spoil the surprise," Dad said. "We'll tell you before we go shopping."

Looking forward to getting the rest of my birthday present, I thanked my family for what they had already given me. Everyone was finished with their pie, so we washed our dishes and gathered in the living room for some games together as a family.

These were an entirely different sort of games from the one I had played all day. Our family did still pull out our board games from time to time, but our favorite was to play various sports against each other on our gaming system.

We laughed together as one after the other of us would line up for tennis, boxing, snowboarding, car racing, and more. Of course everyone looked ridiculous standing there in our living room boxing (or swinging, or jumping) away at nothing. On the whole, I think Dad won more than anyone else, looking the most ridiculous in the process, though everyone won at least once.

All too soon Mom reminded us, "As much as I hate to end the fun, it is a school day tomorrow and we should start heading for bed."

After only a few light complaints we were all putting the games away and making our way upstairs to get ready for bed. My brother, sister, and I took our turns at the sink in the bathroom we shared and one by one went off to our rooms.

As I climbed into bed I thought about how strange my day had been. I'm not sure how it happened, or when, but I felt a little different getting back into bed than I had when I got out of it.

I paid little attention to that, however. The fun of playing games with my family made the events of the day a distant echo in my mind. Content and happy, I laid my head on my pillow and quickly fell asleep.

That's when it happened.

Chapter Three

Rebellion

"Who is he? Where did he come from?" said an unfriendly, husky voice.

"As I already told you, I do not know who he is. He appeared suddenly before me and was clearly more confused about how he arrived there than I was. There was nothing to be done but save the boy from being trampled and bear him away as quickly as possible" said the voice of the horseman who had rescued me.

"It's all just too much coincidence, I say," said the husky voice. "He appears out of nowhere just as we're really beginning to press the attack, and of course he appears right by you of all people. I think they knew you would pick him up and hold yourself back in the charge for his sake, if it really was for his sake and not for your own. They knew they'd be defeated today unless they did something and so something they did!"

"Watch yourself, Borgas," said a third voice, deep and growling, "if you accuse the High King of being a coward; you know his ferocity in battle."

I was slowly regaining consciousness from my swoon in the battle, coming through that strange place where you cannot separate dream from reality or interact with either. As of yet I had no control over my body and could only lay still and listen to the conversation going on around me.

"I agree with Borgas," a fourth voice said, this one high and weak. "He's sure to be a pawn of the enemy sent by some magic to spy out our weaknesses. If we don't deal with him now he'll run off as soon as he's discovered something that'd be of use to his masters."

Another voice responded, "Listen to yourselves! Have you no reason? Even if the enemy had such powers, would he send such a young spy right into the middle of a battle? And if he belonged to the enemy then why did the warrior try to kill him before attacking our King?"

"The warrior might not have known of the plot," the first voice said, "The best spies are sent out in secret. And spies are chosen for their cunning. He might have been acting the whole time, and even now he might be listening in on us!"

"What then?" the last voice replied, "Shall we kill him simply because he is surrounded by a shroud of mystery? Shall we cut off his voice before he is given a chance to tell his story? Let it never be so!

"Certainly, we know nothing of this lad, yet we cannot destroy him simply because we are shaken by the circumstances of his appearance. Suspicion and obscurity are no just cause for punishment, and no wise counsel for action."

Several voices growled their disapproval at these words and the husky voice answered, "Yet they seem plenty of cause for inaction, ruining our attack against the barbarians! I say we end this foolishness now and kill him!"

"Enough!" the Horseman declared. "Are you not noblemen? Are you not kings? The lad is certainly mysterious for now, but we have no proof of evil intent. Our responsibility is to watch over his recovery and do whatever we can to help him on his way wherever that may be, even if it is with us. But hush, now, he is beginning to stir."

The voices had slowly grown clearer as I recovered from my swoon. As consciousness returned to me my arms and legs started moving involuntarily. Apparently they'd finally found life after becoming paralyzed on the battlefield and now, when I might have wanted to lay still, I couldn't help but begin to move.

I opened my eyes to see that I was in a large red tent, surrounded by a group of men. I was lying next to one of the walls on a soft bed made from a plant I didn't know and had a fur blanket over me. The room gradually came into focus and I startled as one of the men rushed to my side.

"Have no fear, my friend, for you are safe here." It was the Horseman, now changed from his battle armor into very different attire. His clothes fit the same historic period as his armor and style of war, but what I noticed most was the crown on his head. Now I understood why the warrior had ignored me on the battlefield when his first attempt to kill me failed – He saw a chance to attack the King – and it was this same King who now knelt at my bedside to comfort me.

"Aerlic, bring him some wine, please," he said, helping me to sit up some. A man rose and poured the deep red drink into a cup from a skin near where the men were sitting and brought it to me.

"Here you are, lad," he said. He was the second one I heard defend the King. He lifted the cup to my lips and gently poured a little into my mouth. I'd never had wine before and the strong drink surprised me. It was quite smooth, more sweet than bitter, and greatly refreshed me.

My nerves began to relax, but I was not fully recovered from my shock and had not yet found my words, so I sat there staring at the group around me. Many of the men had friendly faces. These smiled compassionately at me, even though they probably knew as little about what had happened to me as I did.

Others in the group, however, scowled at me suspiciously, and when they looked at the King it was with great disdain. They clearly thought very little of him, at least for the way he was helping a young man he did not know.

The horseman King ignored their disrespect; instead he asked me, his eyes looking deep into mine, "How are you feeling?"

I looked back at his eyes and they pierced through me. I quickly looked down, though I didn't know why. "I don't know where I am," I said, fidgeting with my blanket.

"That might be expected, lad, since you appeared from thin air on the battlefield and fainted, not awakening until just now. What is your name?" he asked.

"Michael," I replied.

"Michael, you have a strong name, and a mighty one. I am sure that you are destined for great things. It is an honor for us to have you with us for whatever reason you have come."

Seeing that I had no words with which to respond, he went on, saying, "My name is Fidelas, and I am the High King of the land into which you have come. These men you see around me are all also kings, each of their own realms, and it is my honor to join with them in uniting our land under one banner.

"You came to us in the middle of a great war that is now all but finished. I had hoped that today would have been the end of it – we put much planning into today's attack that will not surprise them again – but we will have to endure it for at least one more battle, which I expect will come tomorrow. I shall spare you the details for now, but I am thankful that you are safe so that we may have the pleasure of your company. Truly, I think that brute warrior was not prepared for you to appear right in front of him, or your time with us would have been short indeed!"

"Thank you, your Highness, for saving my life," I said with a slight bow of my head, my senses starting to return to me. I still had no idea where I was or how I got there, but I could at least try to do what I thought was right for the situation.

"Of course, Michael," said King Fidelas, "I could do nothing less. It would have been a shame on us to allow you to suffer such a fate. Let me ask you, lad, how old are you?"

"I'm 13, Sire. Actually, my birthday was just yesterday, or maybe it's still today, I'm not sure," I told him.

"What's that, lad? How is it that you're not sure?" asked Aerlic, still standing at the King's side with the cup of wine.

"Well, it was my birthday where I came from, and I was just going to sleep for the night when I appeared here," I said.

"Do you hear that, gentlemen?" said the King, turning to look at the men, "He has just come of age! We must celebrate with him as best we can!"

"What?" asked Borgas indignantly, "We don't even know who he is! We have a battle tomorrow we have to plan, wounded men to tend to, and if there's a feast to be had it should be when we celebrate our complete victory!"

"Yes, all those things will be done, never fear. And do not worry about provisions for the feasts; we have plenty for both," the King said with a smile, standing up from my side.

"But the men should keep their wits keen for the battle and not waste them with a feast," Borgas continued to argue.

King Fidelas became stern and answered, "Truly, there are prudent measures we must take. Nevertheless, it will do the men good to feast and remember that they fight not only for land and treasure, but for things of true consequence that set us apart from our enemies and sanctify our land. You would do well to remember this, too, as you hold a place of leadership and must demonstrate these values to those under you. No, we will honor this young man tonight and remember that for which we will fight tomorrow. I can conceive no better way to prepare for battle. Let each of you be off to his men to care for them and announce the feast!"

The men began to shuffle out of the tent, some merrily and some grumbling, but all obedient to their High King's command. King Fidelas remained by me and, turning to me, said, "Michael, I must see to my men and a few details of the feast, please excuse me. My personal attendant will hearken to your call and give you anything you need. Do not fail to ask for anything you desire!"

"Thank you, Your Highness; you're very gracious," I said, impressed with myself that I seemed to be saying the right things.

King Fidelas left the tent, leaving me alone with my thoughts. Noticing that Aerlic had left the cup of wine, I took another sip, thinking to refresh myself further. This time, however, I winced as it burned going down my throat and made my head spin. *Maybe I won't drink anymore of that right now,* I thought, and set it down next to my bed.

Gazing around the room, I began to take in where I was. I admit that I had little experience by which to judge anything that I saw in that tent in order to know its significance. My experience with camping went about as far as a four person nylon tent we used on family trips. This tent was huge compared to any I had been in, more than twice the size of my bedroom back home. It was made from canvas and supported by ropes, with soft rugs laid out over the ground.

There was a table set up in the middle of the tent where the men had been sitting, with a variety of things on the wall opposite where I had been laying. I rose from my bed and walked around the table to get a better look at these things.

Two ornate maps caught my attention. The first one was of several islands all in a group. The islands varied in size, some of them were very small, but most looked like they were probably about the size of Great Britain, though it was hard to guess without a legend. One island in the center was largest of all.

This island was pictured by itself on the second map. Cities were marked out all over the island and I assumed the ones written in larger script were the more principal cities.

The map was like nothing I had ever seen. Whenever I continued to look at any given place for a moment the initial image would change, growing more detailed until I could see towers on castles and chimneys on the row houses. I looked at the forests and suddenly the picture would change so that

I knew I was looking at the actual forest, not merely general map notations to say where a forest was.

Interestingly, when the images did change it never looked like anything but a map. It was not like looking at satellite pictures. It never even turned color.

My thoughts were interrupted as a voice called from the door, "Ah, I see you've found our maps!"

I turned to see a young man only a few years older than me coming into the tent. He was light skinned and had straight, dark brown hair neatly trimmed around his neck. He wore a thin chain of gold, which shone brilliantly against his deep red tunic. A belt the color of new spring leaves was fastened around his waist and he had pointed leather shoes on his feet. I fought away a sarcastic thought about how a beardless blend of Santa and one of his elves had just walked through the door and managed instead to get out, "Um, yeah; I've never seen anything like them before."

"King Fidelas had his seer bless them so they could serve him should he ever have to journey apart from his most trusted advisor."

"His seer? What's a seer?" I asked.

"Oh, a seer is someone who receives dreams and visions that help direct their lives according to the plans of the one who gives them such abilities. In the case of the King's seer, however, he doesn't just get dreams and visions about his own life; he also gets them for the King and the whole kingdom."

The young man was helpful, no doubt, since I could hardly misunderstand his explanation, but this was not exactly a conversation I was used to having every day. I asked him, "So, who is it that gives these dreams and visions?"

"They can come from two sources, one good and one bad. In my experience, it is usually easy to discern whether you're getting them from the good source or the bad source," he answered. "The good source is generous with the dreams and visions he gives, as he truly cares about you and wants to help you. But the bad one makes you do all kinds of things that give him more power over your life before he'll tell you anything.

"Both of them require equal amounts of surrender and give revelation and power in return. However, the good source genuinely causes his gifts to make you free while the bad one uses his power to control both you and anyone he can through you."

Questions swirled through my mind, but one seemed most important in that moment. "Which source does King Fidelas' seer get his dreams and visions from?" I asked.

"Oh, the good one, of course!" the young man answered. He paused for a moment and I could tell this conversation was not progressing as he had expected.

He said, "I apologize, this all must be very new to you. I don't know where you've come from, but everyone here learns these things when they're young. That's why it caught me a little off guard when you ask questions like these. I'm afraid I've done a poor job of answering them for you."

"No, um, it's okay, really," I said. "You've done a great job answering my questions. It's just that I have so many more. There's so much here that I've never seen or heard before that not all of what you say makes sense to me yet."

"I suppose that is to be expected no matter how well I answer your questions. Nevertheless," he said, "are there any more questions I can answer for you right now?"

"Yes," I said, trying to think of which one I wanted to ask first, settling on the somewhat obvious, "What's your name?"

"Ha! I really have done this poorly, haven't I? My name is Perilan, and I am at your service for anything you need. The High King has told me that I am to get you ready for the feast tonight and let no service to anyone else take higher priority, unless he himself calls for me."

"And," he added, leaning closer, "I can tell you that if he feels that strongly about it then he won't be interrupting us."

I was curious about the feast and wanted to ask him about it, but one question had been burning in me since I first woke up in this place: "Where am I?"

"Ah! Well, you began looking at those maps," Perilan replied, "Let's look at them again."

We turned again to the maps on the tent wall and Perilan pointed to the first one I looked at, the one with a bunch of islands. "This is the world to which you have come," he said. "These islands are called *Cotheria*, and they have ever been separate and in competition with one another. We are now on the principal island of them all, the large one right in the center of the group. This island is called *Unitia*.

"Much of the competition between these islands is over Unitia, for its size and centrality of location place it along the trade routes to all the smaller islands. Kings have always thought that they could become the richest and mightiest of all the kings of Cotheria if they simply controlled this island.

"The hunger of the kings for such prestige has kept the islands in a state of war for as long as anyone can remember. None of us were born in time of peace. And to make matters worse for Cotheria, when a small island's King was away invading Unitia he left his own land mostly unprotected.

"Often raiders would come to spoil the land and take what treasure they could find. Sometimes soldiers would return to their homeland from their conquests only to find their wives stolen, their houses burnt, and their children dead, gone, or starving among the ruins.

"This history repeated itself many times on each of the islands. Our kings rarely lived long enough to learn any lesson from the past, for soldiers who find ruin at home after fighting for wealth that only their king would possess are not very faithful. The mightiest soldier would rally other discontents to himself and together they would rise up against their own king. They would murder him and establishing a new king, more selfish and broken than the last.

"Our most ancient stories tell us that these islands were once all one land, a land that prospered and had peace. But one by one, islands somehow broke off and took names for themselves, raising up kings to govern them. People forgot old allegiances and finally Unitia was abandoned completely because of continual war. Division has consumed our lands, robbed us of hope, and nearly brought all Cotheria to utter destruction.

"But then, in my father's generation, all the seers throughout the islands started speaking of a coming reunification. They saw signs in the stars they could not explain and heard wonderful things in their dreams. 'A man is coming,' they said, 'who will unite this land in peace again. He will be a King unlike any other, and the peace he brings will never end.'

"Most of the small kings did not like these words, and many seers lost their lives for the message they gave, but for the people of the land these words were hope and life themselves.

"The seers also gave us signs by which we would recognize the one who was to come, and these signs we have all now seen. One of the chief signs they gave was that the man would come from Unitia and that his past would be unknown.

"Since that sign was given, parties have gone to search the whole island of Unitia, looking for this man. Some looked to kill him, not wanting his peace. Some looked that they might see their hope in living flesh before their eyes closed forever in the long sleep. Years passed while people searched this long forsaken island for any sign of the man, yet they found nothing until one day a stranger appeared to a group of refugees who had taken shelter on this island.

"They had fled to this island to find peace from the constant attacks and scheming on their home island, establishing a small village in a secluded part of the woods. Indeed, they hoped they would never be found again, but this stranger approached one of their humble shacks and asked the woman there if she would give him some food. This she did, and before long the whole village had gathered to see the man who had come to them.

"The curious stranger stayed with them that night, but in the morning he was gone and they could find no trace of him. However, reports of this man began spreading through the search parties and excitement grew among the people.

"Finally, as several kings arrayed themselves for battle, each one against the many others, this man appeared right in the middle of them all. He stood in the center of the battlefield with so many armies encamped about him and he waited. He waited until someone came to greet him. The kings refused to lower themselves from their thrones, each one thinking it was a ploy to lure them into an attack. Finally a lowly page risked the wrath of his king to go discover who this stranger might be.

"The kings watched as the page approached the stranger, each one of them expecting cunning and villainy. But as the page neared the stranger, he saw a great smile spread across the man's face and a light in his eyes of pure joy. Such a countenance was not found in all Cotheria during that time of war, for no person's spirit rose enough to create it.

"At the sight of the man's face, the page immediately knelt upon the turf and offered whatever service he could. The man, his very presence radiating gladness, raised the page to his feet and embraced him in a crushing embrace.

"'My name is Fidelas,' the stranger said. 'You shall be great among the people of this land. Will you take me to your king?'

"The page was afraid of his King and said to Fidelas, 'My Lord, the king I serve is not a good man and I fear for both our lives if we appear before him.'

"'Do not fear,' said Fidelas, 'I will speak for you and he will in no way cause you harm. You will yet see him become a true king.'

"The page could not help but trust the stranger and so took him to his king, but he could never have imagined what happened next. Fidelas approached the king and the two looked at one another for a long time. As the king looked into Fidelas' face all the roughness melted off of him. Anger, suspicion, and contempt left him while peace, trust, and generosity rose up in him. A deep transformation took place before all the people's eyes.

"Finally, the king rose from his throne and knelt before Fidelas. 'Please, sir,' he said, 'I do not even know your name, but I know that you are fitter for my crown than I. Will you please take it and rule over my land?' He then took his crown from his head and offered it to Fidelas.

"Fidelas looked upon the king and said, 'My good King, I have not come to demote you. On the contrary, I intend for you to become greater than you are now. Keep your crown and your throne, but I receive your allegiance. Rise and follow me, for there is much to do.'

"Much there was to do and much they did do. Before the day was over all the other kings on the field of battle had also offered their thrones and crowns to Fidelas and, as with the first, he accepted their allegiance but not their position.

"Word of this spread quickly to all the islands and soon all the kings had placed themselves under Fidelas. He became High King over them all.

"Not all the kings, however, delighted in this the way the first had. Many, though not most, had only agreed because they saw how large an army the united kings mustered. They feared that if they did not offer their crown freely then it would be taken by force, and that they would lose their lives as well.

"It has now been five years since High King Fidelas appeared, and in the early part of that time much was rebuilt on the island of Unitia. Prosperity began to return to the islands and people started to feel secure in their homes again.

"But at the end of the second year of the High King's reign – in springtime, when we were only beginning to plant our fields – the barbarians began to raid the islands. We have been chasing them from island to island for three years since then, and that is why we are fighting now," Perilan said, turning to me again.

I realized suddenly that as he spoke the map had become alive and I had seen all that he said. In fact, it had become so real that it was as though the dream world had faded away and all I could see was the map world, moving at every word Perilan spoke. But now, as the images of the map returned to normal, I came to myself again.

I shook my head to clear up my thoughts and said, "Who was the page? What happened to him?"

"I was the page," Perilan answered cheerfully, "And as for what happened to me, I think you can see for yourself.

"Now I must not forget myself again," he said before I could ask any more questions. "We must prepare you for the feast before you are called upon!"

With that he started busying himself about all sorts of things I have not had anyone do for me since I was a baby.

"Remove your clothes, please," he said as he wet a cloth with water from a skin, "We must give you as good a bath as we can."

I protested, "But I just bathed this morning – well, took a shower actually – but I'm sure I don't need a bath again already."

"Ah, but you were in a battle, remember, and battles have a way of getting people messy no matter when they last bathed."

I looked at myself for the first time since I woke up in the tent and realized that I had blood spattered all over me. It is amazing how quickly my desire to keep my clothes on changed and how badly I wanted a bath of any kind.

Perilan was very good at his job and was finished almost before I realized he had begun. He gave me a towel to dry myself and excused himself from the tent. A moment later he returned holding clothes similar in style to his own and like nothing I had ever seen before in their extravagance.

He helped me put on the breeches first, which were a beautiful deep red, redder than the wine I had been given to drink. He then gave me an undergarment and a tunic as shirts to wear. The undergarment was the finest linen and the tunic was silk.

I held the tunic for a moment to look at it before I put it on. It was a marvel to my eyes, deep blue like that place in the ocean just before light cannot go any further. Yet it was deeper in color than that so that the blue shone from the tunic almost with a light of its own, as though it were woven from spun sapphires. Interwoven with the blue was silver thread, creating intricate designs that played tricks on your eyes as it appeared and disappeared in the blue.

I had never seen, let alone worn anything like it and when I put it on I felt as though I was wearing the night sky. I started to move about the tent, looking for a mirror, but Perilan called me back to him, saying, "Do not wander off yet, my friend, we are not quite finished yet!"

He took a belt of silver rings about as wide as my hand and bound it around my waist. Finally, he had me sit on my bed again so he could put shoes on my feet. Like his, these shoes had pointed toes and seemed to be made of leather, but mine matched my outfit, being blue in color.

"There," he said, "Let us find a way for you to look at yourself!" He again left the tent and I was just going to follow him when he returned with a large sheet of polished metal. It wasn't exactly as clear as the mirrors I was used to, but what I saw still amazed me. I definitely had never looked this wonderful before, even if it would never do for me to show up at school looking like this.

"I believe you are ready to feast with the High King now." Perilan commented as he examined his work. As if on cue, trumpets sounded outside and Perilan said, "It is time!"

He held back the flap of the tent for me to step through and for the first time I really saw where I was. The camp was laid out on top of a hill in the clearing of a forest. Trees were all around as far as I could see, which was very far because the clearing gave us a commanding view of all the land for miles around.

I looked west into the setting sun and the gentle breeze that greeted me was a refreshing change from the somewhat stale air of the tent. I had no idea what time of year it might be, but it felt like a beautiful late August night in Minnesota, the time of year that is not too hot and not yet cool; it is just perfect for being outside.

"Follow me, Michael, if you please," said Perilan, "I will lead you to the feast."

He guided me past rows of tents and through small groups of men, all headed the same direction, and before long the groups became a crowd. It actually was not all that different from the rush to get in line for a school lunch, except it was outside and the men somehow seemed both hungrier and more patient than any junior higher I had met at school.

We rounded a bend in the tents and a space opened before us that was filled with tables. Not exactly like a picnic area in a state park, my guess was that these tables were the best these men could do in a camp that needed quick set up and tear down, in case they had to move quickly to pursue the enemy. Each table was a simple board set up on a couple of crates, or maybe a large rock here and there. There were no chairs, except at the High King's table, but the tables were short so the men could sit on the ground. They made their best attempt at setting up rows considering the terrain, but a hillside is not necessarily conducive to order and neatness.

It took us some time to file through the tables, mill through the crowd of men all finding a seat with their comrades, and finally arrive at the head table where the High King stood watching for us.

"Ah, here you've come, at last!" he said. "Everything is prepared for you."

"For me, your majesty?" I asked.

"Of course for you," King Fidelas declared, "It is your coming of age feast, after all! Now come and sit with me at my table."

At this I saw several of the other kings exchange uneasy glances and I guessed that these were the kings who thought I must be a spy.

Other kings approached me and greeted me, grabbing my hand and thumping me on the back, congratulating me for "coming of age." I was not sure what this meant, but apparently it is a big deal with the people of Cotheria.

King Fidelas put his arm around me and guided me away from the kings, saying, "Here, Michael, your place for tonight is next to me. Since your father is not present to honor you, then – if you will allow me – I will take his place for the event."

It's definitely true that my dad isn't here, but somehow I think he'd fit right in, I thought with a little smile. I said to the High King, "I am very honored by your offer, and though I have no idea what is taking place tonight, I will gladly sit by you for whatever it may be."

"Good! Then let us call the men to order." With that he gave a glance to a man in waiting, who, having received the signal, struck a large bronze shield that served as a gong. The army of men stretched before us grew silent and all turned to look at their King. King Fidelas alone remained standing and he addressed the men gathered:

"You men know what mysterious thing happened today as we fought upon the field of battle, how, as we pressed our attack and released the full strength of our might against the foe, indeed just as we turned to trample them as one under our horses, there appeared before me a young man.

"This young man had an appearance like none I have seen before, and he showed quick instincts as he ducked a fatal blow from a barbarian sword. Seeing that this mysterious guest was about to be trampled by our charge, I quickly rescued him from the oncoming tide and bore him away to safety.

"As your kings and I gathered in counsel to discuss the significance of such an event and what is right to do for the young man, he awoke and revealed to us that he has only today turned 13.

"Today is his coming of age birthday! And it is our corporate honor to do for him together as each of you has done for your sons and as each of your fathers did for you.

"Actions such as this are what set us apart from the barbarians who have invaded our land. These barbarians know nothing of honor or nobility. They care only for treasure that shines and land they can defile. By celebrating with this young man tonight as we are doing, by welcoming him as one of our own, we distinguish ourselves from our foe.

"We will share freely from the bounty we have been given so that we may help this young man become a true man indeed, and in so doing we will prove the true men we have become.

"Let the feast begin!" the High King dramatically concluded, thrusting his hands into the air.

The gong sounded again and instantly lines of servants poured onto the field, finding their way through the tables with plates piled high with food. I saw plates with different kinds and cuts of meat, plates of fresh bread, and pitchers filled with something that the men greeted with particular enthusiasm. I looked for where the pitchers were filled and saw barrel after barrel lined up in a row at the edge of the field.

Within moments a servant brought some to our table and asked the High King, "My Lord, do you desire beer or ale?"

The King responded, "Tonight is a light night, and with pleasantly warm weather; I shall have ale, thank you." Turning to me he asked, "Which shall you have, Michael?"

"Um, well sir," I stammered, "I'm not accustomed to either, actually, or even know the difference. I usually have water or milk with my dinner."

"Truly?" the King asked with surprise. "You must dwell in a land of rich abundance indeed to have milk at every meal. I do not think we have milk, and our water is not likely fit for drinking, but I will see if we can find either to suit you."

King Fidelas nodded to the servant with the drinks, saying, "Edwil, please leave your pitchers on the table and see if you can find any milk or water for our guest to drink."

Turning back to me, he continued, "In the mean time, Michael, enjoy a small cup of ale with me; only be sure you fill your belly with meat and bread before ale and beer!"

That was not hard for me to do, for the meat was like none I had ever tasted. It was so fresh and full of flavor, so tender and juicy that I continued piling helpings on my plate well into the evening. I even learned to sop up the seasonings with my bread as I watched the men around me do, which kept the bread from drying out my mouth and making me overly thirsty.

Finally, when the din of the feast seemed to be abating, King Fidelas stood to address the men again.

"My good men, hearken to me once again before the repose of satisfied bellies fully comes upon you. As you already know, this feast is to honor the young man, Michael, who appeared in our midst today from an unknown place.

"In truth, we know very little about Michael, though certainly the manner of his coming indicates that there is some great importance to his presence with us. Yet we will not allow the mystery of his arrival to abate the bounty of our hospitality, for to do so would be to confuse cowardice for prudence.

"It is right that we think this way, for we must consider honor to be our great duty, not that we aim to receive it, but that we are generous to give it. For as we give honor to others we will cause them to become greater. This in turn causes our land, our people, and even ourselves to become greater as well.

"For this reason, I wish at this time to present our guest Michael with a gift befitting the glory of this kingdom."

The High King turned and received something from Perilan, holding it at his side so I could not see it, though I heard gasps of astonishment from many men and kings alike.

"It is our tradition that a father give his son a gift on his coming of age birthday that will help prepare him for manhood," King Fidelas continued. "Michael, I am confident, will be a great leader and warrior, strong in counsel and noble in character. Therefore I have chosen to give him a sword."

Turning to me, he lifted the gift from his side and laid it across his hands, presenting it to me, and said, "Michael, today you have become a man!"

The scabbard was leather, bound with bronze at the top and bottom. The throat of it was set with gemstones and the tip was engraved with an intricate design.

The sword itself was even more impressive. It had a bronze plated hilt. The cross-guard was made so the tips pointed back toward the blade, and words in strange letters were inscribed upon it. The grip had four strips of leather braided around it, two white and two black. Each color started in a point at the top of the grip and wound around it in corkscrews going opposite directions. The effect of this was quite a striking appearance.

In the diamond-shaped gaps of the braided leather, the bronze had been fashioned to look like precious stones in a way that somehow also radiated fire just like a gem would. The pommel was crafted in the shape of a lion's head which had red diamonds for eyes.

The setting sun, red with its own fire, shone upon the sword, making the lion's eyes blaze and the hilt dazzle. I drew the double-grooved steel blade from its sheath and held the sword before my face. I felt as though the strength of the sword were somehow seeping into me and for the first time I felt like I belonged among these warriors.

My reverie was interrupted by the gruff voice I had first heard in the tent. "I will not stand for this! Fidelas, you have always been a fool and now you have gone too far!"

Aerlic stood, "Borgas, watch your tongue! You are speaking to the High King."

"He's not my High King, not anymore – I won't have him. I won't serve a man who honors strange boys who are as likely to be spies of the enemy as friends, all while he's surrounded by kings who fight every day for him, risking their own lives and the lives of their people. If anyone deserves honor it's us and our men, not this boy who shows up out of nowhere in the middle of a battle and stalls our whole charge just because the 'High King needs to get him away to safety.'"

I could hear the mocking tone in Borgas' voice and was unnerved when his declaration received murmurs of agreement from several other kings around the table.

"You gave him your pledge," Aerlic countered, "You owe him your allegiance."

"For what?" Borgas demanded. "What has he ever done for us? Didn't he come with all these promises? He promised us peace, right? Well, I don't know about you, but I'm standing on a battlefield. That's no different than before he came, except before he came I was fighting for myself and my own people and now I'm fighting for him!"

"You are fighting for yourself, Borgas, you only forget," said Aerlic. "You forget that you used to fight against fellow Cotherians and now you fight against the barbarians who pillaged your land while you left it unguarded. The honors you now earn you get to keep, while anything you earned before was lost as soon as you returned home."

"At least before I received honor. Now honor is given to worthless strangers and children by this fool," Borgas said, pointing sharply at King Fidelas. "He wastes time involving himself with people and tasks far below his office, abandoning the things he should be doing. This will only lead our people into weakness and expose us to our enemies even further."

Aerlic shot back, "Does it not make sense that different actions are necessary to accomplish something our fathers never could? If the leadership we have seen before only brought suffering, then perhaps we have never learned what leadership should look like."

"You are as much a fool as he is and I will not abide such foolishness any longer," Borgas said. "I will take my men and leave, and any other kings who are wise enough will do likewise."

Borgas turned to leave the table and several kings stood up to go with him. A number of other kings stood to restrain those who were leaving and just as some began to draw their swords King Fidelas said, "Let them go."

"Let them go?" asked Aerlic.

"Let them go," Fidelas confirmed resolutely. "I did not begin my reign by force and I will not maintain it by force. I will rule a people who desire to be ruled."

Borgas and his crew left the table and began calling their men to follow. The rest of the army sat in stunned silence, watching their comrades leave from the tables around them, shocked by what was happening.

I suddenly remembered the sword in my hands and looked at it, not knowing what to do now. King Fidelas turned to me and said, "Michael, I knew this might happen when I chose to give you that sword, yet I chose to give it to you anyway. That sword belongs to you. It is rightfully yours and you are worthy of it. Do not let these kings' actions cause you to think otherwise."

Turning to Perilan he said, "Take Michael back to the tent and help him into bed. He has had a trying day and I want him to get the rest he needs."

"Yes, your Majesty," said Perilan, and he gestured for me to go with him. I sheathed my sword and quietly followed.

We arrived at the tent and he helped me out of my clothes, carefully folding them and setting them aside. He then gave me a gown to wear to bed, saying, "This will keep you both comfortable and warm."

"Thank you," I said, putting it on. He offered me another sip of the wine, which I accepted, and soon I was feeling quite sleepy. He left the tent as I got into my bed, leaving me alone with my thoughts yet again.

Why would King Fidelas do this for me? I wondered. *He just lost half his army because he gave me a sword, and he doesn't even know me!* "I knew this might happen when I chose to give you that sword, yet I chose to give it to you anyway." *That's what he said, but I don't understand.*

Sleep was overtaking my thoughts, but just before it fully descended on me I heard someone cry out, "Attack! It's an attack! Sound the alarm!"

I sat bolt upright in my bed as the commotion outside the tent rapidly grew. Then in the distance I heard a horn sound out high and shrill – *BOWWWAAAAA – WA – WA – WA – WA – WA.*

My alarm was going off. I smashed my clock and it stopped. Sitting up in bed I looked around my room trying to figure out where I was. A voice called from outside my door, "C'mon, Michael, get up! You're going to be late for school!"

No way, I thought, *that could not have just been a dream!*

Chapter Four

A Mysterious Find

"Michael William Nyquist! Are you awake?" Mom let herself into my room and turned the light on as I sat in my bed, blinking and trying to figure out what was going on.

"C'mon, Michael, you've got to get going. It's time for school!" she said, throwing some clothes at me from a clean pile I hadn't put away yet. "Get in the shower and don't dilly-dally. I'll run downstairs and make sure you have some breakfast you can take with you. Hurry or you'll miss your bus!"

I looked at my clock and saw that it was already 7:00. Somehow I had slept an hour late and my bus was due in ten minutes. I jumped out of bed and ran through the shower, barely getting wet. Bolting downstairs I said, "Where's my backpack?"

"I don't know," said my mom, "Where'd you leave it?"

"I don't know! Agh, I'll go check my room," I said, running back upstairs.

What was that? Was all that just a dream? That had to be more than a dream; it was way too real to just be a dream. But it happened while I was sleeping, and ended when I woke up. That's what dreams do. Geez, where is that backpack?

I searched every inch of my room, throwing things all over and making a complete mess. I heard my mom ask my dad downstairs, "Have you seen Michael's backpack?"

"Um, I think so. Hang on, let me think." That's my dad, unflappably steady and peaceful in the middle of a chaotic you're-going-to-miss-the-bus-if-you-don't-find-your-backpack-right-now frenzy.

"I think I know where it is," he said and I heard the door to the garage open and shut. A few seconds later it opened and shut again and my dad said, "Here it is! I used it yesterday for our lunches."

"Oh, good!" my mom said as I reached the bottom of the stairs, having run from my room as soon as my dad said he had it. I grabbed the backpack from my dad and my arm flew up in the air because it wasn't as heavy as I had expected. "Dad! Where are my books?" I asked.

"I put them in your room. Didn't you see them while you were looking for your backpack?"

"No, I wasn't looking for books. I was looking for a book bag!" Exasperated, I ran upstairs again and rearranged my room a second time trying to find my books under the mess I had created looking for my backpack. Finally, I found them lying just underneath my bed, stuffed them in my bag, and ran back downstairs.

As I took a couple pieces of peanut butter toast from my mom I heard the bus drive by my house. "No!" I shouted and bolted out the door only to see my bus stop empty and my ride to school disappearing around the corner.

I shook my head and sighed a frustrated sigh as I walked back inside. *If I just hadn't had that dream I'd have been on time,* I thought. *How in the world did I sleep through an hour of my alarm going off? I never oversleep like that!*

"My bus is already gone," I said in a huff. "I'm sorry, I don't know what happened this morning."

"It's okay, honey, we'll figure out how to get you to school," my mom said, a little out of breath. I knew she was upset that I missed my bus, but was trying to make the best of it.

"John, can you take Michael to school on your way to work?" she asked my dad, "I'm not exactly dressed for public yet." It was true. She was still wearing her pajamas and bathrobe, but my dad was ready to walk out the door anyway.

"Sure!" he said, "You ready to go, Michael?"

"Yeah, I'm ready."

"Alright, well let's go then," he said as he started heading for the door. I followed him out and we got in the car just as we had the day before, reminding me of everything that happened on our little road trip. Thinking of the conversation with my dad and my dream was too much to process all at once. I am sure the weight of my confusion showed on my face.

It must have been obvious, because as my dad pulled out of the driveway he wasted no time in asking me about it. "So what's going on? You seem a little preoccupied, and I don't think it's just that you overslept and couldn't find your backpack."

I was silent for a minute, not sure how to answer. Honestly, how do you tell someone about that kind of dream, if it even was a dream? If I didn't know what had happened to me, how could I tell someone else?

"I don't know, Dad. Yesterday was really weird. I mean, it was great, but there were a lot of weird things in it, too. But then…" I trailed off, not sure how to say what came next.

"Yes?" my dad prodded.

"I had a dream last night, I think," I said.

"You think you had a dream last night? But you don't remember what happened in it?" he asked, obviously confused.

"No, I remember what happened in it, that's just the thing," I answered. "The dream I had felt more real than real life, and it was really long. I've never had a dream like that. I've never even heard of a dream like that."

"Well, what happened in your dream?" he asked.

"I don't know. It was like I was in a whole other world. I saw maps of places I've never seen before and met people there – Kings and their armies. And right when I got there, or right when the dream started or whatever, I appeared right in the middle of a battle and nearly got killed!

"But then someone rescued me, and after the battle all these Kings were around me talking about what to do with me. Some of them thought I must be a spy and wanted to kill me, but others were kind and wanted to take care of me. The High King ordered them to take care of me and even threw a feast for me, a coming of age feast, because I told them that it was my 13th birthday. They said they did that for all their children, giving them something that would help prepare them for manhood, or womanhood, too, I suppose.

"And the High King gave me a sword, and the Kings that thought I was a spy all walked out and said they wouldn't serve the High King anymore. But even after half his Kings and armies left he told me, 'Michael, I knew this might happen when I chose to give you that sword, and I chose to give it to you anyway.'

"I was laying in my bed in that world about to go to sleep, trying to figure out why this King would choose to give me a sword even if it meant losing half his men. And then an alarm sounded because the camp was under attack. But the alarm in my dream turned into my alarm clock and I woke up with

Mom at my door. I mean, I just woke up from this, like, 15 minutes ago and it was so real. It was more than a dream, Dad but I don't know what it was. Maybe I'm just going crazy."

"No, I don't think you're going crazy, Michael," Dad said reassuringly. "It does sound like you've had a very significant dream, though, but I don't really know what to make of it either. Maybe we can talk more about it later if you want and try to figure it all out."

"Yeah, maybe that'd be good. We'll see," I said halfheartedly.

Really I didn't want to figure it out. I wanted the dream to just be a dream. I didn't want to be so weird that I had anything so abnormal happening to me. Puberty was bad enough; did I have to deal with something else too, a something that I couldn't explain? Why me? Where did it come from? Why now? What does it mean? Or does it mean anything at all? Maybe it was just some weird mutation of my game and conversation with Dad spat back out in dream form. How could I know?

I don't know, I thought as we pulled up to the school. "See you later, Dad. Thanks for the ride," I said, getting out of the car.

"No problem, Michael, see you later," he called back. "Try not to let it trouble you too much!"

I shrugged my shoulders as I walked to the doors, thinking a bit sarcastically, *Yeah, I'll work on that.*

When I got inside the school I realized that I had actually beaten the busses. *Ok, Michael, let's start being smart about this,* I thought, *You've got some time. Just head to your first class early and see what you can figure out.*

So that's what I did. I picked up what I needed from my locker and went to my first hour class. When I got to the classroom, however, the door was shut and locked. *Great. So much for that idea. Maybe I can find Mr. Gustafson.*

Mr. Gustafson was the seventh grade social studies teacher, and everybody loved him. He had a way of helping you know why history was important, not just in general, but by demonstrating with specific events. He could help you see how history helped shape the parts of culture we have now that are important to seventh graders.

I wandered over to the teachers' lounge and found him sitting behind his desk. "Mr. Gustafson," I said as I knocked on the door, "Could you –"

"Oh, Michael!" he said, interrupting me, "Hey, missed you yesterday, but happy birthday. Did you have a good day?"

"Um, yeah. Yeah, it was a good day. Hey, could you unlock the classroom, by any chance?"

"Sure! That's no problem. You going to do a little catch up studying?"

"No," I said flatly, "I just wanted a little kinda quiet space to think for a bit." I hesitated, not sure if I should tell him or not, but my thoughts were like a roiling volcano inside of me. My words tumbled out of my mouth before I could hold them back, "I had a really weird dream last night. It made me sleep an hour late this morning and miss my bus. My dad brought me to school and I just wanted to sit and try to figure out why it's messing with me so much."

"Ah, so that's the look I see on your face," he said with a smile. "Can I help you figure out something about this dream of yours, or would you like to wear that look all day long? I mean, I assume you don't want your friends asking you, 'What's wrong?' all day and then not believing you when you tell them, 'Nothing.'"

"Um, sure," I stammered, "But, um, how are you going to help me?"

"You might be surprised," Mr. Gustafson said, "I have quite a bit of interest in dreams."

"Why's that?" I asked, feeling weird talking with my teacher about something that felt so personal.

"Well, obviously I enjoy history," Mr. Gustafson answered, "And there's a lot that dreams have done to shape history. In fact, for the vast majority of the world's history, people of all cultures considered dreams to be of huge importance, and everyone from emperors to peasants would make life altering decisions based on them."

"Really?" I asked.

"You bet!" he said, "In fact, it wasn't really until the Enlightenment Period in the mid to late 18th century that any people as a whole started to reject things like dreams. That's when society started putting their trust in reason and intellect, making things like dreams irrational and thus irrelevant. Does that make sense?"

"Um, I'm not sure I get it yet," I replied.

"That's okay. What I mean is that people started to value intellect and reason over more abstract things like dreams, visions, or other immeasurable experiences. Science advanced enough that we didn't need a pantheon of gods to be in every tree, rock, and stream there is in order to explain it. We no longer needed to credit things we didn't understand to something supernatural; we just assumed that we didn't have the explanation for it yet.

"So if someone had a dream, they didn't think of it as divine communication anymore, and they didn't look for any more meaning in it than what they ate before they went to bed. Am I making more sense now?"

"Yes; well, I get what you're saying about history, I think, but what does that have to do with my dream?" I asked, "Are you saying that my dream is just spaghetti and pumpkin pie?"

"No, that's not what I'm saying. Remember that I said the Enlightenment Period came only a few hundred years ago, but we have a few thousand years of recorded human history.

"I believe there is a reason that people for so many years put their trust in dreams. It just doesn't make sense to me that the practice of pursuing and interpreting dreams would have endured for so many years through so many diverse civilizations if there wasn't something legitimate there."

"So you think there probably is something significant about my dream," I said, trying to understand.

"I think there may be," he said. "As I look at records throughout the years, there are a handful of times when a ruler had a truly impactful dream so that no matter how hard he tried to shake it off it would haunt him with a sense of its significance. Those cases stand out from the rest as perhaps more significant than an ordinary dream, though I'm not saying that ordinary dreams are unimportant, because they are. Just maybe they're not as important, like the person who gives the dreams knows when to shout and when to whisper."

"What do you mean, 'The person who gives the dreams?'" I asked.

"Well, you don't think you give yourself your dreams, do you?" he asked in return.

"Uh, no; I suppose not," I answered. "But I still don't understand how someone else could give me the dreams either. I mean, is there some person who wanders into my room at night and sprinkles some sort of magic dust on my brain that makes me dream?"

Mr. Gustafson chuckled, "I don't think it probably happens quite that way, no, but think about it logically for a second. It makes sense that we don't give ourselves dreams. At least, I will say, that we do not give ourselves all of our dreams; meaning that some of our dreams come from another source. After all, there are many records of people who had dreams from which they gained knowledge they had never known before. And if it was new knowledge to them, then they could not have given themselves the dream.

"If we do not give ourselves dreams, then who does? Certainly it is not another human who can enter the private chambers of our sleep and implant such mysteries inside of us."

"Then who does give us our dreams, Mr. Gustafson?" I asked impatiently.

"I believe there is more than one source," he answered, "Though I think we will not have time to talk about that much more today."

I heard the bustle of students in the hallway and the clang of lockers shutting, which meant that the busses had arrived and other students would soon be pouring into the class.

Mr. Gustafson continued, "Michael, I'm sorry that we may not get to talking about your actual dream today. It sounds like it really is an important one and I would keep trying to figure out what it means if I were you. I will try to encourage you with this, though, that if someone gave you a dream with that much significance, it is probably important enough to them that they'll help you understand it, too."

"But who gave it to me?" I asked with exasperation.

"I don't know, Michael," he answered. "But I bet that if you just keep paying attention, whoever it is will keep talking to you to help you understand your dream.

"Also, just my two cents, but you're not crazy. Not in the least. Rather, I'd think the opposite, that you've been chosen to have this dream because you are someone extremely special."

Mr. Gustafson's words encouraged me to a degree, but in that moment what I really wanted was answers. I let out a deep sigh and asked, "You really think so, Mr. Gustafson?"

"Absolutely! Here, think of it this way: Pretty much all our lives we'll feel the pull of what the majority of people around us are doing. That pull makes us all more comfortable being just like each other. On the other hand, deep inside, each of us knows we were born for greatness. None of us as little kids wanted to grow up to be a nobody; all of us wanted to grow up and be significant.

"The trouble is that this creates a conflict on the inside of us, the part that desires to be great warring with the part that longs for acceptance from the people around us. This conflict comes from the fact that to do something special you have to do something different than the majority of the people around you. In fact that's kind of the definition of 'special' – that it's different than the norm.

"So you think of the people who made history – George Washington, Winston Churchill, Martin Luther King Jr., and all the other people who have brought the world to where we are now – all of them had to step out into what made them special in order to leave the mark they did. And in stepping out they had to break the pull to be just like the majority.

"Everyone is made to be special, Michael. I'm sure this dream of yours will help point you toward what makes you special, toward the way that you will leave your mark on the world and what you'll be remembered for in history books. Keep after it, and if you're willing to share, I'd love to hear what you come up with when you figure out your dream."

"Thanks, Mr. Gustafson; that helps," I said as the first students came into the room.

I had never thought of it that way, that somehow having this dream was an indication of being significant. I had also never thought about how being different is a good thing, at least not like that. I mean, I had heard a lot that you have to be who you are and all that, but I never thought about how our differences are actually what make us special.

All this didn't get me any closer to figuring out my dream, though. While Mr. Gustafson's words helped me feel better about myself, they did not give me the answers I needed. In fact, they gave me even more questions! More than all the rest, one question scared me – Who is this person that is trying to talk to me through my dream?

Thoughts of my dream faded some as the day went on and I had to concentrate on my classes. I was definitely convinced that something big had happened to me, but since I had no grid for explaining it then I was not able to unravel what it was all about.

Not knowing what to tell my friends yet, I tried to avoid telling them anything about my dream. The last thing I wanted was to have them think I was weird or crazy and be unable to explain it to them.

When lunchtime came, I was first at the table since I did not have to go through the line for a school lunch. A minute later Matt sat down across from me and immediately greeted me, saying, "Hey, happy birthday!" Matt was loud and outgoing, with sun-bleached hair and freckles that stood out on his tan face.

"Thanks," I said as Liz and Austin joined us.

Liz was not exactly a tomboy, but with five older brothers and no sisters she definitely had a rough and tumble way about her femininity. She smiled through her braces and asked, "Hey Michael, how was breakfast with your dad?"

"Good," I said through a bite of my sandwich.

"What else did you do with your day off?" Austin asked, brushing his straight black hair away from his eyes. It was always falling down over his face.

"Oh, well, actually my dad took me on a little road trip after breakfast and we played Risk all day in this really nice park," I answered, leaving out all details of the conversations we'd had.

"Wow, that's cool," said Dylan, my quiet friend with a short, nappy afro as he sat down. "My parents didn't do anything like that when I turned 13. It was just another birthday for me."

"Yeah," I said, "My parents said something about how they wanted this one to be different because they think it's special somehow. They didn't really explain it to me yet, so I don't know what they mean."

"Hey," Matt cut in, "speaking of not being here, where were you this morning?"

My heart beat a little faster for a moment as I tried to think of some way to not tell my friends about talking to Mr. Gustafson or about my dream.

"Oh," I said, "I overslept and missed my bus. My dad had to bring me in this morning so I just went straight to class. What did I miss?" I asked, hoping to turn the conversation away from myself. It worked.

They told me that nothing had happened that morning, but that I had missed some fun when Nick tried to pick on them at lunch while I was gone. Nick was an 8th grader who had a knack for finding people who had things he wanted and then using creative (and sometimes violent) ways to get those things. Of course, just like any bully, the only reason he got away with it was because of his size. He was at least six inches taller than anyone in his grade, let alone ours, and looked like he probably worked out every day to fill out his frame.

He wore old clothes that usually did not fit and had a band of thugs who followed him simply because he was the best at finding ways to manipulate circumstances for his good. They stuck to him like parasites riding on the back of a shark, desperate for the scraps he occasionally passed down and the feeling of importance that came from being close to someone with a form of power.

It was a fairly routine occurrence for him to bluntly invite himself to our lunch like a cloud of locusts in human form. He would take the best parts of our lunches and leave us hungry. It was especially frustrating because none of us understood why he could not just buy his own lunch. That is why I was confused when my friends told me that I had missed some fun when he came by while I was gone.

"Fun?" I asked, my eyes wide with surprise. "When has it ever been fun when Nick comes to our table?"

"Yesterday!" said Matt. "He kept trying to come mess with us, but every time he got near our table a teacher would show up. So he just kept wandering around the lunch room. He looked like he was lost and couldn't find his table! It was hilarious!"

"Yeah, and one time," Austin added, "he came by the table and we thought he was going to finally get away with it. But right then Ms. O'Connor walked up and gave him that look she has."

"No!" I said, slightly horrified. Ms. O'Connor was one of the computer teachers, and though she was short and otherwise nice, she was like an angry leprechaun when she was crossed. Most students liked her, unless they had gotten on her bad side; then they were afraid of her.

"Yes!" Austin said, giddy as he finished his story. "Nick made some comment to Liz about her braces, about how bad it would hurt if he hit her so she'd better just let him have her food. But before he could even grab a French fry, all of a sudden Ms. O'Conner showed up and gave him a look so dirty it made even him blush! He walked right back to his chair and never came back."

We all laughed at Nick's expense, glad that he had finally been caught. That peaceful victory fueled our conversations for the rest of lunch, keeping my mind far from both my dream and my weird conversations with Dad. As the bell rang and we started heading to our afternoon classes, Austin called, "Hey Michael!"

"What's up?" I asked, slowing down in the hallway for him to catch up.

"Do you want to see if we can hang out tonight?" he asked.

"Yeah, that'd be great!" I said excitedly. "I'll ask my mom as soon as I get home and call you with what she says."

"Awesome!" he said, smiling as he turned to go to his class. "See you later, Michael!"

"See ya, Austin!" I replied.

I navigated my way to my locker to get what I needed for my last few classes, anticipating when school would be over and I could hang out with Austin. I was sure my mom would let me since it was a Friday night. *Maybe she would even let Austin sleep over!* I thought, and was even more excited for school to be done.

When the last bell rang, I hurried to my locker, stuffing what I needed for the weekend into it, and then raced out to my bus.

I sat next to Brandon, a heavyset boy who was hoping that adolescent growth spurts would make his weight and size perfect for football. He moved into my neighborhood when we were both 11, after which it was rare for many days to go by without us playing together.

We got off at our stop and I waved goodbye to him as I ran for my house. Bursting through the door, I called, "Mom! Can Austin come over tonight?"

"Well hello to you, too," she replied, coming around the corner with her phone held to her ear. "I'm talking with your dad, honey; hold on a sec."

"Oh," I interjected, "ask him if Austin can come over tonight!"

She scolded me with her eyes for interrupting and said, "Just a minute, John; Michael has a question for you. I'm going to put you on speakerphone."

She took the phone from her ear and pushed the speakerphone button. "Go ahead, Michael; what did you want to ask your dad?"

"Hey Dad," I said, "Can Austin come over tonight?"

"Well, your mom and I were just talking about maybe making other plans for tonight that we thought you might enjoy," his voice crackled up from the speaker. "How would you like to go shopping for your birthday present tonight?"

"Yeah!" I blurted excitedly. "Let's do that!" With everything else that had happened I had somehow forgotten about shopping for the rest of my birthday present. Dad's reminder excited me, in sort of the same way as when you find money you forgot you had.

"But couldn't Austin come with us?" I asked, looking from the phone to my mom and back again.

They were both quiet for a moment. Dad broke the silence first, saying, "Well, Babe, what do you think about it?"

Mom shrugged her shoulders and said, "I guess I don't see why Austin couldn't come along. What do you think?"

"I was thinking the same thing," Dad said. "Sure, Michael, Austin can come over tonight."

"Awesome!" I said, and then pressed further. "Do you think he could maybe spend the night, too?"

Mom and Dad both laughed as they understood what I was really asking the whole time. Mom said, "How much homework do you have? Could you get it all done this afternoon?"

"Why would I have to get it all done this afternoon?" I objected.

"Well, if Austin spends the night then you won't get any of it done tomorrow. And if we get you your birthday present tonight, then I don't think you'll want to do any on Sunday either."

"Oh, right. Um, yeah, I can get it all done this afternoon," I said.

"How about we do this," Dad proposed, "let's say that Austin can sleep over tonight as long as your homework is done before he gets here and as long as his parents are okay with it. If your homework's not done then we'll take Austin home on the way back from getting your present. Sound good?"

"Deal," I said.

"Alright," said Mom, "now let me finish talking to your dad a bit." She took him off of speakerphone and returned the phone to her ear. As she wandered to a farther away part of the house I heard her say, "John, are you sure it's a good idea to give him that?"

Curiosity held me where I was, hoping to hear more. Mom only said, "Alright, if you really think it's safe, then I'll trust you. I had better let you get back to work…Love you, too; bye."

I was concerned now, as well as curious. "Mom, what are you guys getting me?" I asked.

She replied a little flatly, "Birthday presents are a surprise, Michael; you're not supposed to know what they are."

"I know," I said, "but what are you getting me that you think might not be safe?"

"Oh, you heard that part, huh?" she said. "Well, your dad says you'll be just fine, and I'm sure he's right. He asked me to not tell you what it is, though; he wants to tell you when he gets home."

"I really have to wait until he gets home to find out what I'm getting?" I begged.

"Yes, you really have to wait until he gets home," she answered firmly. "Now, you might want to call Austin to let him know he can sleep over tonight and get working on your homework so that he really can."

"Yes, Mom," I conceded, and quickly called Austin with the news.

"Hello?" he answered.

"Hey!" I said, "My parents said you could come over! And I asked them if you could spend the night, too, and they said yes!"

"Really?" Austin asked excitedly. "Let me ask my dad quick if I can."

I heard muffled talking on the other end of the line. A moment later, Austin returned, saying, "He said, 'Yes!'"

"Alright!" I exclaimed. "My parents said I need to get my homework done before you come if you're going to sleep over, so I'd better go."

"Okay," Austin said. "Call me when you're done, and hurry!"

"Right. See you later," I said.

"See you later," he replied.

I hung up the phone and headed to my usual spot for doing homework – on the floor of my bedroom – only stopping long enough to tell Mom that Austin's dad said he could sleep over.

Homework always seemed easier, somehow, when it stood between me and time with my friends. At any rate, I could always work faster under those circumstances than I normally could.

I was just finishing up when I heard Dad walk through the door, followed by a mumble of voices greeting one another.

There was a rush of feet on the floor that I knew was Amy charging at Dad to give him a hug. Finally, I heard Dad's heavier footsteps making their way up the stairs and down the hall to my room.

He knocked on my door, opening it slightly, and greeted me, "Hey Michael, how's it going?"

"Good," I said, smiling back at him. "I just finished my homework. When do you think Austin can come over?"

Dad laughed at me and said, "Well, why don't you call him right now while I change my clothes? He can join us for dinner. But after you get off the phone, come see me in my room for a bit, okay?"

"Okay," I said, getting more excited about my present. I put my books away and called Austin. He was packed and ready to go, so after agreeing that his parents would drive him over we got off the phone and I hurried to meet my dad.

I knocked quietly on his door and he answered, "Come on in!"

"Grab a seat in the chair," he continued as I entered the room. For as long as I could remember, my parents had a giant plaid overstuffed chair in their bedroom. I went over to it and sat down, sinking deeply into its well worn cushions.

Dad grabbed a seat on the corner of the bed and asked, "How was school today?"

"Good," I said. "It was pretty much a normal day."

"You didn't have any trouble after missing the bus?" he asked with a tinge of concern in his voice.

Oh yeah, I thought. I had almost forgotten everything from the morning, but at Dad's reminder my dream came rushing back to me. "Um, no, I didn't have any problems," I answered, shifting uncomfortably in my chair. "I just went early to my Modern History class to think for a bit, but Mr. Gustafson talked to me instead."

"What did he have to talk to you about?" Dad asked.

"Well, for some reason I mentioned my dream to him, so he was telling me about how dreams have played an important role in history."

"Really?" Dad replied, "I would have never thought of that, but that's interesting." He stared through the floor for a moment, and then came back to our conversation. "Hmm, well, anyway, I'm glad that your day went well. I asked you to come in here, though, so I could talk to you about your birthday present."

"Mmhmm?" I answered, my feet twitching with anticipation.

"Michael, your mom and I believe that your thirteenth birthday is a very special birthday, so we want to give you something this year that is different from anything we would normally give you. But before I tell you what it is, I am going to tell you why we are doing this. Sound good?"

"Sure," I said, settling back a bit into my chair.

"Son," he began, "there're a lot of cultures throughout history that have chosen an age in their children's lives to celebrate more than any other. It varies from culture to culture in what age that might be and in how they celebrate it, but the common thing in all of them is that it has to do with something called, 'coming of age.'

"That term means something different depending on the needs of the cultures. In a lot of places it means that the child, if it's a boy, will no longer stay at home with his mother, but instead will go out to work with his father. In some places it's the age when apprenticeships are arranged so that the boy can begin to learn a trade that will provide for him when he becomes a full grown man. And for girls in a lot of cultures, it's even the beginning of the time when they can get married."

"That's really weird, Dad." I said.

"I know, isn't it? Don't worry, though, we won't make your sister get married when she's 13," Dad said with a wink, as though he had needed to reassure me.

"Right, well, that's good. But what does this have to do with me?" I asked.

"What it has to do with you," he said, "is that you just turned 13, which, as your mother and I talked about it, we decided was the right age to celebrate your coming of age."

Seeing that he had not answered my question he went on, "Coming of age for you will not mean that you're going to start coming to work with me or that we're going to ship you off to some job. It just means that we want to do something significant for you that will help prepare you for manhood – and I mean that specifically. We don't just want to prepare you for adulthood; we want to prepare you for manhood.

"We wanted to give you something that was a symbol of strength and honor and other values that we want you to embrace as a man. Our hope is that giving you this gift will help you begin to walk more in those things now so that by the time you move out and have a family of your own you will have already been living as a man for many years.

"From this point on we will look at you as a man, no matter what the world says about your age. We will be teaching you things that you will need to know to be not just a successful adult that makes it in life, but things that you will need to know if you are going to change the world.

"This won't happen all at once; it'll happen bit by bit, but we're going to honor you as a man. We will do this first because we believe you're worthy of that honor, and second so that by the time the world recognizes you as a man you will have five to seven years of experience living as one and you'll be able to lead anyone else your age.

"We really believe that your teenage years are a gift, despite what our culture says they are. They are a gift because these years are a very special time for us to build you up in who you are, to make sure you know who you were made to be, and to do whatever we can to help you become that person."

Dad looked at me for a second and asked, "So what do you think?"

"I don't know, Dad. I mean, I'm excited. It all makes sense. I guess I'm a bit nervous and I don't know what it really means, but it sounds good."

"I understand, son," Dad said, "This isn't normal and you haven't seen it before, so you don't know what to expect. That's okay; we've never seen it before either, but we're very sure that this will be a good thing.

"So," he said in a tone that sounded like a change in subjects, "We want to give you something that will symbolize the importance of this birthday. Up till this morning, we didn't have any ideas that made us really excited, but your dream gave us one that we like a lot."

I gulped back fear and disappointment. *My dream? Why does it have to come from my dream? Why can't my dream just go away!*

Dad continued as though he didn't notice, "We're going to give you a sword, Michael."

I sat dumbfounded, not knowing what to say. When I found my ever changing 13 year old voice again, I cracked, "A sword?!"

"Yep, a sword," Dad replied, leaning back with a smile.

Still in shock, I asked again, "A sword? You're really giving me a sword, like, a real one?"

"Yes, a real sword!" Dad answered, laughing this time. "Why wouldn't we give you a sword?"

"I don't know," I said, shrugging my shoulders. "I mean, it's a weapon. It's dangerous. You always taught me how careful I need to be with knives, but now you're giving me a sword. I guess I never thought you would give me something like that."

"You know, Michael," Dad said, "that's kind of the point. A sword is dangerous, so you have to know how to use it and be careful, but manhood is the same way."

"Huh?" I asked, totally confused.

"Manhood – womanhood, adulthood, just being a person – really is a dangerous thing," Dad said. "I'm not saying that it's dangerous to us, but it can be dangerous for other people. Just like with a sword, if we start flinging it around without being mindful of the people around us then we will hurt them – and the closer the people are to us the more severely we will hurt them.

"The damage that manhood can inflict looks different, but it can destroy someone's life just as badly. For example, part of being a man means that you have the physical ability to have children. But if you throw that part of your manhood around without thinking about other people then you can destroy both a child's life and the life of that child's mother. If you do that over and over again then you will leave a path of destruction in your wake that affects more lives that you can count."

I squirmed in my chair uncomfortably. "Wow," I said quietly, "I never thought of it that way."

"And unless we teach you, there's no reason you would think that way. That's why we are going to teach you.

"Michael, a sword is a symbol of strength and honor. It is connected with many stories that give us pictures of different aspects of true manhood. We'll give you a sword and then every time you see it you will remember what it means, and the more you think about those things the more you will become those things.

"Yes, a sword is a weapon, which means that it hasn't always been used for good purposes. But the problem was never the sword. The problem was the heart of the person who wielded the sword. Many noble things have been accomplished with swords, just as many terrible things have been done with them. We will train you to use yourself as you would use your sword – only for good and with all your might. Do you understand?"

I nodded and Dad said, "Good! There will obviously be a lot more later, but we don't need to talk about everything all in one night. Did you get a hold of Austin?"

"Yeah," I said. "His parents were going to bring him over right away."

"Oh good," Dad said. "Then we'll be able to eat dinner and go get your sword right away."

"Um, Dad, where are we going to shop for a sword, anyway?" I asked.

"You know, your mom and I wondered the same thing," he said. "There are tons of online stores for them, but we didn't want to wait for one to be shipped. So I looked for one that had a physical store we could go to and found a memorabilia shop in the Mall of America that sells them."

"Go figure," I said. "What can't you find at the Mall of America?" This mall, also known as The Megamall, has over 2.5 million square feet of stores, not to mention its own movie theater and amusement park. Before you could find anything you wanted on the internet, you could always count on the Mall of America.

"So we'll go right after dinner?" I asked.

"Unless there's some reason to wait," Dad said.

Just then, the doorbell rang. I gave Dad a quick look to make sure he was done talking to me and his nod told me he was, so I ran downstairs to get the door.

I pulled the door open and greeted Austin, "Hey, come on in!" His dad followed him up the walkway so I held the door open for him, too. He was wearing sweat pants and his hair was untidy, making him look as though he had just gotten out of bed.

"Hi Mr. Thompson," I said as he came in the door.

"Are either of your parents around, Michael?" he asked without looking at me.

"Um, yeah, both of them are. Dad's upstairs and…"

"Can I talk to one of them?" he interrupted.

"Sure," I said. "Let me just go get my dad; I'll be right back." I turned to head up the stairs, but saw that my dad was already on his way.

"Oh, hey, Dad. Mr. Thompson wanted to talk to you," I told him.

"Hi Dave," my dad greeted him. "What's up?"

"Hi John," Mr. Thompson said. "Can you guys bring Austin back tomorrow?"

"Sure, that's no problem," Dad answered. "Does he need to be home by a certain time?"

"No, just whenever. I don't care when he comes home as long as he still has time for his homework," replied Mr. Thompson, looking passively at Austin. Austin gripped his bag and looked at the floor.

"Alright," said Dad with his usual cheer, "we can do that. You have everything you need, Austin?"

"Yup," he answered.

"We'll see you tomorrow, Austin," his dad said abruptly as he opened the door. "You be sure to thank them for dinner."

"I will. See you, Dad," Austin said, watching the door close.

I looked at Austin, wanting to ask him what had just happened, but my mom called us from the kitchen.

"Michael and Austin, dinner is pretty much ready. Do you want to take your things upstairs and then come eat?"

"Yes, Mom," I said, and I led the way to my bedroom. Austin dropped off his bag and we headed back downstairs.

Mom had made meatloaf with mashed potatoes and corn for dinner – a family favorite – and we all had second helpings except for Austin.

"You sure you don't want more?" Mom offered for the third time.

"No thanks," Austin said.

"Don't be shy if you're hungry," Dad said. "You can see there's plenty more to eat."

Whether from hunger or because of my parent's persistence, Austin finally helped himself to seconds. As he plopped a spoonful of mashed potatoes on his plate, Dad asked him, "So, did Michael tell you what we're going to do after dinner?"

Austin looked at him confused, "No, he didn't. Are we doing something special?"

"We are doing something special," Dad said. "Do you want to tell him about it, Michael?"

"Yeah," I said, sipping some water to help me swallow a big bite. "Mom and Dad are going to get me a sword for my birthday and we get to go shop for it tonight!"

Austin almost choked on his food. "Really?" he said, "a sword?"

"Yeah!" I said, "a real one!"

"Mom and Dad are getting you a sword?" Steve asked excitedly. "That's so cool! Can I get a sword, too?"

"No, Stevie, you can't get a sword," Mom answered. "At least not until you're older. We'll see about it then."

Steve would hardly stop talking the rest of dinner and as we hurriedly cleaned up the dishes. Austin was particularly quiet, but with Steve's noise and the general excitement none of us really noticed.

As soon as we finished cleaning up, we climbed in our van and drove to the mall. I could hardly wait as we got through the door and was the first to find the kiosk with the mall directory so we could go right to the memorabilia store.

"The map says it's this way!" I said excitedly and took off to find it.

"Hold on, there," Mom said laughing, "Wait for the rest of us."

We wandered up two floors and a third of the way around the building before we finally found the store. It was filled with all sorts of things from various movies. They had everything from Marilyn Monroe wigs and Chewbacca costumes to Harry Potter magic wands and Avatar action figures.

Wandering through the store, we found the back corner was lined with swords. Some swords had pictures next to them of the characters who had used them in the movies. As I scanned the wall to see which one I might like the best I suddenly stopped, paralyzed by what I saw.

It's not possible, I thought.

"What's wrong, son?" my dad asked with genuine concern in his voice.

I could tell that my face had gone white and I felt sick to my stomach. My eyes just kept staring at the sword right in front of me. I pointed to it and said, "That's the sword from my dream."

My dad looked where I was pointing. "This one?" he asked, "Are you sure?"

"I'm positive, Dad, it's pretty distinctive." I looked around at the other swords and gestured to them, saying, "There's not exactly another sword here like it."

He looked at the sword again and asked me another time, "You're sure you're sure, this is the sword from your dream."

"Yes, Dad," I said a little exasperated, "It's the exact same sword! The lion's head with the red eyes, the white and black leather on the handle braided just like that, the bronze hilt, the writing that I can't read, the scabbard with the bronze and precious stones, everything! It's all just exactly like the sword I got in my dream. That is the same sword!"

"What are you talking about?" asked Austin.

"I had a crazy dream last night, and a king in my dream gave me a sword just like that one," I said, too shocked to care if Austin found out about my dream. "But if I saw it in a dream then what's it doing here?"

"Can I help you?" asked a man whose nametag said, "Manager."

"I don't know, Michael" my dad said to answer my question, "but I'm going to try to find out."

"Hi," he said to the store manager, "What can you tell me about this sword?"

"That one?" he said, looking at the one from my dream, "I can't tell you anything, unfortunately. It looks like a great sword, but I've never seen it before in my life, don't know how it got in my store."

"Really?" said my dad. He turned to me, bending down to my level and asked quietly, looking right in my eyes, "Michael, do you want this sword or do you want to look at the others?"

"No," I said firmly, looking right back at him, "I want this sword." As much as part of me wanted to run away and pretend I had never seen it, something about that sword captivated me. Whether I liked it or not, I knew it must be important.

"Ok, that's all I needed to hear." Turning back to the manager he said, taking the sword from the wall, "I'll take this one."

"That sounds great to me," the manager said, "But I'm not sure that I can give it to you. See, I don't know where it came from. I order all the swords that come into this store and I know our catalog very well. I can tell you with full confidence that I have never seen that sword before anywhere."

"Why would that mean you couldn't sell it to me?" my dad asked.

"Well, for one, it's not in the computer system," he explained, "So there's no price on it and if I just make up a price then it'll throw our numbers out of balance and make a mess for us."

"Oh, but you're the manager," my dad said, "And very experienced in the business. I'm sure you can make up a fair price for the sword and find a way to enter it in your system that it won't throw your numbers off.

"Besides," Dad pressed further, "If you didn't order this sword then you didn't pay for it either. Anything I pay you for it is pure profit. Now that's a good sale, and one that you won't get if you force us to look at your other swords.

"So tell me," he said, heading for the checkout counter, "How much do you want for it?"

The manager followed my dad and I caught a smile on my mom's face. The two of them haggled at the counter for a few more minutes before I finally heard the sounds of a checkout in progress.

At last my dad came back over to us and handed me the sword. As he placed it in my hands he said, "Michael, happy birthday. Today you have become a man!"

I was stunned at what I heard, though maybe by now I should have just expected the unusual to happen. Shaking my head I mumbled, "That's what the High King said to me in my dream when he gave me this sword, too." Having a dream like I did was one thing. Having that dream start to invade your real life is another thing completely!

Tears welled up in my eyes and my dad knelt by me to wipe them away. As he looked gently into my face I asked, "Why is this happening to me?"

"I don't know, son, but I'm proud of you. All day long I've watched you demonstrate incredible strength, strength that will make you a leader and help you know what to do in hard times. Having something happen to you that you don't understand can be very hard, but you've just gone along with it, trying your best to figure it out. And you've still been responsible with everything else you had to do like going to school and finishing your homework. Michael, that really is incredible and makes you a leader because you're doing things that real men do.

"I don't know what your dream means, and I don't know why things from your dream are showing up here, but I love you. You are my son and I am so proud of you. I'm here for you and everything's going to be okay."

He wiped another tear from my eye and gave me a big hug, saying, "Why don't we head home now and have some leftover birthday pie and ice cream?"

"That'd be great," I said, starting to cheer up. "Thanks, Dad, I love you, too." I added, giving him another hug.

"Ah, no problem," he said. "Now let's hurry home so I can look at that sword!" He raced out of the store with my mom calling after him, "Honey, wait for the rest of us!" But she was too late, I was hot on his heels, with Austin and Steve right behind me – we wanted to look at the sword, too.

We let them catch up outside the store, but kept a quick pace back to our minivan. I held my sword the whole way home, just looking at it and feeling in my hands. I remembered the strength that I felt come into me from holding the sword in my dream and wondered whether anything like that might happen with the sword in real life.

I did not know why all this was happening to me, but as I looked at my sword I realized that what my dad had said on my birthday was true. Turning 13 wasn't an ordinary birthday for me; something special had happened that day.

It seemed that none of us knew what that special thing was, exactly, but I did know that in just two days something had happened to me that made me feel like a different person. I did not know who this new person was yet, but I felt stronger and braver than I had before, and not just because I had a sword; something on the inside of me had changed and I knew it because I had started to view life differently.

Austin sat next to me, glancing over at my sword. I would sometimes look over at him, but he would quickly look away. None of us spoke, except for Stevie, who wouldn't be quiet. When finally no one would talk to him about the sword, he resigned himself to a conversation with Amy.

We pulled into the driveway and Steve asked me, "Can I look at your sword first?"

"Well," I said, "I'm going to look at it first, but you can look at it with me as long as Dad and Austin can look at the same time."

"Alright!" Steve said with a little fist pump as we piled out of the van turned around as soon as his feet hit the garage floor and I said climbing out of the back seat, "Dude, keep moving! I know you're excite we're not going to look at my sword in the garage."

Dad, Steve, Austin, and I gathered around the sword in one corn dining room table while my mom dished up pie and ice cream. Amy very girly girl, was not interested in my sword, so she helped Mom.

I drew the sword out of its sheath and we marveled at how it gleamed in the light of the chandelier. Cradling it in my hands, I gave it to Dad and he sort of flicked the edge with his finger, but cut himself it was so sharp.

"Yikes!" he said as he handed the sword to me and went to the bathroom for a tissue to put pressure on the cut. "Michael, you're going to have to be very, very careful with that sword," he said. "I know how to test a blade to see if it's sharp without getting cut and that thing still cut me."

I set it down on the table when our dessert came and as we ate we talked about different parts of the sword. Looking at it now I began to realize how incredible it really was. In my dream I had not had the chance to look at it very much, but as I considered the craftsmanship of it and how gemstones were set in both the sword and the scabbard, I realized that I had not just been given a sword, I had been given a treasure.

When Austin and I set out sleeping bags on my floor I was glad that he did not ask me about my dream. I might have brought it up, since I had already told him about it, but I did not know what I could tell him about it since I could not explain it myself.

We found conversation, instead, about normal things that felt lighter and helped distract our hearts from the unanswered questions we had. Hours passed as we talked about teachers we didn't like and girls we thought we maybe, if we could work up the courage to admit it, might someday like.

It was around midnight when we finally laid our heads down to sleep. Before I closed my eyes, I saw my sword one last time, leaning against the wall where I had set it. The precious stones gleamed out at me even in the dim light and I marveled even more at what the High King had done for me in giving me such a treasure.

I was a little nervous about trying to sleep since the last two times I tried I had awoken in a whole other world – once waking up to a battle raging all around me and once waking up to missing my bus.

It turned out that I had no need to fear, for nothing disturbed my sleep that night. What would happen the next day, however, was even stranger than my dream.

Chapter Five
Picking Apples and Hunting Boar

I woke up late in the morning around 10 o'clock with the sun shining brightly behind my window blinds. It was a relief to me to have a normal night's sleep. Even though only one night had been affected by my dream it felt like a lot longer because of everything that had happened since then.

Austin was still asleep, so I got up quietly and went downstairs. I found the rest of my family already awake and lounging around, enjoying a lazy Saturday morning. Dad was still eating breakfast and greeted me first, "Good morning! What time did you guys go to sleep last night?"

"About midnight, I think," I said.

"You think you might be up for another little outing today?" he asked.

"Um, maybe? What were you thinking?"

"Well, we saw the sunshine this morning and got talking, thought it was a beautiful day to go to an apple orchard," he said.

"Really?" I asked, "Awesome!"

If you have never been to an apple orchard then you have to understand, there is no better way to enjoy a beautiful fall day in Minnesota than to go to an apple orchard.

For one, depending on where you go, you get to sample dozens of different kinds of apples, all for free. That way, you know which apples you like the best and can go to the part of the orchard that grows them. Once you decide then you can either walk or take a tractor ride out to that part of the orchard and pick your own apples. You can gather incredible amounts of apples, taking them home and making wonderful things like apple pie or cobbler or even homemade apple sauce, all of it packed full of the taste of fall and the memories of picking apples together with your family.

The best part is getting a special treat from the orchard's very own bakery. My favorite at the orchard we go to is the apple fritter, covered in warm, gooey caramel and big enough that even a 13 year old is satisfied by the end of it.

"When can we go?" I asked.

"As soon as everyone is ready, I suppose," Dad answered. "Though, we'll have to wait for Austin, obviously."

Of course this was true, but waiting for someone when you are excited is very difficult. To take my mind off of the orchard, I snuck back into my room to look at my sword until Austin woke up.

This did not take much time, however. Despite my best efforts at drawing the sword silently from its sheath, it rung quite loudly and Austin woke with a start.

"Oh, geez, Michael! You scared me half to death!" he said.

"Agh, I'm sorry, Austin. I was trying to do it quietly," I apologized. "But, um, hey, my parents want to take us to an apple orchard today. It's really fun. We should go!"

"Um, sure," he said sleepily. "Are we going right now?"

"We'll go as soon as everyone's ready," I answered, grabbing some clothes to wear for the day. Austin followed my example and we were soon headed downstairs together.

We left the house by 11 and made it to the orchard not half an hour later. Climbing out of the van, we made our way into the old barn that had been converted into the orchard's shop/restaurant/processing area. We had been to the orchard enough times to know by heart which apples we wanted to pick, but we sampled what they had out anyway and took a cup of cider for our trip out to the apple trees.

There are so many different kinds of apples that a decent orchard is a very large place, and finding where your particular apple trees are can be pretty tricky. Fortunately for us, though, it was a busy Saturday morning and the tractor regularly ferried people into the orchard.

Hopping up into the trailer behind the tractor we managed to grab six seats together on the crowded bench. The smell of diesel exhaust drifted back to us as the tractor noisily powered us down the paths through the trees. Here and there the driver stopped to let passengers off or on.

Finally, we arrived at the most popular section of the orchard: The Honeycrisp Apples. More than half the trailer unloaded and reloaded here, with those getting off quickly dispersing among the trees to find the best apples.

My family was among this group, but we were in no hurry to find apples close to the tractor road. Knowing that the least harvested trees would be the ones farthest from that road, we started walking down the lane between rows of trees, past all the people trying to grab for whatever they could find quickly.

There were only a few other people who did the same as my family and all of us together quickly put the noise of the crowd behind us. It was only a faint clamor by the time we stopped to pick our apples, starting a small din of our own. We called out as we found good ones, competing for who could find the largest and best looking ones.

"Austin, let's go over here," I said, pointing through the trees to another row, thinking that those might be even more untouched and have even better apples.

I heard him say, "I'm right behind you," as I ducked under the low hanging branches. But as I stood up to look for more apples, I found that there was no other row in that direction as I thought there was. In fact, it was like I walked right into a forest.

That's weird, I thought, *I could have sworn there was another row of trees this way.* I turned around, expecting to see Austin right behind me still, but Austin was not there. The apple trees were not there either. Instead I saw thick brush, showing no signs that I might have just trampled through it on accident.

I looked in every direction, turning completely around, and I did not see apple trees anywhere. I did not see cultivated rows of trees anywhere. All I saw was wild forest, thick and close. I paused and realized that I did not hear any sound from the orchard, neither the far off noise of the crowd nor the nearer calls of my family.

"Dad?" I said, quietly at first, and then listened for a response. There was no sound but that of a bird that stopped singing when I spoke. "Dad?" I said, more loudly and urgently, hearing no reply. "Dad! Mom! Austin!" I called out, trying to stay calm.

That orchard has to be right there; it can't just disappear! I started to go back the way I thought I had come, finding my way through or around the brush as best I could. I walked about 20 feet and stopped. *I must have gone the wrong way,* I thought, *I know I didn't walk this far from the orchard.* I went back through the brush again and found roughly the spot I had started from, pausing to look around and consider my way.

I heard something off in the distance that made my ears perk up and all my senses worked together to make my hearing as strong as it could be. I waited, hoping to hear the sound again.

Suddenly I did hear it. Something was coming through the woods. It must have just moved a little at first, but now it was crashing through the trees at high speed. The sound grew louder and louder and I realized that whatever made the noise was coming right at me!

Without thinking I started to run, trying to find any place that could be a refuge from the beast running after me. Dodging trees and trying not to trip on the undergrowth, I ran a rough zigzag, doing anything I could think of to shake off whatever was coming behind me, hoping that it was not really chasing me and that if I just was not in its path then I would be okay.

I slipped on a fallen branch that rolled under my feet as I stepped on it and fell headlong into a small clearing. In that brief moment of lying on the ground I heard the crashing behind me continue off to my right, circling around me. Soon it was right in front of me again and headed my way. I started to scramble up to my feet in near panic, but it was too late.

As I turned to run back the way I had come I heard the animal behind me cry out a harsh squeal and felt the ground shake as it burst into the far side of the clearing, a mere ten feet from me. Without looking, I began to run again, but halted after only a small distance. There was no more crashing behind me in the woods. Whatever was chasing me had stopped.

Cautiously, I hid behind a tree and looked toward the clearing to see what might have happened to the beast. There were so many trees blocking my view that I could not see anything, so I moved slowly forward as quietly as I could. Creeping low to the ground to the clearing's edge I saw the beast lying on the ground with a long spear in its side. It was a giant boar; huge, over seven feet long and round as a barrel.

Voices spoke at the far side of the clearing, "Good aim, Delthun! It is no wonder that you are so fierce in battle when you are so deft in the hunt!"

I knew that voice. It was the voice of the High King!

Suddenly, without knowing how or why I was doing it, I stood up, stepped to the edge of the clearing, and said, "Hail, High King Fidelas and his mighty company! Thank you for delivering me from this wild beast!" I was shocked at the words coming out of my own mouth.

The High King stood in the middle of a group of men, only five or six in all, who looked like the kings I had seen before. He stood next to a towering giant of a man and had, from the looks of things, been slapping him on the back. At my appearance his countenance changed and he asked "Why, Michael! Is it really you? I thought that we had lost you in the battle the night of your coming of age feast."

"It's true, my lord, that you lost me, but not to the enemy. I don't know that I can explain what happened yet, but it was as though I woke from a dream and was no longer here. In fact, I don't know where here is at all or how I got here again."

I will never forget the way the High King looked at me. Somewhere deep inside me I knew that it looked bad for me to disappear with a treasure sword in the middle of a battle and to now appear before the King alive and well. I knew this might look like confirmation that those who thought I was a spy were right. Yet when he looked at me, though I saw questions in his eyes I knew they had nothing to do with me personally. I knew that he was as sure of me as he ever had been and that, if given the chance, he would give me the sword all over again. Seeing such trust in me did something in my heart and I knew that from that day on I would strive to be worthy of such trust.

He asked me, "How is it, Michael, that you have disappeared from us for so long, and now have reappeared in different clothes that we did not give you, yet still wearing your sword?"

I looked at myself for the first time since I stumbled into the woods and saw that I indeed was wearing different clothes, not just from what I last wore in the dream but from what I wore to the apple orchard. When exactly this transformation happened I cannot say, but I was dressed in hunting clothes just like the High King and his company. Not only that, but my sword hung from my side, even though I had left it at home that morning.

"I wish I could tell you, my King, but I have no answer, for I do not know myself how this has happened."

King Fidelas appeared to think for a moment and then said, "It is certainly a peculiar situation, Michael, yet I do believe you. I am only trying to discern what lies behind your mysterious visits with us. You are a curious fellow indeed, but I do not think there is any evil purpose in your heart."

"Your Majesty," I said, stepping to the King and kneeling before him, "I assure you that my heart is as faithful as I can make it, and I would never betray you. Please, here is my sword as proof of my loyalty." I drew my sword from its sheath and held it up to him, holding it by the blade and bowing my head.

King Fidelas grasped the hilt of my sword and said, "Michael, I take your sword as a symbol of taking you into my service, and I give it back to you, so that you may serve me freely." He turned the sword around and held it out to me again, now holding it by the blade himself.

I heard the kings around him holding their breath and somehow knew that the High King was placing himself in a most vulnerable position. By holding the sword to me hilt first, he pointed the blade at his own heart, and as sharp as the sword was he would not be able to stop it if I were to thrust it toward him. He was placing his life in my hands.

The feeling of being given such trust was like a narcotic. It made my head spin with wonder and yet at the same time washed my mind clean so that I could see and feel that this is the way life should always be.

Taking the sword in my hand again I said, "Thank you, Your Highness; I will serve you faithfully."

I stood, sheathed my sword, and said, "I thought that boar was going to run me down and kill me. I sure am glad that one of you got it before it got me!"

The kings laughed and the tall one said, "Surely you were safe wandering through these woods until we roused the boar. We were probably chasing it right at you without knowing it, so I am also glad that I got it before it got you or your blood would have been on our heads!"

I recognized this king's voice as one that I had heard in the tent as I came out of my swoon. When I had heard it before it was like a bear growling to threaten an enemy away, but now this deep voice boomed to shake the forest like a voice coming from the very roots of the mountains. This must be the Delthun I had heard the High King address.

"Yes, this day is twice blessed," laughed King Fidelas. "We have not only hunted well and harvested a generous dinner for the men, but we have found a lost friend whom we can again welcome into our company for however long we may have him."

With that he smiled at me and said, "Here, Michael, we have a spare horse you can ride. There is only a small saddle on it, as we had only intended to pull our quarry from the woods with it, but that will suit you fine – for though you are indeed a man, you are yet light in the saddle."

At the High King's words, a man dismounted from his horse and untied the spare from his own saddle. I recognized this man and called out, "Perilan!"

"Aye, Michael, it is I, and good it is to see you healthy and well, I might add," he said as he began readying the horse for its traveler and tow. "You may want to come help me with the horse, Michael, unless you desire to help the others in cleaning the boar."

Cleaning the boar? I thought, *What, they're going to wash it?* But then I saw what he meant, for Delthun had also dismounted and drawn a large knife while other kings positioned themselves at each leg, turning the boar upon its back and exposing its underbelly to Delthun's knife. As he placed the knife against the beast's hide he turned and said to me with a grim smile, "It is the messy duty of the one who makes the kill to also remove what will not be eaten and lighten the load for the horse to tow."

With understanding I never wished to have, I hurried over to Perilan and said, "I think I'll help you with the horse, and maybe we could do whatever needs done a little farther away."

"Certainly, Michael, we can do what needs done a little farther away, but we must stay near enough to respond to their call in a timely manner, for that is the duty of those who attend to kings." Leading me a short distance away, he showed me how to tie the rope in such a way that it would cinch tightly around the saddle and the boar, so that the act of pulling the animal only increased the security of the harness.

I was glad that words had jumped out of my mouth of their own accord when I first heard the High King because it helped me get through my initial shock. Now, however, my head was beginning to think clearly again, leaving several mysteries swirling in my mind.

First, where was this place and how did I keep ending up here? It is easy enough to explain away a dream as just that, a dream, and then move on with life no matter how real the dream is.

I knew that my dream was significant and that I needed to figure out what it meant. But now that I knew these people and places were simply part of my dream, I did not know how to relate with them. Should I treat them like real people or should I not care because I know that I will wake up eventually and not have to worry about anything that happened in the dream?

The trouble was that I did care about these people. I felt badly for leaving them in the middle of a battle and for how foolish that probably made King Fidelas look.

King Fidelas. Just thinking of him did things in my heart that I had never experienced. It didn't matter if he was just part of a dream, he had already impacted my life perhaps more than anyone else. There was just something about the way he spoke to me and the trust that he gave me. When I looked into his eyes it was somehow like looking into my heart, and the longer I looked the stronger my heart became. The more he spoke to me, the more my heart stirred to be trustworthy and faithful. Every action he took toward me was pure; there was no selfish motivation in him. I had never met a person like that who inspired so much in everything that he did.

That thought led to my second line of questions – What had happened in that battle? Who attacked? Was it the barbarians or was it the rebellious kings? What happened after the battle? Were they still at war? And whatever happened to the rebellious kings? Had they come back? Were they punished?

All these questions weighed on me so that I was glad when Delthun called out in his booming voice that they were ready. We led the horse over to the kings. They encircled the boar, which now lay on its side and was much thinner than it had been. Perilan produced some skins of water and handed them to the kings, who all drank thirstily from them in turn and then washed their hands or blades as needed.

Finally we all mounted, the rope having been secured, and we made our way back out of the clearing down the trail they had made while chasing the boar.

Fear sprung up in my heart as we began to leave. I knew that I had come out of the orchard the other direction and was now riding away from where it should be. Unfortunately, I had little else to do since I had already looked for the orchard and could not find it. I really did not believe that it was there anymore at all, though I didn't know what had happened to it. Maybe I had somehow fallen asleep while looking for apples and this was all a dream.

Maybe something else was happening altogether. I did not know, but I had to trust that I would wake up from it eventually just as I had awoken from my dream.

We rode in two columns with me in the front since I was towing the animal – this seemed backwards to me, but they said that you want the bulk of the party in the rear so that if help is needed it can be more readily given – which placed me next to King Fidelas. I was glad for this arrangement, not only because of the admiration I had for the man, but because I wanted to ask him the questions that weighed on me.

I was just going to ask what had happened in the battle that night when the King spoke, "Michael, forgive me, I am sure you have many questions that you want answered, but before you ask them I must try to answer some questions of my own."

It was a revelation to me that someone so perceptive might have questions about anything, so I just said, "That's okay, Your Majesty; I can wait to ask my questions."

I never imagined that he might need my help to answer his questions. I only thought he was telling me that he did not want to talk while we rode because he wanted to think instead. That is why it surprised me when he asked, "Michael, where did you go the night of the battle?"

His question took me off guard and I was afraid to answer, since it meant telling him that I thought he only existed in a dream world. Of course I had to answer, so I swallowed hard and said slowly, "Your Highness, I really don't know where I went that night. I know it probably sounds very strange, but what I experienced was like a dream."

I looked at him to see his reaction and could tell that I had not said enough yet to make myself clear, so I went on. "I mean, I live a life in another place, a whole other world where Cotheria doesn't exist. I'd never heard of it until I came here. And…" I trailed off, afraid to say what I had to say. "And my last time here seemed like a dream – a very real dream, more real than any dream that I've ever had and in a lot of ways more real even than my normal life – but still like a dream."

I could see that King Fidelas was thinking hard, so I tried to explain more. "What I mean is that I came here as soon as I was asleep the night of my 13th birthday and I suddenly woke up from here when the alarm sounded for the attack. It was as though that alarm woke me up from my dream and I was back in my normal home. The dream even made me oversleep so that I was almost late for school."

His eyes were fixed on the rough path through the woods in front of us. As I waited for him to respond the boar caught on a tree trunk. I needed help to back my horse up and watched as the men wrestled the beast back onto the path.

As we renewed our pace, King Fidelas said softly, "Michael, this is very strange to me, though our land is not wholly unfamiliar with the inexplicable appearance of persons. I have not yet revealed to anyone the land from which I come, for instance.

"I do not mean to worry you with my questions. I do not doubt you, as I said before. What you have said only confirms my belief that you must be here for a purpose. Indeed that much is obvious, and I desire to know the purpose so that I can help fulfill it."

"Your Majesty?" I asked so as to say that I did not understand.

"Everything about these circumstances has something to tell us. We are not to overlook the mysterious nature of your appearances and disappearance simply because we do not understand it. Rather, we can be sure that you are here for some great purpose. My only question about it is whether that purpose is for you to aid us, for us to aid you, or for both in some measure.

"And since I do not know the answer for certain," he continued, "then I will assume the last of these options and continue to look for what ways I can best help you so long as you are with us, expecting that you will do the same."

I wondered at this, about how I could possibly help them. I considered how little of their world I knew, how I did not know how to do any of the things I had seen them do. Fighting, hunting, mapmaking, and anything else I could think of that I had seen in this world. All of it was so foreign to me that I did not think I knew any way to really help them. Not only that, but they were all grown men, brave and strong. I was only a small 13 year old, and barely that, who had all the constitution necessary to faint in the middle of a battle.

"Did you have questions for me?" the High King asked, interrupting my thoughts.

"Um, yes, I did," I said as I came back to reality. "If I can ask, Sire, what happened in the attack that night?"

A shadow came over King Fidelas' face and sorrow filled his eyes. He sighed and said, "Michael, I knew that the kings who rebelled were plotting against me. They were the ones who held their own purposes from the beginning and nothing but fulfilling their own desires would satisfy them.

"They agreed in the beginning to follow me because they feared the size of my following among the other kings, but they never gave me their hearts. Consequently, when the union of all the kings brought heightened attacks from the barbarians, their hearts turned against me even more. In the end they chose to prefer agreement with the barbarians to agreement with me or their fellow Cotherians.

"Even as they fought by my side they were conducting negotiations with the barbarian leaders. When I chose to honor you with a feast and the gift of a sword it so violated the values they hold that they betrayed us utterly. They killed our sentries and sent immediate word to the barbarians, calling on them to attack the camp.

"Their plans were well laid and we fought hard just to survive. If it had only been the barbarians we fought then the battle would have been short and easy. However, the rebellious kings directed their armies to attack as well. Had all of their men had followed that command then we likely would have all perished. Blessed hearts that many of those men had, though, for they fought against their own brothers on our behalf, and those who did not die that night now follow us."

I did not know what to say. My face was strained with the weight of my guilt. *All that happened because of me!* I thought. It mattered little to me that this might all be a dream and therefore the people who died were not real. What mattered was that I felt the reality of this world more keenly than anything I had ever known, and that reality said that people had died because of me.

Struggling to keep my voice from cracking, I asked, "What happened after that?"

"We hastened to save the families of those who had remained loyal to us who were living on the lands of rebellious kings," he answered. "We knew that it would be a race to each island, for punishment would surely fall severely on those who had, in the eyes of those kings, rebelled.

"The barbarians harried our steps and made it hard to move quickly. Those were very difficult days, for with my seer Vemrilun on a journey, we could not know to which island this punishment would come first. We were forced to decide simply based on numbers and distance – which island was closest and had the most family members on it.

"This meant that we did not get to all the islands in time and some of those who had risked everything to stay loyal to us also lost everything. They returned to their villages to find their homes and all their family burnt and destroyed."

The High King's voice was strained in saying this. I could only slump lower in my saddle as he continued, "We grieved as best as we could with those suffering such loss, but had to continue moving to rescue those who might still be alive, sometimes succeeding and sometimes failing.

"Finally we managed to gather all of our surviving families and army together into an ancient fortress on the island of Unitia. It has been uninhabited for years beyond memory and its decrepit walls gave us little cheer. Yet what remains of its strength has been a great relief from being nipped at and chased from island to island, always running to rescue others and losing more men in each venture.

"Winter is coming now, and this hunt is to provide food for us through the cold months. Usually winter is a dreaded time of cold and hunger, but we are looking forward to it because the seas will become too dangerous to sail and the land too cold to encamp. This means that we will have peace to heal our bodies and grieve for what we have all lost, at least so long as this hunt is successful. We need this meat because we have little grain from a summer harvest. Running for your lives and the lives of your loved ones leaves little time to gather grain for bread and ale."

I wanted to disappear. I could not imagine a worse feeling than what I felt in that moment. It sounded as though I had caused the destruction of an entire nation including the deaths of many whole families! I didn't know what to say, but as tears began to flow down my cheeks I managed to sigh, "Your Majesty, I am so sorry. I didn't choose to come. And I didn't mean to cause so many terrible things to happen. For your sakes I wish that I had never come!"

"Michael," the High King said soothingly, "All this is not your fault. Those kings were already laying their plans well before your appearance and only accelerated their plans when they grew jealous of your treatment."

"I know," I said, "but you were so close to a final victory that maybe if I hadn't shown up then the barbarians would have all been defeated and those other kings would have made real peace with you."

"What you are saying sounds like good reason, Michael, for looking only at the actions that were taken," he said. "But there is a reason those actions were taken. All men take action based purely on what is in their hearts.

"As Perilan told you, few kings in this land inherited their position from their father. Most of them usurped their crown from the king before them, who also usurped it from the king before them. All of them were treacherous murderers; not one of them kept themselves from this cycle of selfish bloodshed, including those who are now loyal to me."

We reached the place where they started the hunt. I saw that they had left a cart here to help transport whatever game they caught. The High King said no more as he dismounted to help lift the boar onto the cart. It took them little time and soon we were underway again.

I was still trying to understand how the kings' rebellion was not my fault, so I asked, "But King Fidelas, if you knew that's what was in their hearts then why did you give me the feast and the sword? How could you do that when you knew what it would make them do?"

The High King said, "Michael, let me explain their actions to you; then you will understand mine.

"Most importantly, know that every person is responsible for their own actions. There is nothing I did or could do to force them to take any particular action. They always had a choice. They could have just as well chosen to humble themselves and rejoice in the honor that I gave you as they could have chosen to do what they did.

"Second, consider what they said. 'We're the ones who have been fighting. We deserve to be honored, not some strange boy.' You may not know this, but the coming of age feast and gift are so important to our people that warriors are even excused from the army to go celebrate with their son or daughter and then return to duty.

"That means that each of those kings had already received the honor that I gave you. I could not honor them in that way because they had already been honored in that way by their fathers. They were jealous of you even though you were simply receiving something they already had. They perceived that they were suffering injustice, that they were being denied something that was due to them, but the reality is that it would have been unjust to deny you the honor that I gave you.

"More than that, the reason they felt that they deserved honor was because they fought for me. Many of them had fought in a way that was worthy of honor, and all of them would have received honor and gifts from my hand, but their service to me in that area was not yet fulfilled. Our enemy still encamped in our land, defiling it wherever they went, and honors for battles are not given until the final battle has been won."

As the High King spoke, it felt as though explosions of thought were going off in my brain. When he said these things I knew he was right, and they seemed so obvious that I wondered how I had not thought of them on my own. I began to sit taller in my saddle.

King Fidelas continued, "Their statement betrays another thing in their hearts that led to their treachery. It shows that they forget it is an honor simply to ride into battle with so many great kings. This land has not seen so great a host gathered together since time beyond memory, with gallant kings and knights arrayed together in united company. To be a part of this army, especially as one of the kings in this company, is truly an honor to be guarded and cherished.

"But they despised this honor in their hearts, noticing instead that they were not the High King and, hating to serve another man, they saw shame in their position where they should have seen honor.

"In addition to this they measured honor by the physical treasure given to the one being honored. When they saw me give you that sword, they knew that none of them possessed a sword half as great, and jealous anger burned within them.

"They proved that the treasure of their hearts was whatever possession they could hold rather than the company they keep. That is why, for the sake of their treasure, they betrayed the company of kings to embrace the company of barbarians."

"But you said the coming of age gift is an honor," I interrupted, "and you did give me this treasure sword. So, I don't understand, is giving treasure not a sign of honor?"

"You are right, Michael; or, mostly right at least," he answered. "The coming of age gift is not honor all by itself, but rather it is a way of expressing honor.

"To honor someone simply means we cause that person to become greater in the eyes of the people around them, adding more weight to the presence they carry. This can be done by granting possessions or titles, but it can also be done by a few kind words spoken in the company of others.

"Therefore, when we honor our children as they come of age, the honor is in the new title they carry – man or woman – and the privileges that go with it that causes them to be more greatly esteemed in society. Usually, the gifts we give are only a celebration of this. In your case, however, I desired to give you a gift that befits who you are and would elevate you more in the eyes of this nation than coming of age alone could accomplish."

"I see," I quietly replied, feeling that King Fidelas might have a higher value for me than I had for myself.

"Perhaps," said the High King, "but I think I can help you see more clearly. There is one more piece you must understand in order to realize that you are guiltless.

"I have told you what honor is and how the kings grew jealous when I gave it to you. However, note that honor is not the same thing as authority. Honor is the character of those with noble position; it is how true nobility behaves. It is what qualifies a person to carry authority and is the measure of faithfulness with whatever authority you have.

"However, these kings gained positions of authority through treachery rather than honor, and therefore did not know how to use their kingship. They forgot that a king's greatness comes from his people, so they used their people to exalt themselves instead of exalting their people."

King Fidelas glanced at me to see if I understood and I slowly nodded, still thinking. He continued, "Only if they had honored those under them would they have become truly glorious, for the glory of a king is in his people. If his people dwell in rubbish then his glory is small, but if his people dwell in palaces as though they were kings themselves then his glory is great. It is the duty of a true king to exalt his people from the rubbish heap to the palace, but to do this he must truly set aside his own glory in his heart and purpose wholeheartedly to exalt those below him. We must learn that honor is not a limited commodity, and that giving it away is the only way we will ever receive it.

"Unfortunately, lacking a change of heart, they continued to look for opportunities to usurp and honor themselves instead of honor others. In truth, unless they changed their heart toward those above and beneath them, it was only a matter of time before they rebelled, for an ignoble heart can only bear with true nobility for so long. A selfish heart cannot abide generosity.

"So you see that it is selfishness and self-deceit that caused those kings to make the choice they made. Those things were in their hearts, which explains their actions.

"However, if I choose my actions based on what lies in their hearts then I can only imitate their actions instead of demonstrating the true heart of nobility. And if I do not demonstrate the heart a king should have then I cannot exalt the kings under me into the same nobility and our people will remain in the terrible cycle in which they have lived for centuries.

"Michael, that is why you have no guilt in what has happened, because you honestly had nothing to do with it. I did not choose my actions because of you. I chose them because of what lies in my heart and because I could not act out of what lies in the hearts of those rebellious kings.

"That does not mean you are unworthy of the honor or gifts that I gave you. On the contrary, you very much are worthy of them, and shall only grow more worthy as you see yourself in the same way that I see you."

I shifted uncomfortably in my saddle, not entirely because of the ache growing in my legs. King Fidelas turned to look at me and said, "Michael, when I gave you your sword I said that you will be a great leader and mighty warrior one day. I meant those things or I would not have said them. That is why I chose that particular gift for you, because I know that it will serve you in your future.

"And why did I honor you as I did, exalting you before my entire army?" he asked, reading the question on my mind perfectly. "I honored you because everyone needs to experience what it is like to be honored. The honor that I gave you is to prepare you for your future just as much as the sword I gave you.

"That is why the coming of age feast is so important for all our children, so that they know they are important not only as children, but as men and women. They need to know that their adulthood is celebrated and welcomed, that those who have gone before them are proud of them and filled with anticipation of all the great things they will do.

"When these things are expressed to one who is coming of age, it causes confidence to grow in them. Then, where before there was a child unable to meet their potential, there is now a man or a woman who has the courage to become all that they were made to be."

King Fidelas reined in his horse, coming to a stop at a bend in the trees. The path some time ago had become a small road, only a little wider than two horses or a small cart, but no longer tangled with underbrush and fallen branches. Autumn leaves carpeted the path before us and a quiet fell as the rest of our company paused behind us.

"Michael, do you understand what I've said to you?" the High King asked me.

"I think so, Your Majesty," I replied, "But all of this is so new to me that I'm not sure I really understand it yet."

"You speak with good insight. Understanding will come in time, yet I believe that your heart understands better than your head, Michael. As you let your head believe what you already know to be true then you will fully understand what I am saying."

He paused to let what he said soak in and then spoke again, spurring his horse to continue walking, "Let us put off any further questions for another time. We both already have much to consider, and are now nearing the castle where we must part. There are many other matters concerning our preparation for winter that require my attention."

As he said this we rounded the bend in the trees and quite suddenly came out of the forest into a wide open space, in the center of which rose enormous walls, high and thick, with a second ring of walls beyond that rose even higher.

This must be their stronghold, I thought. *It looks like a crown on top of this hill.* Indeed that is exactly what the castle looked like, with the two mighty walls and the inner buildings and turrets that rose from the very center of it all. The open space we entered looked freshly cleared, as though the forest had grown right up to the wall itself. In fact, there were a few places where men busied themselves with repairing the walls where trees or vines had begun to break them down.

As I looked I noticed that repair work was being done all over the place. Rough scaffolding rose all around the walls, both inner and outer, and crews of both men and women worked diligently to repair or rebuild as was necessary. Most of the base of the wall had been finished and the work left was mainly to build up the tops of the wall so men could defend from there. As it was there was no place to stand.

"There is much work left to do," the High King commented, "and we must all help as we can. You will have to excuse me, Michael, but I must aid in the rebuilding and see how the other hunting parties fared.

"However," he said as we passed under the great archway, "There is someone I want you to meet."

Chapter Six

THE SEER

We passed a giant gate as we entered the archway, with beams like trees bound together with iron. These appeared to be newer than the walls and must have been one of the first repairs done. Looking up as we rode through the gate I saw the portcullis hanging above us – a web of thick, interwoven iron bands – and what looked like cauldrons for oil and small windows from which to shoot arrows.

As we passed through one wall and into the other there was yet another massive gate and another portcullis like the first, and yet another that looked more like a thick wood and iron wall that could be lowered beyond the portcullis. I shuddered to think what it would be like trying to invade this castle.

The walls themselves were at least 50 feet high and 20 feet thick, with about 30 feet in between. I thought, *There's no way an invading army could break through all this. No wonder King Fidelas picked this stronghold for the winter. I wonder what it looked like before they started repairs.*

When we finally exited from the walls we were met by a group of boys who were ready to take our horses. King Fidelas asked the head boy, "Where is Vemrilun?"

"I believe he is overseeing the repairs on the outer wall, Sire, in the west quarter," said the stable boy.

"Thank you, lad," said the High King.

Perilan stepped forward and King Fidelas nodded to him, saying, "Perilan will take you to our seer, Michael. His name is Vemrilun and he is a good man. He may speak to you in ways to which you are not accustomed, but do not let this alarm you; it is simply part of the gift he is to us. I will tell you that I am sending you to him for both our sake and for yours. You mentioned that your previous time with us was like a dream to you, but that you do not know how you arrived here this time. Vemrilun may have answers for you in this matter, and the more we all know the better," he concluded with a smile and a hand on my shoulder.

To Perilan he said, "Vemrilun will know that I sent you. He likely already knows that you are coming and may know why, but tell him anyway of the things I have presently spoken to Michael."

"Yes, Sire!" said Perilan happily. Turning to me he asked, "Shall we go find Vemrilun?"

"Yes," I said to Perilan, and then turning to the High King added, "thank you so much for all you've done, Your Majesty."

"You are very welcome, Michael. Please come find me, if you like, after you have talked with Vemrilun and we will have dinner together again."

The mention of dinner made me realize how much past meal time it must be and I suddenly felt very hungry and thirsty. "That would be wonderful, Your Majesty. I will come find you then. Thank you."

Perilan and I parted ways with the High King and went off to our right toward what I assumed was the west quarter. There was a lot of bustle inside the castle walls, too, as men and woman went to and fro with various bundles in their arms or repairing certain buildings. Remarkably, much of what was in the courtyard was still in fairly good condition, just needing a new thatched roof mostly.

It occurred to me as we walked that the stable boy had said Vemrilun was working on the outer wall, yet we were in the courtyard with the high inner wall between us. I expressed this concern to Perilan, "How are we going to get to Vemrilun when he's on the outer wall and we're in the courtyard?"

"Don't worry," he said, "The inner wall will give us a better view of where he might be and there are ways other than the main gate to get from wall to wall."

He led me to a stair that ran up the inside of the wall and as we neared the top we took care of our steps. Many stones were broken or loose and could easily have slipped from their place. We picked our way to the outer edge of the wall and looked out.

I was amazed at the view of the land that we had from here. Between the height of the wall and the height of the hill you could see for miles and miles around.

"Is that the sea?" I asked Perilan, pointing to the horizon.

"It is," he said, "and we have many ships anchored there. You might notice as well that there are beacon towers between here and there, indeed on all sides of this stronghold. They are manned even now and the lookouts give us advance notice of attack. This is especially important for the harbor because it would be easy for an army to invade and burn our ships before we could bring any defense from here. But with notice from that beacon we can mount an army and ride to the harbor before enemy ships are within bowshot of the bay."

Perilan turned his eyes to the work being done on the outer wall and after a moment of searching said, "Ah, there he is! Follow me."

He turned and walked carefully to a parapet in the wall with a door in its side. The door itself had rotted away long ago, but there were hinges still hanging from the stone. We passed through the doorway and began descending a long, winding stairway back to the base of the wall. Very little light filtered all the way down from the door up above, so we paused to let our eyes adjust to the darkness.

"What are we doing down here?" I asked in a low voice, though I didn't know why.

"You will see, my friend. Can you see me well enough to follow again?" he asked.

"Yes," I answered.

"Then come this way," he said, and led me to the back of the staircase to what looked like another rotted door. He pulled it open with a rattle and paused again.

"When this stronghold is fully restored, the whole base of this tower will become a storehouse for weaponry that is used in defending the wall. Wood for the fires that heat the oil, countless arrows, spare swords, spears, and shields will all be kept in this place. Should an invading army come as far as this tower, they might come in to raid it. In that event, they would likely see a door like this and assume more stores of weapons are in here.

"They will be right, for more weapons will be kept in this room. However, there is something more special about it." He entered the room and bent close to the floor.

"You see, Michael, the whole floor of this closet will be covered with dirt, and even with torchlight it will not be much brighter than it is now in the corners of this small room." Perilan reached out his hand, only a moving shadow in the dark, and lifted a trapdoor in the floor. "This is where we're going, Michael. I'll lead the way, but be sure to follow closely behind me, for it will be very dark."

To say that it *will be* dark implies that someplace could be darker than where we were already. Nevertheless, Perilan was right enough, for at least in the little room I could perceive his form as a shadow, but after passing through the trap door there was no more light than in a cave.

"Where are we?" I whispered.

"We are in a secret tunnel," he replied. "It goes between the outer wall and the inner wall, and it is one of our greater defensive schemes. Tunnels like this one connect the towers in both walls so that if the outer gate is breached the men on the walls are not stranded. Or if we prefer to engage them between the walls then it provides a way of bringing reinforcements to the battle without opening the inner gate. Ideally, we could rain down an endless shower of arrows upon them from both walls and avoid either of these, but the tunnels, so long as they are known only to us, provide us with great opportunities in battle."

I held on to his shoulders so as not to lose him in the dark and we walked slowly. *What I wouldn't give for a cell phone right now*, I thought, remembering all the times I'd seen one used as a flashlight.

Time passes more slowly in the dark, and so it seemed like an eternity until we reached the far end of the tunnel and climbed out into a similar room in the outer wall. We made our way out of the room and up the stairs where we stood for a moment in the doorway, blinking in the bright light.

After our eyes adjusted, we looked out upon the wall and I recognized that this wall had indeed been repaired significantly more than the inner wall. Though the top was still much broken down the scaffolding rose in some places right to the top and it would not be long before they worked to repaired that as well.

Perilan led me across the rubble to a silver haired man who squatted on the broken stones. I heard him speaking very quietly while writing on small pieces of paper. The scratch of his pen on the parchment seemed to go in rhythm with the words that he spoke. When he was done he took the paper, rolled it up, and placed it carefully in the wall so that it would not blow away.

As he put away his writing things he spoke, without turning, and said, "Greetings, Perilan! It appears that the hunt went better than expected today, for you have brought with you something of far greater value than the boar Delthun speared."

I tried to keep my composure as he stood and turned around. *How did he know about all of that,* I thought. *He maybe could have seen us coming into the castle, but that wouldn't have told him that Delthun killed the boar.*

"Michael," he said in a voice both light and firm, "I am glad to finally meet you. I told the High King this morning to be wary in the hunt, for he would be meeting more than game in the forest. I told him that a friend was coming who would do great exploits for this kingdom. Are you that friend?"

"H-h-how do you know who I am?" I stammered, not from fear, but from depth of perplexity.

"I know many things, Michael," he answered, standing and fixing me his penetrating gaze, "but so do you. You just haven't learned to trust yourself yet, but I will help you with that. My name is Vemrilun, and I am the High King's seer."

"I-it's good to meet you," I said, quite intimidated.

Perilan said, "The High King has sent us to find you so that you may speak with Michael about certain experiences he has been having. He believes that your gifting may provide insight that will benefit both Michael and us."

"I suspected as much, though I was not certain of what would be the content of our conversations," Vemrilun said. "Well, Michael, are you ready to talk with me? Perilan, we will stay here. Please inform the High King if you see him that I will join him for dinner."

"With pleasure, my lord," Perilan answered. "Michael, it is good to see you again." With that he turned and made his way back to the door in the ruined tower, leaving me alone with the seer.

Vemrilun's eyes followed him through the door and lingered there, as though he was watching something there that I could not see. He stood tall and straight on the wall, thin of frame, yet I knew that he must be quick and strong. His dress was like all the men in this Kingdom, though more brightly colored, and he had a silver beard that curled close to his pointed chin.

At last he turned to me again and said, "The High King has sent you to me so that I may answer your questions, and in so doing, answer some of his as well. You need not fear me, Michael, for I know you will be faithful to us; it is not in your heart to be otherwise.

"There is, however, some mystery about your seemingly random appearances with us, and understanding that mystery will help us to know how to best serve you in accomplishing your purpose with us.

"So, Michael, why are you here?" he concluded abruptly, sitting down.

I was not ready for that question, especially considering that I hoped talking with Vemrilun would help me to answer it. I sat down next to him thinking, *I don't know why I'm here. I don't even know where here is or how I got here.*

Shaking off these thoughts, I collected myself for a moment before asking, "By 'here,' do you mean here in Cotheria or here on this wall?"

Vemrilun answered, "Michael, you have asked a good question. Let us address the latter half of it first. Why are you on this wall?"

"I am on this wall because King Fidelas sent me to you," I said.

"Yes, and why did King Fidelas send you to me?" he asked.

"He sent me to you so that you could help me understand what I've been experiencing."

"Ah! So we are getting to something real now. What are these experiences you have been having that are so mysterious that no one can help you but me?"

I looked and could tell from his smile that he was using some lighthearted humor. Whether he intended for it or not, his teasing put me at ease in trying to answer him.

Still feeling strange about my dream, I took a deep breath and told him about what had happened the last time I was here, from my perspective, making sure to note how much I liked the maps that he had made.

I concluded the story and he looked at me silently. After a brief moment of consideration he asked me, "What happened then? Is that truly the end of your story?"

"I don't quite understand," I said. "That was the end of my dream. Are you asking about what happened after I woke up?"

"Yes," he said, "what happened after you woke up."

"Well," I started, "I missed my school bus because I couldn't find my backpack or my school books. My dad took me to school and I told him about my dream. I told a teacher about my dream, too, and they both told me that they thought it meant I must be very special to get a dream like that."

My mind scanned through my whole day, highlighting anything that seemed important, and then it hit me. The sword! Of course there was something more to tell Vemrilun.

"Oh!" I said, "There was something important that happened! See, my parents had promised to take me shopping for a special birthday present and they actually wanted it to be a coming of age gift, just like here in my dream. And when I told them about my dream they liked the idea of giving me a sword, so they took me to get one that night, the night after I had my dream.

"When we got to the store we looked around at all the swords, and there, right in the middle of the store, was the sword that King Fidelas gave me. The exact same sword! This sword," I said, pointing to it at my side.

He looked at my sword with recognition in his eyes and I saw that this filled in much of the puzzle for him. "I knew the High King gave you that sword," he said, "yet it is an entirely different thing for it to appear in your world as well. Was there any explanation for how it came to be in the store?"

"No," I said. "The manager who does all the ordering was working that night and told us that he'd never seen that sword in his life; he had no idea how it got there. "

"What happened in the store?" Vemrilun asked.

"Um, well, the store manager didn't want to sell us the sword, but my dad kinda just didn't give him another option. They haggled over a price and my dad bought it for me. We went home and looked at it until we went to bed."

"So you now possess this sword in both your world and ours?" he asked.

"Yes," I said.

"Now about this morning; do you know how you got here today?" he asked.

"No, I have no idea how I got here today," I said.

"Tell me what you were doing when you found yourself here," he said.

I shrugged and said, "I was just picking apples at an orchard with my family and a friend of mine. I thought that maybe if I walked through the trees to the next row over that I would find some better apples, but when I came to the other side of the trees I found myself in a dense forest.

"I thought that maybe I'd somehow been on the edge of the orchard and accidentally walked out of it while I wasn't paying attention, but when I turned around I couldn't see any apple trees. My friend had been following me, but he wasn't there. I retraced my steps for about twenty feet and still didn't find anything. I called out for my dad and mom, but they didn't answer.

"Finally, I heard something move in the woods, but then the thing came crashing through the trees right at me and I ran. It turned out to be the boar with a whole hunting party right behind him. That's when I met the High King in the woods and joined his party."

"I see," he said. "So in entering into this world today you never fell asleep, so that it seems as though the two worlds are the same world, yet they are not. Does that describe what you are experiencing?"

"Yes, that's it exactly," I said. "And that's the hardest thing for me right now because I don't know what's real." The words left my mouth and I became afraid, for I had done what I meant not to do: imply that this world might not be real and offend anyone who belonged to the unreal world.

Vemrilun perceived my heart exactly and said, "You have no reason to be afraid, Michael, for I understand what you are saying. How do you know what is real when you have an experience like this one? In some ways the less logical experience feels more real than the life you grew up with, yet so much of your life is anchored in that place that you cannot simply leave it behind as fantasy. I know that realm well, for that is the realm of a seer.

"Michael, I will explain to you what will be most helpful to you now, though I am sure we will speak again on this matter.

"First, the matter of what is real. We live in the realm of the natural world, the place of physical things that we experience with our senses, but there are other realms around us that are beyond our normal ability to experience. These realms are not closed to anyone, but different people interact with them in different ways. Often this is done in complete ignorance as people engage in things of greater significance than they realize or take credit for things with which they honestly had very little to do.

"The gift a seer possesses allows him at times to cross right into those realms that are somewhere beyond the natural, sometimes seeing literally what is happening in those realms and sometimes seeing only what some divine hand desires to show them. To help make this explanation easier, I will use the word 'revelation' to describe anything a seer perceives from other realms.

"Revelation can come from more than one source, so a seer must be discerning to know which source is speaking, for there are both good and evil givers of revelation. The good source gives revelation to empower those he has gifted so that they may know him and become a blessing to all mankind. The evil source uses his form of revelation to manipulate and control, to cause division and bring darkness upon the people, but he is crafty and can disguise himself well when it suits his purposes."

"How do you know which one is talking to you?" I asked.

"That is a very good question, Michael," Vemrilun said. "Let me use what has happened among the kings of Cotheria to illustrate.

"These kings have heard the voice of the one who gives evil revelation, though they do not realize it. He whispered in their ears words of jealousy and envy and pride. He gave false revelation to them, teaching them that they deserved greatness and showing them a vision of gain to dazzle their eyes against the true riches offered to them.

"Contrast this revelation with that possessed by King Fidelas, who so exudes goodness that he produces it in those who have gathered to him. He has seen a vision of true nobility and become convinced that the sole purpose of his position is to exalt those below him.

"This includes defending them, certainly, which is why he goes to war, but he primarily concerns himself with teaching his kings how to honor their subjects so that they become people of the highest quality and greatest productivity. Note, Michael, that the productivity is a byproduct of the quality of the people, that as people become truly who they were made to be they will contribute more to both themselves and those around them.

"So you can tell which source of revelation you are hearing by the kind of revelation that you receive. If what you hear speaks to you of how great you are in a way that enables you to help others then it is almost certainly the good source. But if what you hear speaks to you of how great you are in a way that alienates you from others and makes you jealous of them when they receive honor then you have certainly heard from the evil source."

The sun was getting low in the sky, shining the last yellow rays of the day. Soon it would set into the western sea, far off in the distance. Vemrilun remained silent for a moment, letting me think, and finally asked me, "Does that help you understand?"

"I'm pretty sure I understand about the whole good and evil sources of revelation thing," I said, "but I still don't understand how to know what's real."

"Ah! I never did finish that point, did I?" he laughed. "Well, as I said, sometimes a seer will see exactly what is happening in the other realms, seeing the actual beings who live in those realms who are the good and evil givers of revelation and their servants. In this case a seer is seeing something that is truly *real* even though it is not *natural*.

"Sometimes, however, the revelation given to a seer is not real in itself, but rather it is something that represents values the source wants to communicate. The important reality in this case is the lesson being taught, for the revelation is not to entertain the seer, but to train him according to the values held by the one giving the revelation.

"My dreams and visions are a classroom for my life. What matters most is not what is real in them, but what I learn from them, for what I learn will become real within me, and through me can become real in the natural world. What I see may be real, but that does not specifically help me know why I am seeing it. Does that make sense?"

"I think so," I said. "What you're saying is that, from my perspective, it doesn't matter whether what I see and experience here is real or not, the only thing that matters is what I learn while I'm here so that I can apply it in my normal life."

"Correct, or mostly correct at least," he replied. "There is some importance in knowing whether what you see is real or not, but I think that when it truly matters then you will be given grace to know.

"You are here for a purpose. The Divine Hand has moved you here and is moving things around you so that he may teach you something important. How he teaches you is not nearly as important as what he teaches you – particularly what he teaches you about himself – but the lessons you learn are vastly more important than the world in which you learn them."

"Okay, I think I understand," I said, trying to wrap my mind around what Vemrilun said. This conversation would have seemed insane to me only a few days before, but my experiences were undeniable and I was glad to have some explanation for them.

"Good," he said. "The second thing I will explain to you, then, is about your experiences. You are right about your first time here; it was a dream, and you need ask no more questions about it in that way. It was a dream, a very special dream, but nothing more than that. Dreams are very significant, however, and are not to be ignored. Much is spoken to us in our dreams that can help shape our lives for good if we will learn to listen and interpret what we hear.

"But what you are experiencing right now is not a dream; it is an open vision. There are other kinds of visions that do not seem so real. These might feel like just imagination or they might overlap with your normal world in some way, but an open vision is like a world of its own, as though you were having the most vivid dream you can imagine while you are yet wide awake.

"Open visions are rare, and very important because of that. Sometimes the Divine Hand whispers and we learn to notice the whisper, but sometimes he shouts when he is really saying something important. An open vision is never a whisper," he said laughing and putting his hand on my knee.

I laughed with him and it felt like the first warm day of spring. I had been so serious since I had my dream that it was refreshing to laugh.

The sun was touching the horizon now, its red light shining across the island. The sound of hammers working on the wall had slowed in the dimming light and now voices called out to one another in greeting below us. It was clear that friends were meeting after a hard day's work and happily going together to a well-earned dinner.

"We must soon join them, Michael," Vemrilun said, "but let me say just a few things more."

I nodded to indicate that I was listening and he said, "Look out across the land. Tell me what you see."

Lifting up my eyes from the castle wall I really looked at my surroundings for the first time. "I see a whole land," I said. "I see trees and I hear the birds that live in them. I see other birds flying in the sky to warmer climates for the winter. I see the sun setting over the ocean and the ships in the harbor. I see the guard towers and I see the castle."

I paused to find something else that I saw, but Vemrilun stopped me. "That's enough," he said; "you've done well.

"I point these things out to you so that you will notice that none of them exist in your world. It is not a small thing that you are seeing all this right now. All of it is important, so as long or often as you are here keep your eyes open to whatever you might see.

"There is a whole world around you, and whenever something ordinary becomes extraordinary for a moment then take notice, because in that moment you are to learn some of why you are here.

"Also, I would say to you that what you have told me of your experiences reveals much to me, particularly about your sword. That part is not important for you right now, I think, for it will be revealed in time.

"What I want you to know is that you are a seer, or at the least you are having experiences such as seers have. This is a gift and not a curse. There is nothing wrong with you. Rather, there is something very right with you, for the Divine Hand sees that he can trust you with whatever he will show you through these dreams and visions.

"It is true that this gift is marked by unusual experiences that could potentially alienate you from people you care about, but I simply advise you to pass on the lessons you learn through your experiences and keep more private how you learned them. There is nothing wrong with speaking of what you see, but it may preserve your relationships more if you keep it to yourself."

These last words he said with a wry smile and a depth in his expression by which I knew that he had learned these things personally. The sun was getting very low now and dusk was settling upon the land. Vemrilun said, "We must get down from this wall while there is light to see or we may have to spend the night here."

With that he stood quickly and gathered his things, helping me to my feet, and speedily finding his way over the rubble back to the tower door.

It was even darker in the tower than it had been before, so we slowly made our way down the steps and along the wall to the inner doorway that led to the tunnel. We entered the storage room under the stairs and Vemrilun held the trap door for me, saying, "I will be right behind you. The tunnel is straight and has no bends or corners so you will easily find your way to the other side."

"Okay," I said hesitantly. I was nervous to go through the dark tunnel first, but had little choice and started making my way.

I walked straight for what seemed like a much farther distance than when I had gone through it before. Brushing away fear, I thought, *It always seems longer on the way back, and distances and times are tricky when it's this dark. The far wall must be just ahead of me.*

Continuing on a few more steps I tripped on something in the ground and fell. Reaching down toward my feet I felt it and realized that it was a tree root. *That's strange,* I thought, *how could there be a tree root right in the middle of the tunnel? They must have just not cleared it yet in their repairs.*

Getting back on my feet I was going to begin walking again, but as I stood up something with dozens of points struck my head. "Ouch!" I shouted and recoiled from whatever I had touched.

Stupid roots, they're even in the ceiling! I stood up again, this time more carefully, with my hand above me to feel what was there so I did not hit my head on it again. When my hand touched it I pulled it back again and said, "That's not tree roots, not unless roots have leaves!" and I noticed the sound of my voice. It did not sound like I was in a tunnel; there was no echo. It sounded like I was out in the open.

I looked around me for some indication of where I might be and saw a light growing somewhere off to my right side. *I have no idea what's going on, but there's nothing else to do,* I said to myself and began making way toward the light.

I pressed my way through more trees, over roots and fallen logs, under branches, just trying to get to the light. I stopped suddenly, the way blocked by a giant hedge. The light clearly got brighter on the other side of the hedge, but I could not see a way through or around it.

Wait! I've got a sword! I thought with excitement and unsheathed my blade. It was the perfect weight for me to handle and easily cut away the hedge as I swung, so after only a few strokes I was already well into it. A few strokes more and I was through to the other side.

Blundering into the light I caught myself from falling and stood there blinking from the brightness. The sound rose around me and I started as I recognized it, for right in front of me was my family, happily hunting for the best apples.

Chapter Seven
Job on the Rocks

I HAD THAT FEELING YOU SOMETIMES HAVE when you go to a movie theater and somehow during the movie you forget what day, time, or even season it is, and you become completely disoriented.

It was worse than that, actually, because at least a movie is not real. A movie cannot swallow you up so completely that you live in it for a time – who knows how long – and then spit you back out as though nothing ever happened, leaving you standing in the theater delirious from the experience and feeling lost in your own world.

That is what it was like as I stood there in the sunshine, watching my family run around from tree to tree like a bunch of bumblebees in a field of flowers. I felt alienated from them and from the apple picking that I had looked forward to so much.

I wanted to be one of those bumblebees, excitedly buzzing around looking for the best apples, but my flight took me into another world. Now I was back, quite abruptly, and was starting to resent the experience no matter how special it said I was.

Someone bumped into me from behind and said, "Hey, don't stop there! I need room to get out from under the tree." It was Austin. I moved to the side and blandly said, "Sorry."

Austin and I looked at one another. He was smiling, apparently enjoying our trip to the orchard as much as I usually do. I, on the other hand, had lost all interest in picking apples, or in being with other people for that matter. I wanted to be alone more than anything, and groaned knowing how impossible that was at that moment. All I could do was stand there and stare at him, dumbfounded as to what I could say.

"Dude, you okay?" he asked.

I answered coldly, "No, I'm not."

"What's wrong?"

Unable to keep looking him in the eye, I stared at the ground as adrenaline swept through my body. Thoughts raced through my mind and I considered how to answer Austin. Just as I opened my mouth to say something, we were interrupted.

"What're you standing around for, guys? Let's find some more apples!" It was my dad, and he had three bags of apples already in his hands.

"We're only going to get a couple more bags," he said, "So you'd better hurry if you want to keep up!" He ducked back under the tree to the row where my sister and brother were picking apples.

I said to Austin, "I don't know, but let's keep up with everyone else." I ran after them, not caring if Austin followed or not, nervous to get too far away from my family lest I disappear into another vision.

My attempts at picking apples were half-hearted at best and in the end I only filled about half of my bag. It looks bad when your seven year old sister out-picks you at all. It looks really bad when she picks three times more apples than you, especially when she can only reach the lowest branches of the trees.

We got back on the tractor and headed to other parts of the orchard for baking apples and eventually back to the barn/store/sample area. The apple laden crowd disembarked from the trailer and we shuffled our way past them to where we could purchase some treats.

I ordered my favorite, the gooey caramel apple fritter, and coupled it with some hot chocolate. Dad purchased various other apple treats for Austin and the rest of my family and we sat down to eat. They were all in high spirits, laughing and teasing each other about their various adventures from picking the apples. Austin kept shooting questioning glances at me, but there was no way I would answer him there.

We finished our treats and went to buy our apples. As we piled into the van to go home, Austin quickly sat down next to me in the backseat. He waited until we were on the highway to talk, and then asked me, "Mikey, what is going on?"

Shaking my head, I said, "I really don't know, Austin. Something weird happened in there; I don't know how to explain it. Just give me some time to think."

Austin looked hard at me, as though considering whether to leave me along or not, but apparently decided to honor my request. He let the issue go and we stayed quiet the whole way home.

I stared out the window, looking at the fall colors that covered the bluffs east of the highway and thinking about what had happened that morning.

Not even awake for four hours yet and I've already had more than a whole day! What is happening to me? Was Vemrilun right? Did I have a vision, given to me by some Divine Hand who's trying to teach me something? Why me? Why now? Why couldn't these lessons have waited until I'm older or something. Dad would do a lot better with this than me. Or Mr. Gustafson, he seemed to think the whole dream thing was pretty cool and important. This should be happening to them, not to me.

The more I thought about it, the more alone I felt and the more I resented what had happened. *I didn't ask for this! I just wanted a normal birthday. What changed that all of a sudden this is happening to me?*

Spiraling deeper into resentment I finally gave up trying to figure it all out. I tried to find something else to think about, but nothing else would stick.

When we arrived home I helped with a couple bags of apples and then ran off to my room. I had not been there long, lying on my bed with my sword, trying to keep the tears from rolling down my cheeks, when there was a knock at my door and the sound of the door softly opening and closing.

I looked up expecting to see Austin, but I was wrong. It was my mom.

"You okay, honey?" she asked as she walked to my bed.

"I'm fine," I said, turning around again, not wanting to talk about it.

"You don't look like you're fine," she said. "You were so excited to go apple picking this morning and then you barely picked any. And you were quiet the whole time that we were together after picking apples. What's wrong?"

She was sitting next to me on the bed now, scratching my back the way moms do. "I don't know. Something happened while we were picking the apples."

Her scratching never slowed. She just stayed quiet, waiting for me to go on.

"I had another dream or something," I finally said.

"Last night? You had another dream?" she asked calmly.

"No, not last night; while we were picking apples. I just walked into another row of trees and all of a sudden I wasn't in the orchard anymore. I was in a forest and was nearly run down by a boar that the High King from my dream was hunting. He took me to his castle and I talked with him and with his seer, who told me I was having an open vision given to me by some 'Divine Hand' that was supposed to teach me something. I was going back with him to have dinner with the men when I was suddenly in a forest again. It was really dark and all I could see was some light behind a giant bush. I used my sword to cut through it and was all of a sudden back in the orchard again as though nothing had ever happened.

"I hate this, Mom. I don't know what's happening or why it's happening to me. I feel like I'm going crazy or something."

"You're not going crazy, honey," Mom said, doing her best to comfort me.

"Then why am I seeing things that aren't there?" I snapped.

The scratching stopped on my back and my mom said, "Honey, look at me."

I rolled over and sat up to face her. She lifted my chin so that I was looking in her eyes. "Michael, I don't know why this is happening to you, but I know you're not crazy. There are a lot of things that happen in this world that we can't explain, but you know what?"

She waited until she saw that I was really listening and said, "It seems like your dreams and visions are trying to explain themselves to you and you should maybe just trust them."

I pulled away from her in disgust at her suggestion. "What?" I asked.

"Michael," she said, "something is happening to make you have those dreams or visions or whatever they are. If *we* can't explain it without calling you crazy, but the people you see in that place can explain it to you, then I think it's worth trusting them. If someone is giving these things to you to teach you something then maybe you should accept what you are taught while you're in that place."

"But what if I don't want to? What if I just want them to go away so I can be normal again?"

"Honey," she said soothingly, "that just wouldn't be like you to run away from something like that."

"But what do I do?" I asked. "If I can't even go to sleep or pick apples without maybe getting abducted into another world then I'm scared to do anything because I don't want to disappear there again."

"You can't live your life in fear, Michael. The only way you grow is if you keep going even when things are hard. You never know when a teacher at school might give you a pop-quiz, but that doesn't keep you from going to school, does it? You don't live in fear of a pop-quiz, right?"

"No," I admitted.

"Well, then you shouldn't live in fear of this either," she said.

"But this is different, Mom!" I protested.

"Tell you what," she said, "if we're going to trust these things that you're getting, these dreams and visions, and you're getting them from a 'Divine Hand,' then why don't you ask him why he's giving them to you and see whether he says anything?"

I couldn't think of anything to say to that. I mean, if we were going to trust the revelation that I was getting, to use Vemrilun's word, then it made sense to just ask why this was happening to me.

"Besides," Mom said, "it might be a good test to see how real these things are. If you ask and someone hears you and responds, well, that's pretty good evidence that you can trust what they're showing you. But if you ask and you don't get any kind of response, that tells us a few things the other way. It's a win-win situation for you."

I could not argue with her anymore. She was right; I really couldn't lose if I would just ask. It might be crazy, but I could pretend to be crazy for a little bit if it might prove that I wasn't crazy for real.

"Alright, Mom, I'll do it, but I think I'd like to do it on my own if that's okay."

"That's totally okay. I'll leave you alone up here for a little bit. Then you can come downstairs for some lunch and a bit more time with Austin before we take him home this afternoon." She smiled comfortingly as she walked out the door and closed it behind her.

I sat there for a moment, not sure what exactly to do next. I had never tried to talk to a "Divine Hand" before. Where was he? Did it matter which direction I faced? Did he even speak English?

"Well," I said to myself, "I guess if he can take me to a whole other world right in the middle of an apple orchard, and he can make the people of that world speak English even when they don't write it, then it probably doesn't matter what I do. He'll just understand me anyway – if he's there at all."

I slid off my bed – taking my sword with me, thinking that it might be kind of important since it had sort of come from that other world – and thought for a second what to do.

Shrugging my shoulders and feeling rather silly, I knelt on my floor with the sword in front of me as a knight might do before his king. It felt more real to me that way, rather than simply talking to the air.

Lifting up my head I spoke whatever came to mind, "Dear Divine Hand – "

Geez, that sounded stupid.

"I don't know exactly what to say. If you can hear me, I'm the one you gave that dream and that vision to. And, well, it's really kinda weird and I don't know what to do with them. I feel like I'm going crazy and I'd like them to stop if I don't know what they're for.

"But if you're there, and you really are giving these things to me, I'm asking that you would just tell me what they're for and why you picked me. Why me? What for? What are you trying to teach me?

"I'm really nervous to say this, but I just feel like I should for some reason, so here goes – I give you permission to give me the answer at any time. Whatever you want to do, you can do it. However you want to answer me, it's okay; just please answer these questions for me, because I feel like I'm going crazy.

"Ok, well, um…Thanks. I guess I'll probably talk with you later."

It felt like such an anticlimactic end to my attempted conversation with the "Divine Hand" that I shook my head as I stood up, thinking how stupid I must be to try something like this.

I put my sword away and went downstairs to join everyone else. We ate a delicious lunch, and then Austin and I left the others peeling and slicing apples.

Taking a football outside to play catch, we were alone together for the first time since the orchard. Austin wasted no time, asking, "So what in the world is going on?"

I tossed the ball to him and answered, "I don't really know. I mean, something crazy has been happening to me, but I don't know what it is. I don't really want to talk about it."

"But what happened?" he pressed. "You were all happy this morning, but then all of a sudden you got really mad and quiet when we were picking apples. And last night, you were your normal self, too, until you saw your sword at the mall and then you freaked out."

"I didn't freak out," I objected.

"Well, you nearly cried about it. Most people don't cry about their birthday presents unless they don't get any," he retorted, throwing the ball to me harder than normal.

"I told you, something crazy was going on; I just don't want to talk about it, alright?" I said, getting a little defensive.

"Right, whatever," he said as he caught the ball. "I'll just leave you alone then. Whenever you feel like talking to your best friend, though, just, you know, remember me, okay?"

"Dude, it has nothing to do with us being best friends," I shot back. "It's just, you wouldn't understand."

"Oh, I get it. I'm the dumb kid of some dumb parents who can't get a job, so I can't understand what you're going through. I see how it is. Thanks, Michael."

"What? Where did that come from? It has nothing to do with your parents, or your dad's job issues, or anything like that. It's that I don't think anyone could understand what's been happening to me. I mean, I don't understand it yet, so I don't even know how to talk about it."

"Well, okay. Whatever," he said, halfheartedly tossing the football back to me; it hit the ground several feet in front of me. "I think I'm done playing catch."

He walked off toward the house without another word. Too angry to care, I picked up the ball and followed him in. When I came through the door he was already talking to my parents about getting a ride home.

"Um, well, sure we can give you a ride home right now," my dad said. "Are you guys done playing already? You weren't out there very long."

"Yeah, we're done. My parents don't like when I stay too long past lunchtime anyway, and we had a late lunch," he answered. All of us knew from years of me playing with Austin that this was not true.

"Well, okay then," Dad said without arguing. "Just go grab your things and I'll take you home right now if you like."

"Thanks, Mr. Nyquist; that'd be great." He turned to go to my room without so much as looking at me.

I wrestled with what to do. Part of me wanted to fight with him until he realized how stupid he was being and another part of me wanted to stay with my family and let him go without speaking to him. *Fine,* I thought, *if he doesn't want to talk through things or try to understand how hard all this might be for me, then let him run off and not talk to me.*

In the end, though, I knew that I should do something if I valued our friendship. I did not see a good future there if both of us pulled away, so I followed him upstairs. He was almost done packing his things as I came to my door. Not knowing what to say, I stood there quietly, awkwardly staring at him as he stuffed his things quickly back into his bag.

Finally looking at me when he was done, he opened his mouth as though we were going to say something, but stopped. He only shook his head angrily and then picked up his things, shoving his way past me as he walked out the door.

Again, I slowly followed him back downstairs and said goodbye as he left. He returned my goodbye and walked out the door ahead of my dad.

"What was all that about?" Mom asked. "Did something happen while you were outside?"

"I don't really know," I answered. "He asked what had happened at the orchard. I said that I didn't want to talk about it, and all of a sudden he flipped out, like I was keeping things from him because his dad doesn't have a job or something. Then he walked off and wouldn't talk to me anymore."

Mom stood silently in the kitchen for a moment, weighing how I was doing. She came near and asked, "You want a hug?"

I didn't want to admit it, maybe, but yes, I did want a hug. I leaned into her shoulder and heaved a giant sigh.

"Mom, I didn't ask for these things to happen to me," I whispered, trying not to cry or let my siblings hear. "I didn't do anything to get them. I don't understand them. And now Austin's not talking to me just because I don't want to talk to him about it. If it was happening to him then he wouldn't want to talk to me about it either!"

"I know, honey," she said, "I know. You didn't do anything to get these things, and maybe they'll just go away now. Whatever happens with what you've been going through, I'm sure that Austin will calm down and be his normal self when you see him at school."

"Yeah," I said, feeling somewhat comforted. "I hope so, anyway."

"Why don't you join us getting the apples ready to bake; it'll take your mind off of everything else," she suggested.

I nodded and pulled away from her hug, wiping my nose a little with my sleeve.

"Alright, c'mon then," she said, beckoning me to follow her with a nod and a smile. She put me to work next to Stevie and Amy, cutting apples into small pieces to boil for applesauce.

As the day went on, I was glad for the chance to work quietly with my family, but my heart felt tortured with anxiety over both Austin and my strange experiences. Paranoia filled my mind. I kept expecting to disappear into a vision or thought maybe the High King would ride his horse through our kitchen window and slice some apples with his sword. Or maybe helpful Perilan would come with a tray of something special to drink and then I would have to talk with him in front of my whole family.

For all my fears and expectations, nothing happened the rest of the day, or the day after that either. We had a great time baking as a family and enjoyed wonderful apple pie for dessert after dinner. Our Sunday night ended the way it always does and we all went to bed on time to be ready for school and work the next day.

It was with some disappointment that I went to bed that night, wondering if my prayer of sorts had not worked or if the "Divine Hand" just had not heard me, did not care, or whatever. I really expected that he would have answered me by then.

In a way, though, I was glad he had not, since it maybe meant I could be normal again. *Better not get your hopes up too high, there, Michael,* I thought. *You'll probably have another dream as soon as you fall asleep.*

That is what I thought, but nothing disturbed my sleep all night long. I woke up at 6:00 am with my alarm and it felt like I had just put my head on my pillow as though no time had passed at all.

I went to school and, ironically, had a couple pop-quizzes – a terrible thing for a teacher to do on a Monday – but no visions interrupting my classes. On top of that, while Austin was not exactly enthusiastic around me, he did talk to me. I began to hope that those things were gone for good and I was back to normal, and that my life might be able to return to normal, too.

My spirits were high as I came home. Even homework sounded wonderful to me because it was normal and I was growing confident that I might be able to just expect normal again. It did not take me long to finish my regular assignments, but since I was enjoying my homework so much I decided to keep going and work on some projects that I soon had coming due.

I was sitting in the office on the computer when Dad came home from work and gave a, "Hi, Love! Boy, is it good to see you," greeting to my mom.

She came out of the kitchen to welcome him home and said, "That was a little more enthusiastic than normal, did you have a rough day?"

"Oh, just the same as it's been," Dad said, "Today was just particularly heavy with it."

"Hang in there, honey," she said, "You just keep doing the right thing and they'll come along eventually."

"Thanks, hon. I love you," Dad said. "I'm going to go change."

He headed upstairs like he always does when he gets home from work. When he came back downstairs he saw me in the office and came in to say hi to me.

"Hey, Michael! What'cha working on there?" he asked.

"Oh, just a project for school," I said. "Mr. Gustafson gave us a list of 'heroes in history' and we're supposed to pick one and write a paper on what made them a hero."

"That sounds like a good project," Dad said. "Who'd you pick?"

"Well, I was one of the last to get to pick, so the only ones left were ones I didn't know anything about. I picked Mother Theresa," I said.

"Really, Mother Theresa? I think I like Mr. Gustafson if he put her on a list of heroes in history. You'll have to tell me more about what you write as you get into it."

"Ok, Dad, I will," I said as he left to go help Mom with dinner.

As I sat there I thought of what he had said to my mom when he came in the door about how things were rough at work. I had not ever heard him talk like that. I wanted to know what he was talking about, so not long after we sat down for dinner I asked him.

"Dad, I heard you talking with Mom about your work when you came home. What's going on?" I asked rather bluntly.

Dad stopped mid-bite, putting his fork down on his plate. He was silent for a moment and it made everyone else quiet down, too. Finally, he took a drink of water and said, "Well, Michael, it's kind of hard to explain."

He exchanged looks with my mom before he kept going, but then asked, "Do you know what I do at work, Michael?"

"Um, not really, I don't think. No," I answered.

"Well, my title is Director of Retail Management Training, and that means that I'm responsible for the training of all the district and store managers in the retail side of the company. My job is to make sure that they have everything they need to manage their store or district well according to the management philosophy of our company.

"My boss is the Senior Director of Human Resources. He is over all the different aspects of HR – human resources – for the whole company, including payroll, benefits, and management training for both our corporate headquarters and our retail locations. His position gives him the authority to choose whatever management philosophy he wants for the whole company. Because I train the managers, I am supposed to use that philosophy when I do my job, training the local level managers to do the same. Does that much make sense?"

"What's a philosophy?" Amy asked.

"Good question," Dad said. "A philosophy is sort of a way of thinking about something. 'Management' means to take care of what we have by leading a staff and being responsible for all the details under our authority. So when I talk about a management philosophy, I'm talking about what different people believe is the best way to lead the people and take care of the details given to us by the company. Does that help?"

"Yeah, that makes sense," I said, putting a bite of chicken in my mouth.

"Alright," Dad continued, "well, sometimes it can be tough at my work because my boss has a very different management philosophy than I do. We have different opinions of how to best lead a staff, in particular.

"That means that I'm in a hard place at work right now because my boss can tell me to do pretty much whatever he wants to, so far as it concerns the company, and I'm supposed to do it. But what he wants me to do as I train the managers, teaching them to do the same, just isn't a good way to treat people, which also means it would be very bad for the business."

"What do you mean?" I asked.

"Oh, I just mean that if we don't treat the people who work in the company well then we'll start having some serious problems. If we don't treat our employees well then we might start losing them, which means lots of wasted time hiring and training new ones, which also means having an inexperienced staff in our stores that we can't always depend upon. If we can't depend on our staff then neither can the customer. If the customer isn't confident in the staff we have in our stores then they won't shop there as often. And, of course, if customers don't shop as often in our stores then the company doesn't make as much money.

"Or what might happen if we don't treat our staff well, just in case they do stick with us, is they probably will develop a poor attitude toward work. Then when they come to work, they'll complain. Or maybe they'll just pick up the bad management philosophy that's caused them to be treated poorly and they'll treat each other or the customer the same way. In either case our stores become a negative place to be, which isn't good for the customer experience. If a customer doesn't have a good experience in our stores then they won't come back.

"What would probably happen in reality is a mix of these two options, but the result is the same – the company loses money, which means they can't afford to pay all the people they have and they have to shrink the size of the company, even laying off some of our employees or closing some of the stores.

"All of these things are bad for our company, and all of them stem from our management philosophy. So I have a very important job, because I help to keep all of these things from happening. But at the same time I'm in a hard place, because my boss wants me to train people to manage in a way that just doesn't treat people right."

The room was quiet for a moment; the only sound was the clinking of silverware on plates.

"Are you going to lose your job, Dad?" I asked.

My mom stiffened and dad got a sad look in his eyes. He heaved a slow sigh and said, "You're thinking of Austin's dad, aren't you, Michael?"

Looking away, I said, "Yeah, I'm thinking of him, but there are a lot of people losing their jobs right now."

"I know, son; there are a lot of people out of work right now, but I don't think I'll become one of them. I really don't think so, but yes, it is possible. Right now I just have to be very careful in how I relate to my boss. I'm working to prove my philosophy to be the better one by using it when I talk to him. I encourage him and tell him the things he's doing well, even when those things are small. I thank him for the good things he does for me and point out the good parts of his character.

"He really seems to appreciate all those things, so in that way he likes me, but he doesn't understand what I'm doing. He just thinks I'm being nice. But as my department of HR continues to perform above average I'm confident that he'll see the benefit of my philosophy and come around."

"But what if he doesn't?" I asked. "Or what if he doesn't give you enough time to show your department's performance? What if he fires you before then because you aren't doing what he wants you to do?"

"Then he fires me and loses the chance to learn something better than he's using now, which would be unfortunate for both himself and the company. There's really nothing more I can do about that than what I'm doing now. I honor him the best that I can because of his position and follow his instructions as much as I can without sacrificing what I know to be right. But if doing the right thing means that I lose my job then I have to be okay with that and trust that there's something better out there for me."

"But –" I started in again, but my mom interrupted me.

"Now, Michael, you know your dad," she said, "and he's not going to lose his job. He's been with that company for a long time and they know him very well. Staying faithful to one job has a lot of benefits, and job security is one of them. A company isn't nearly as likely to ask you to leave if you've worked well for them for a long time."

"But," I tried a second time and Mom stopped me again.

"Michael, let's just finish our dinner, eh? There's nothing to be worried about and we'll let you know what you need to know if something important happens."

I looked at Steve and Amy and saw the same fear I felt written on their faces. Like my mom said, I know my dad, and I had never seen him look as sad and stressed out as he did in that moment. However, the conversation was obviously over and I would have to be content for the time being.

I waited until I was just going to bed and saw him walk past my room by himself. *This is my chance,* I thought. *I bet he'll talk to me if Mom's not around.*

"Hey, Dad!" I called.

He turned around in the hallway and poked his head in my door. "What's up, Michael?"

"Can you come talk to me for just a second, please?" I asked.

He took a couple steps into my room and asked, "Is this about my work?"

"Um, yeah," I said sheepishly, adding quickly while I could, "but it's just that I know there must be more going on than you said at the table because I've never seen you look so worried before and I'd feel better knowing the whole truth than being given some half fake answer that's supposed to comfort me."

"Michael, you're mom and I didn't lie to you; we don't think I will lose my job. Sometimes, though, there are just things that are better for moms and dads to keep to themselves. I'm sorry about that, but it's true, though I know it doesn't make you feel any better about it."

"Dad," I pleaded, "You said that I'm a man now. Please talk to me like I'm a man."

My dad stopped now; I had hit the mark. He looked at me steadily, searching my eyes as though he were gauging whether I was truly ready. I looked back at him, trying to look as grown up as I could.

Finally, he said with a sigh, "You're right, Michael. I said you're a man now, and it's true. I'll tell you more about what's going on."

I sat up eagerly as he sat down on my bed. Taking a deep breath, he said, "Son, there's more going on at work than just what's happening with my boss. Like I said, I'm the Director of Retail Management Training, in charge of training all the district and store level managers in the retail side of our company. That gives me a very big and important job, but there are three other directors who report to my boss.

"Those three people are over other equally important aspects of Human Resources in our company – payroll, benefits, and corporate management training. Does that make sense so far?"

As far as I understand what those three things mean, I thought, but said, "Yes."

"Good, well, the trouble I'm having at work is coming more from the three other directors than from my boss. You see, they've all kind of gathered around the one who's in charge of training the corporate managers. She's relatively new, doesn't like me, and fully embraces our boss' management philosophy.

"The problem is that the philosophy our boss has chosen uses manipulation to control people into the actions you want them to take. It can be summed up by the phrase, 'Do it this way or else.' That kind of environment just makes employees walk around in fear, wondering when they're going to get caught doing something wrong.

"It doesn't allow us to engage employees at the heart level, opening them up to ingenuity and creativity, instead keeping things very shallow. When people are allowed to take what's inside of them and use it to make a significant contribution to the company then it transforms work into a whole new thing for them. It makes work into something in which they can see themselves and the part they play, and it makes them feel important.

"Are you following me so far?" Dad asked. I thought for a second and then nodded. "Good," he said before continuing.

"Now, I said that the other three directors have united against me, so to speak, all of them embracing this management philosophy and using it in their particular areas. The problem for me really comes in that all of them work in corporate headquarters, while I train the managers in the field. This really has isolated me at corporate as the only one not in line with this style, which makes me stick out like a sore thumb. My coworkers frequently complain to our boss about me and accuse me of things I'm not doing."

"Like what do they say?" I asked, feeling defensive for my dad's sake.

"Oh, just stuff like, 'He's trying to undermine your authority,' or, 'He's after your job; you'd better watch out,' or, 'He's not following procedure; he needs punished.' Those kinds of things."

"Oh, I get it," I said. "So how come your boss hasn't punished you if that's what he says managers are supposed to do?"

"Well, he has punished me, Mikey; he just hasn't fired me. For the past three years I've received little to no raise while the company as a whole is doing pretty well and giving standard raises. My reviews – kind of like a yearly report card – always focus on ways that I could follow policies more closely. And, believe me, I try every day to find new ways that I can do what he wants me to do without sacrificing what I know is right. I try to convince him that there's a better way than the way he does things, never arguing with him, of course – that wouldn't help me at all – but he hasn't come around yet."

"Sometimes I struggle to keep hope that he ever will come around," Dad said, trailing off and staring down at the floor.

I did not know what to do with the heavy silence that followed. Dad had never spoken to me this way before, and it scared me. Yet at the same time, something inside me came alive to be trusted like this, to be given a measure of respect as a grown up.

"I just want to see people really come alive," he said quietly. "I want them to know who they are and feel how full life can be when we live out who we are. I want them to see how much better everything is when we help the people around us become excellent in their strengths instead of mediocre in their weaknesses. I want them to see what happens when we focus on and guide people into what they do well instead of punishing and imprisoning them in areas at which they continually fail."

He grew silent again, but the sadness had left his eyes. They now glowed with a hint of passion, opening a window to the fire that burned inside of him.

"Michael," he said, "I want to tell you one more thing that I think is important for you. Do you remember when I told you in the park that I want you to conquer the world, but not like we do when we play Risk?"

Now there's a change of subject, I thought. "Yeah, I remember," I said.

"Well, what's going on at work is a good example of what I meant."

"I don't understand, Dad," I said.

"That's okay, just follow me for a second. See, my boss' management philosophy is a lot like Risk – it uses brute force to impose its values on everyone in the company.

"But my management philosophy is what I want to see you use in your life – it uses honor and encouragement to bring out who people were born to be and woos them to embrace the same values of their own free will.

"A person who does this has conquered the world in a way. I mean, they're not the supreme ruler of the world or anything, but they've established the values that govern each person from within so they influence every decision that people make without having to lift a finger to force it to happen. Does that make more sense?"

"I think so," I answered.

"Good," he said. "Then you know how I told you that in order to conquer the world you have to change people's identities so that they're glad you conquered them? Well this sort of does just that, except that instead of changing a person's identity I simply want to help them find the one they already have. Once they discover who they are, I can help them live out that identity while teaching them to do the same thing for other people. That teaching process explains them the values that 'conquered' them and by which they now live, while at the same time setting them free to fully express their own culture and personality.

"So, tying all this back in to my work situation, I'm trying to 'conquer' my boss and fellow directors according to this method. I'm trying to help them see that they have such awesome strengths and talents that it's silly for them to resort so quickly to punishment and manipulation to manage the company. If I can win that battle then I can win the whole company and I will have 'conquered' just a little more of the world, so to speak."

He used the quoting gesture with his hands whenever he referred to conquering someone, presumably so that I would better see his heart.

I thought for a moment and asked, "Dad, if they're trying to conquer you in a way and you're trying to conquer them, isn't it all the same when it really comes down to it? Like, aren't both of them bad, even if one seems to do good things?"

"That's an important question, Michael, because you're right, the end doesn't justify the means. If I'm 'conquering,' so to speak, with the same competitive heart that they have then it doesn't matter if my style of management produces good things because it still comes from a bad heart.

"For me this starts with how I live life anyway. I just believe it's the right thing for me to do to lift up the people around me and help them become the best they can be. Honestly, it just makes sense to live life that way. That's part of the reason I can't manage any different way, because it's just not who I am. What I do flows out of who I am.

"Let me say it this way – Conquering by its true definition can really only be done by forcing your will or your values onto other people. In that case, the conquered people have no choice in the matter. They can fight against you, but you overpower them. What I'm doing is completely different than that, because instead of forcing them to adopt my values I'm simply demonstrating a better way and inviting them to join me. They can refuse my invitation, but I'll still give it anyway.

"So what I'm doing really isn't conquering anyone, technically, it's just inviting them to something that simply makes a whole lot more sense than the way people normally do things."

"Then why do you use the word 'conquer,'" I asked.

"I guess I use it because what I'm talking about is something worth fighting for, not in the sense of going to war and having real battles, but in the sense of the way I'm doing it at work. So since I'm fighting for it then it's just kind of using the same language to say I'm conquering the world. Does that answer your question?"

"Um, I think so, but I'm not really used to thinking this way and I'm tired. I think it's all getting a little muddled in my head right now."

"That's okay, son," he responded. "I'll let you go to bed now, but one last thing before I go –"

"Yes, Dad?" I asked.

"Let's keep this conversation as man to man," he said. "Please don't tell your brother or sister what we talked about yet, okay? I think it's probably a bit more than they need to know."

"Okay, Dad. Thanks for talking with me. I love you," I said, giving him a hug.

"I love you, too, son, and I'm proud of you," he replied, hugging me back.

"Thanks, Dad. I'll see you in the morning."

"You're welcome, Michael," he said, closing my door behind him, "See you in the morning."

Chapter Eight
THE ENCOUNTER

It was the middle of the night when something disturbed my sleep. I heard a noise from across my room and, afraid to open my eyes, listened for what might be happening. I waited for what seemed like a long time, telling myself that I probably just imagined whatever it was, but I just could not shake the feeling that I was not alone.

When I finally peeked out into my room I did not see anything out of place until I noticed that my sword had fallen from where I had propped it against the wall. Right away I realized that the way it fell was not normal, for it had not just slid sideways along the wall as it would have if I simply had not balanced it properly. No, it had fallen into my room, toward my bed. In fact, the lion's head on the hilt was looking right at me.

As I looked into those red diamond eyes they flashed and a thought that was not my own shouted in my head, saying, "He's coming!"

Fear gripped me and I ducked under the covers. Wild thoughts ran though my head and I thought how stupid I was for ever getting that sword in the first place. *Why did I have to get that sword? I could have picked any sword in the whole store and I had to get that one! Stupid! Did I think that dream was cool or something? Why did I have to get the one that was weird? I shouldn't have gotten it; someone else should have had that dream and bought that sword. I don't want it! I don't want it anymore! I thought this was done! I don't want all of this happening to me!*

I started to moan these words, whining for whatever was happening to stop, but it would not stop. The angrier I got about my strange experiences the stronger this one became.

More and more uncomfortable, fear growing, my heart pounding in my chest. "He's Coming!" the voice shouted again and I began to writhe on my bed.

"Stop it! I said, 'Stop it!' I don't want this anymore!" I was yelling into my room, my eyes clenched shut, desperate for whatever was happening to stop.

The sense that I wasn't alone increased and I felt a distinct presence growing all around me. Something compelled me to open my eyes. I saw my sword rise up from the floor, leaving its sheath behind as it moved toward me. My breaths came in heaving gasps and I panicked. I lay curled up in a ball with my face half buried in my pillow. The lion's eyes were living flames and I could feel the heat of its breath on my face as it stopped only inches away from me.

"HE'S COMING!!!" the lion shouted, and instantly my room filled with light, intense like the core of the brightest star. The weight of this Presence crushed me and I lost my mind. I spun in circles on my bed like a dog trying to lie down, looking for a place to hide, but somehow I knew that nothing could hide me from the gaze of this Presence. There was nowhere to go and everything was laid bare. I have never been so naked in all my life.

I lay there, afraid, exposed, with no idea what was happening or what was going to happen, and then I heard a voice.

"Michael, I love you."

My fear still strong, my heart still pounding, I now knew even less what to do. This voice was like none I had ever heard before. I am not really sure that I can truly say it was even speaking words, yet I understood it. It was both high and low, stern and soft, powerful and gentle. It shook my room and yet felt like a comforting blanket.

"Michael, I love you, and that's why all this is happening to you," the voice said.

I could not tell where the voice was coming from. Light had swallowed my room so completely that I could barely distinguish the walls anymore and the voice came from somewhere in the light, or maybe from all parts of the light; I cannot say exactly.

Somehow I knew that the Presence was looking for a response, so I whimpered, "Who are you?"

"You know who I am, Michael; who do you think I am?" the voice said.

Trembling on top of my sheets, I answered, "Are…are you the Divine Hand?"

"I am," the voice resounded.

We were both silent for a time. I felt paralyzed and was certainly not going to ask any questions that showed I was angry about my strange experiences, but I did not have anything else on my mind to say to the Divine Hand.

My sword suddenly floated away from my face toward the center of the room where the light was most intense.

"You took this sword and asked me a question, Michael, did you not?" the Divine Hand asked.

"Yes, I did," I answered.

"Michael, I want you to know something about me. I want you to know that I am good, that I will never do anything that is not good or I would cease to be who I am." As the Divine Hand spoke, his voice changed like a symphony, as each part of the orchestra rises and falls.

"You asked me why I chose to give you these experiences that you have had, and the reason is because I love you."

I was too afraid to be very angry, but I felt a spark and said, half crying, "I don't understand."

"Michael, I have seen your life from beginning to end, and I know who you were born to be. I love you too much to not give you what you need to help you become that person. These experiences are necessary for you, to help you, to guide you, and to shape your identity so that you can become the fullness of who you really are."

"But why?" I protested, knowing that I could not hide my dislike of the answer I had received.

"You must learn to trust what I tell you in your dreams and visions, Michael. In them I have already told you that these things are gifts that show you one of the ways that you are special."

"But I don't like being special that way! I just want to be normal!" I said, still afraid, but knowing the Divine Hand wanted to have this conversation.

"Even those people whom you think are normal, Michael, really are not. They may have less dramatic gifts than you, but even though these gifts appear to be less significant they are equally powerful with what you are experiencing."

"Then why can't I have those gifts?" I asked in desperation.

"You can have those gifts, as you honor them in the people to whom I've given them. I have given you this gift so that you may know that I give gifts to people. Those with less dramatic gifts often don't realize that they've been given anything and they need someone to lead them. You are a leader, Michael, and I have called you to find the gifts I have given people, to help them to see them and use them."

"But why me?" I moaned as tears came to my eyes.

"Because I love you," the Divine Hand said.

"I don't understand," I said, the tears streaming down my cheeks now. "I mean, I'm shaking, I'm so scared right now, and don't want to say anything wrong or anything, but I don't understand how making me so weird is a loving thing to do!"

"I know, Michael," said the voice, and I felt it vibrate deep inside me. "I know how you feel, both now and about the experiences I have given you. The fear you feel is because of my jealous love for you. I am jealous for you that you would become all I have seen you to be, and my love for you is like a fire that would burn up everything that holds you back from fully becoming that person.

"The more you become that person the less fear you will experience in this kind of encounter with me and the more it will feel like love should be experienced.

"If you could see yourself the way that I have seen you then you would understand how giving you these gifts is an act of my love. In my love, I work to help you become all that you can be, which sometimes means helping you change from who you are, leaving behind things that are less than you and embracing what will make you fully you. Does this help you understand, Michael?"

"Yes," I said. Knowing why I was so afraid made me feel slightly less afraid and an incredible peace began to seep into my heart.

"Good," the Divine Hand continued, "because there's more to my love than this. These gifts also show that I love you because they help you become truly glorious."

"I don't understand what you mean again," I said sheepishly, wiping my tears with my sleeve.

"Remember what King Fidelas taught you about honor and glory, Michael. Glory is a measure of greatness, Michael, and right now you are surrounded by my glory. You can see and feel it here as I reveal it to you, but normally on earth glory isn't tangible; it is only a concept or idea.

"People have most commonly measured glory by how powerful, influential, or wealthy someone could become. So, if someone became a rich ruler of a large empire, with thousands of servants under them and a massive army with which to subdue other nations and keep his own people from rebelling, then that person would be considered glorious.

"True glory, however, depends on the people who belong to that emperor and not on the emperor himself. You see, any ruler can oppress the people he rules in order to make himself wealthier and more powerful, but this forces the people into poverty. He may live in the grandest palace the world has ever seen, but his people live in mud huts. This is not glorious at all. In fact, it is the exact opposite of glory.

"Real glory comes upon a ruler when he recognizes that his people are what make him glorious and he spends his life working to exalt them. This king's labors decrease the apparent gap between him and his subjects, even so that a stranger might confuse who was actually the ruler, but his glory is greater by far than the oppressive ruler.

"Consider this: Who is more glorious, the king of peasants in mud huts or the king of fellow kings, all of them living in palaces?"

"I guess the king of kings would be more glorious," I replied, the peace settling in more deeply.

"Why do you say that, Michael?" the Divine Hand asked, his voice sounding close to me, as though he had leaned in to listen.

"Well, it just makes sense, if you think about it. I mean, the best teachers I have are the ones that I learn the most from, and they also are usually the ones that I know really care about me and not just what they teach. Coaches are the same way, too. The best coaches are the ones who make their players and teams great, and the great teams get noticed, so I guess that means they get glory. But the coach doesn't get glory if he doesn't make his team great. In fact, if he doesn't make his team great then he gets fired."

I stopped talking and realized that I felt differently then I had ever felt while talking. It was like something inside me gave me words to say that I would not normally think of, but they flowed out of me so naturally that they truly became my words.

The Divine Hand was waiting for me and I felt like I had been exposed while doing something very private. I wanted to hide what I had just done, but despite the peace that had replaced my fear I was no less hidden from his Presence. Everything was still laid completely open.

"There is no need for shame," he said. "That is your gift of understanding coming out in you. Your seer gift is not the only gift I have given you and it feels the way it does because each gift you have from me is actually a part of me. I put some of my traits inside of you so that you can become whom I've seen you to be. Your gift of understanding will help you to take what you learn in your dreams and visions and use them in normal life. Then you can teach others and lead them into the glory I intend for their lives, which will give you the glory that I intend for yours.

"Michael, I am glorious because I give myself wholly to those under me, working to exalt them into all that I have seen they can be. I have seen you as a glorious one, shining even as I am shining now, but to carry this glory you must be a leader who sees the gifts I have given people and then exalts them into who they truly are."

"You mean that if I do this then everywhere I go I'll have this light shining from me?" I asked with a cringe.

"Yes and no, Michael," he replied. "Yes, this light will shine from you everywhere you go, but no, no one will see it. I will see it and you will feel it, along with some others who will also be able to feel it because of the gifts I have given them. But don't worry. After all, if I made you shine like this then your own glory would be a hindrance to you becoming all I've seen you to be simply because no one would come close enough to you for you to help them use their gifts."

The Divine Hand paused after speaking these words and my sword rose higher in the center of the room. The light began to fill the sword so that it glowed from within, growing brighter and brighter as it swallowed the light until all my room was dark except for the sword that hung in the middle.

The lion's eyes glowed like openings into a volcano and light shone from its mouth, casting teeth shaped shadows on the wall. The blade was like lightning bound in crystal and the hilt looked like the sun with faint shadows woven about it.

The voice spoke from the lion's mouth, each word shaking me as the roar of a lion, yet filling me with courage as though I were the lion. It said, "This sword is an image of you, Michael. It is crafted the way it is so that it represents you. As a sword leads in battle and gives victory, so you will lead many and help them to be victorious. And as my light and my presence can magnify the aspects of this sword, helping it to become more than it could be on its own, so can they magnify your gifts and make you greater than you can be on your own."

The voice became silent for a moment and it felt as if the lion were breathing deeply, feeling its own strength and anticipating what would soon come. I let the courage I felt in the sword well up within me and sat up with one last sniffle, looking into the eyes of the lion head. The more I looked, the more lion-like I felt and my breathing became the same.

I considered all that I had seen and how all that had filled my room was now inside my sword. I thought of the words the Divine Hand had spoken and realized that what I saw now was simply the result of my sword taking on the nature of the Divine Hand while keeping the strengths it already had. That union created something more beautiful and wonderful than either of them had been apart from the other.

Realizing these things, I held my gaze into those eyes and said, "If I am like that sword then I want to be like it as it is now, not as it was before. Will you fill me as you filled my sword, so that I can become all you've seen me to be and help do the same for others?"

The Divine Hand responded in a voice that resounded from every atom of my being, "I WILL!" and instantly light shot out from the lion's mouth into me and a wind rushed through my room. My sword fell from where it hung and I collapsed onto my pillow.

Staring at the ceiling, my world spun around me. It's hard to describe, but I felt the way my sword had looked. Joy, peace, and hope filled me till I thought I was going to explode. My mind rang with clarity of thought, free from all distraction and double-mindedness. My eyes saw more clearly and I perceived my surroundings more fully than I ever had. I was changed, and in comparison to my life before, truly it was like being alive for the first time.

As I lay there in my euphoria, with unfading smile on my face, I wiped a tear of joy from my eye and marveled at the roiling explosion of life that I felt inside of me. I felt HIM inside of me – that Light, that Presence, the Divine Hand himself! He somehow really was inside of me; everything that had been in my room was now in me!

Waves of peace swept over me and I felt sleep creeping in. And as my eyes closed on a new world I said, "Oh, Divine Hand, thank you. Please never leave me again!

Chapter Nine
A Difficult Choice

When I woke up the next morning I felt surprisingly refreshed. After turning off my alarm I just laid in my bed for a moment trying to figure out whether what I remembered happening that night was real.

I let my eyes casually look over my room, as though looking for some sort of residue from my encounter that would confirm my hope. Then I saw my sword lying at the end of my bed where it had fallen and I quickly checked to see that the sheath, too, was where it had been as well, right in the middle of my floor, empty and abandoned by the sword that had floated away all by itself.

Crazy, I thought, *It really happened!* I shook my head in wonder at it all. While seeing that my sword really had moved all by itself was definitely a comforting confirmation of my experience, I hardly needed the proof. Clenching my eyes shut, I rubbed my chest over my heart and knew that something had happened, not because of any outward sign of it, but because I could feel *Him*.

I knew my experience was real because I still felt it. I was full of it! The light, the presence, the voice, it was all still with me, inside me, making everything new all the time and I couldn't get enough of it!

He didn't leave me! I thought excitedly and I jumped out of bed. I looked around my room, in a daze over what to do next. I felt so different that I was disoriented, completely distracted and having trouble remembering my normal school-morning routine.

Moving by impulse, I saw my sword and picked it up, feeling it settle into my hands so naturally it was as if I had used it in battle for years. Like an old friend reacquainted, I looked at it with new eyes and said, "Hello, you. So you're made to be like me, eh? Then I will look to you and remember who I am, and we will remember together this night that changed our lives."

I took a deep breath of exhilaration and began to come back to myself, remembering that I did not want to be late for school. Taking a last look for now at my sword, I turned and put it away in its sheath and set my thoughts toward the day ahead of me.

Rifling through my closet and drawers, I found some clothes and headed to the shower, turning the water extra hot. I could hardly keep from laughing as I stepped into the tub, not for any reason in particular, but just because I had so much joy bursting inside me.

Knowing how ridiculous I was being, and laughing more because of it, I said to myself, "What do I do now? I'm totally different than I ever was before and I don't know what to do with myself!"

I laughed at the question, but was serious about it at the same time. My friends certainly would not understand what had happened to me, especially considering that I never even told them about my first dream, let alone anything else that had happened to me. Even Austin, who knew I'd had a dream, though nothing about it, could not understand.

My family might understand, or at least my parents might, since they knew about my experiences, but what about my siblings?

"Well, Stevie and Amy probably won't really care anyway," I said to myself as I shampooed my hair. "If I'm happier all the time anyway then it probably means I'll be nicer to them than I was before, too, so they won't mind the change. But what about my friends; how do I explain this to them, or do I have to?"

To be honest, I wanted to somehow just be different without having to explain why I was different. I spent the rest of my shower trying to figure out the answer to my situation, comforted in my new reality by the security that came with this joy-filled Presence. While what my friends thought about me was still important to me, I was amazed how different my emotions were than I would normally expect them to be.

Instead of fear coming in and paralyzing me from doing anything for which they would make fun of me, my concern was more because I valued them so much. I truly cared about them and that is why I wanted to make sure this change in me only made our friendships stronger.

In any case, while I love my friends, there was no way I was giving up what had happened to me just to keep things from getting weird between us. If anything, I had to figure out how to get them to have the same experience that I'd just had.

As I stepped out of the shower a thought came to me. I remembered that after I had my dream I talked to Mr. Gustafson about it and he actually thought it was a good thing. *Maybe I could talk to him about this, too, and he would have some advice for me.* I decided to see if my parents could give me a ride again so I could hopefully beat the busses and have more time to talk with him.

I went downstairs and found that my dad was making us a special breakfast of pancakes, eggs, and bacon. He greeted me, saying, "Hey, Michael! How many pancakes do you want?"

"Umm…wow, are you making them as we order them? I think I'll have five, since there's eggs and bacon, too. What's this for?"

"Well, I woke up a little early it just sounded good to me this morning, so I thought I'd shower early and just get going on it so it could be ready for everybody else when they needed to eat. And I'm making them fresh for everyone because all you kids eat at different times." He smiled at me and added, "This'll just take a couple minutes. Would you like cheese on your scrambled eggs?"

"Yes, please; and thanks," I said.

I let him pour out the pancakes and then asked, "What are the chances that you could give me a ride to school again today so I can be a little early. There's something I want to talk over with Mr. Gustafson."

"Well, I'd have to check with your mom to see if she can finish up here for me," he said," since Stevie and Amy still need to eat, too. You know what, I think they'll be down and I can get them started in time to still get you to school early, so I think that'll work. What do you need to talk to him about; that Mother Theresa project?"

"Um, no, actually," I answered and wondered just how much I wanted to say to him right now, deciding to go the simplest route and give him a summary. "I had another weird thing happen to me last night and he seemed to have some good insight on that sort of thing when I told him about my dream. I just want to see what he thinks about it."

"Oh, really? You had something else happen to you last night? What happened?" Dad asked, tinges of both concern and curiosity in his voice.

I glanced at him just to double check that he looked up for it, realizing that it's totally different telling someone about a strange experience that you think might have just been last night's dinner than about one that you are sure changed your life forever. I chuckled to myself and thought, *Well, ready or not, he asked.*

"You know how my dream and vision talked about a Divine Hand, Dad?"

"Yeah."

"Well, after I had my vision – which, Mom told you about it, right?"

"She told me as much about it as you told her, at least, though I'm sure we only got a pretty short version of the whole story," he said.

"Yeah, I'll have to tell you the whole story sometime, but anyway, when I talked to Mom about that vision she said that if some 'Divine Hand' was trying to talk to me then maybe I could try talking back to see if he would tell me what he was trying to say. So I did that after she left my room. I got my sword out and said some kind of prayer, I guess, asking the Divine Hand to speak to me and tell me why all these things have been happening to me so that I could know that I'm not crazy. "

"Uh-huh," Dad said to show he was listening as he flipped the pancakes.

I paused, with no other way to say it but to just jump off the cliff, "The Divine Hand showed up in my room last night."

Dad put the spatula down after only flipping half my pancakes and looked at me. "You mean you had another vision last night, but this time you saw the Divine Hand?"

"Well, I'm not sure exactly," I said. "I suppose it was a vision, since my first one felt just like normal life, too, except that this one happened in my room and not in the world where I went in my dream and first vision."

Slowly picking up the spatula, Dad recollected himself somewhat and finished flipping my pancakes. When he was done he leaned against the counter and cautiously asked, "So what happened? What was he like?"

I was still a little nervous to tell him the story, but my excitement flooded out and I blurted the whole encounter, gesturing more and more wildly as I went on. "It was incredible, Dad! I woke up in the middle of the night, I don't even know what time, because I heard a noise in my room. I looked around and saw that my sword fell into my room, towards my bed, which was really weird and I got a really creepy feeling like I've never had before.

"I was so scared and all of a sudden my sword took itself out of my sheath and flew over to my bed all by itself and I heard this voice in my head shout, 'HE'S COMING!'

"I totally freaked out, but all of a sudden my whole room was filled up with light like crazy and I heard this voice coming from everywhere say, 'Michael, I love you.'

"It was the Divine Hand talking to me, and he was the one filling my room with light. He said that he sees me the same way and that he's giving me these dreams and visions to help me become all that he knows I can be and so that I can help other people become all that they're supposed to be, too, just like you were talking to me about last night like you do at work, Dad.

"And he told me that my sword is like a picture of me and how awesome I'm supposed to be and when he said that, all the light that was in my room somehow crammed into my sword and made it look way cool, like, its eyes were glowing so bright and light was coming out of its mouth and the blade looked like lightning.

"It was crazy, but I started thinking, 'Hey, if I'm supposed to be like that sword, can I be like it as it is now, all glowing and cool and stuff, and not like it was before? So I asked the Divine Hand if he could make me like that, just like he made the sword like that, and he said he would and right away this blast of light shot out from my sword and hit me and I fell back on my bed and, oh man, I just felt incredible, like all this peace and joy and just anything good you can imagine, I was feeling it and the peace just kept growing until I fell asleep.

"And when I woke up this morning I still felt the same way and thought maybe I'd somehow made the whole thing up, but I know that I didn't because my sword fell onto my bed right where it had been hanging in the middle of the air last night, and I know I didn't put it there because I never even got out of bed. The whole thing really happened and I feel totally different and better than I've ever felt in my whole life!

"I know it's really weird and I still don't know what to do with it, but I'm so glad that it happened and I don't want to ever go back to being like I was before. It's like...I don't know what it's like...it's like I have a whole new life, like I'd never been alive before, but now I am, and I don't ever want to go back."

Breathing out a huge breath, I flopped into a dining room chair, exhilarated, but nervous about how my dad might react.

I looked at him and he just stared at me, looking utterly lost. I am sure if I did not know what to do with myself, then he must be even more clueless. Almost absentmindedly, he tossed my pancakes onto a plate and said, "Here, why don't you get started on these while I make your eggs? And the bacon's done already so you can have some of that, too, if you want."

I started on my pancakes while he poured out some of the eggs he had beaten onto the griddle, and we watched together as they bubbled and cooked. The silence felt awkward after my excited explosion and Dad, knowing that he needed to give some sort of response, said, "Well, that sounds like your strangest experience yet."

"It really was, Dad," I said gently, "but it was amazing. What do you think about it?"

He exhaled a deep sigh and said, "Michael, I have to be honest with you. I've never had that kind of experience, or any kind of experience like what you've been having lately. That doesn't mean that I doubt them, because I trust you and I know you're not crazy. It just means that I'm flying by the seat of my pants in what to do with them.

"Before this one they weren't really quite so personal. I mean, the other ones just took you off into another world, which is weird and honestly scares me a little bit. But they just seemed to be trying to teach you something, which feels pretty nonthreatening, so it's not that hard to put up with the weirdness for the sake of the lesson being taught since it didn't seem like anything bad.

"This one is different, though, because it really invaded your world, which means it invaded my world, too. Now I have to wrestle with it and really figure out what to do with it because now you've had an experience that wasn't in another world, it was in our world. And not just that, but your interaction with that other world didn't stop when the vision stopped because, apparently, the Divine Hand did something *to* you that is still doing something *in* you.

"And I don't know who this Divine Hand is, so I don't know if I trust him with my son. He seems to be doing only good things, but since I don't know him then I don't know how to be sure.

"Not to mention the plain old 'weird factor' of the whole thing..." he trailed off.

I could tell there was a lot stirring inside him that he just didn't know how to say. He looked up at me with loving concern in his eyes and I held his gaze for a moment. I tried to think of something I could say, holding my plate out to him to buy some time. He put my eggs on my plate and I started to eat them when a thought suddenly came to me.

"You know, Dad," I said, "There's something you might try."

"What's that?" he asked.

"Well, especially after the orchard I thought I was going crazy and really didn't like what was going on with the whole weird-experiences-at-random-times-that-I-had-no-control-over thing. But when I talked to Mom about it she said I should just ask the Divine Hand to tell me. She said, 'If there really is some Divine Hand who's trying to teach you something, then he would probably answer you if you just asked him.'

"So I did, and when he showed up in my room last night he said he had come to answer my question. I don't know if he'd show up to you like he showed up to me, but I do know that he answers questions, so maybe you just need to ask him to show you something that would prove to you that you can trust him with me. And if he doesn't show you something, then you know that for whatever reason you can't trust him and we'll figure out what to do from there."

Dad was silent for a moment, weighing what he thought of my suggestion. "I'd kind of have to trust him blindly at first," he said.

"That's true, Dad," I said, trying to encourage him, "but how else are you going to get your answers?"

He shrugged, "Well, I'll think about it anyway, Michael. It's a strange enough thing that I'm not ready to go that far quite yet, but I'll let it sit for a while and we'll see what happens."

"Do whatever you feel is best, Dad," I said. "It was just an idea of something you could maybe do to feel more comfortable with what seems to be happening to me, especially after last night."

Just then we heard some footsteps on the stairs and looked to see Stevie coming into the dining room.

"Wow, Dad, you're making pancakes and eggs?" he said excitedly.

"Yup, and bacon. How many pancakes do you want?" Dad said.

"Oh, three or four. Thanks, Dad!" he said.

Dad started to pour Steve's pancakes and said, "Was your sister right behind you?"

"Yeah," Steve said, "She was waiting for the shower when I got out. Why do you ask?"

"Oh, Michael just wanted a ride to school today so he could have extra time to talk to one of his teachers," Dad explained, "So I was just going to get her pancakes and eggs started if she's not going to be long."

"What do you want to talk to your teacher about, Michael?" Steve asked me.

"I just have a question for him about something," I said.

"About what?" Steve persisted.

"Just about something. I don't think I have time to tell you all about it right now, but maybe later," I said, hoping to put him off until I knew more about what had happened to me and could explain it to him better.

For the first time since my encounter with the Divine Hand I felt a little nervous about the whole thing. When I thought in the shower how life might look differently now it was still a distant idea, but now I had just avoided telling someone whose opinion mattered to me. I realized that I was a little afraid.

I told my dad that I would go finish getting ready to leave, and went back to my bedroom. I glanced at my backpack and the books sitting next to it that I needed to put into it, but walked right past them to my sword.

Picking it up, I sat on my bed and held it across my lap. I looked at it, remembering what it had looked like and done that night. Closing my eyes, my heart cried out, *"What am I going to do? Last night was better than I ever thought anything could be, and I want to keep that so bad, but I didn't think about how hard it might be to have my life change so much!"*

I opened my eyes and, looking at my sword again, thought, *Did I really think that things wouldn't change much after I saw what this sword looked like with him in it?*

As I sat on my bed, my teenage emotions caused a tear to trace down my cheek when I suddenly had a thought go through my head that I knew was not mine.

"Do you wish you hadn't asked for this?" it asked me.

No one else was in my room, and I knew that, but I still looked around anyway and asked, "Who said that?"

"Michael, you asked me to fill you last night. All the wonderful things you've been experiencing since then are because I did fill you. You haven't just been feeling emotions; you have been feeling *me*," the voice said in my thoughts.

"Divine Hand? Are you talking to me?" I asked, and then paused to listen.

"I am," my thoughts said all by themselves again.

"This is really weird," I said.

"And me speaking to you by making your sword fly across your room isn't?"

"Good point," I said.

"Do you wish you hadn't asked for this?" he asked again.

I sighed heavily and said, "No, I don't wish I hadn't asked for this. I meant what I said that I don't ever want to go back to how I was before; it really is like I'm alive for the first time ever. It's just that I wish it was easier to just go be a different person without everyone expecting me to be the same."

"You should go talk to Mr. Gustafson," he said.

"Mr. Gustafson!" I said with a start, "Geez, if I want to go talk to Mr. Gustafson then I need to leave!" Just then I heard my bus drive past my house and Dad calling me, "Michael, are you ready yet? If we don't leave soon then you'll be late!"

I threw my books into my bag and ran out of my room and down the stairs. "Sorry, Dad, got distracted in my room, but I'm ready."

"That's alright. You have everything you need?" he asked.

"Yup," I said.

"What about your lunch?" my mom asked, holding my lunch bag out to me. This was the first time I had noticed her.

"Oh, yeah, I suppose that'd be good. Thanks, Mom."

"You're welcome, Michael. Have a great day at school," she said.

"Thanks, Mom; will do," I said and asked my dad, "Are you ready to go?"

"Yep! Let's go!" he said with his odd early morning excitement.

We headed out the door and into his car, pulling out and going down the familiar road to my school. As he dropped me off at the door he said, "Let me know what Mr. Gustafson has to say; it might help me as I think about all this."

"Okay, Dad, I will," I said.

"Love you, son. Have a great day!" he said as I climbed out of the car.

"Love you, too, Dad. See you later," I replied.

I was in a hurry to get to Mr. Gustafson so by the time Dad started driving away I was already past the flag poles and almost to the doors. I walked past the office and down the hall to my locker, getting everything I needed for my first two classes and leaving everything else before going to see Mr. Gustafson.

The busses were not there yet, so the halls were almost empty and I made my way quickly to the social studies area of my school. I found Mr. Gustafson in his classroom preparing the whiteboards with some notes we would apparently need that day.

"Hi, Mr. Gustafson," I said as I walked into the room.

"Oh, hi Michael," he said, looking over his shoulder to see who had come in.

"Are you busy?" I asked.

"Not really, I'm just finishing here," he said as he finished off a line of notes with a flourish and capped his marker. "What can I do for you?" he asked as he turned to face me.

"Well, I wanted to talk to you more about that dream thing we talked about last week," I answered.

"Ooh, more about that dream? What about it?" he asked excitedly.

"Um, well, more stuff like that has been happening since then, too." I left off there, wanting to see how he would react.

"Really?" he asked, sitting down in a desk close to mine, "Like what?"

"Well," I said, still cautious, "on Saturday my family went apple picking and while we were at the orchard I all of a sudden found myself in the same world that was in my dream. I did a bunch of stuff in that world and talked to people and all of that, and then pretty much just as quick I was all of a sudden back in the apple orchard with my family.

"While I was in that world, one of the people there told me that I was having a vision given to me by a 'Divine Hand.' But when I got back I was angry about it because it felt like I had no control over what was happening and, really, I just thought I was going crazy."

"Mmhmm?" Mr. Gustafson encouraged me, "So you're asking me about that vision or is there more?"

"There's more," I said. "I didn't know what to do about it, but my mom said, 'If there's someone out there who's trying to talk to you, they probably want you to understand what they're saying and if you asked them they would probably explain it to you.' So I tried talking to the Divine Hand, asking him to tell me why he picked me and what was going on so that I could know that I'm not going crazy."

I searched Mr. Gustafson's face for anything that might tell me that he thought I was crazy, but he just looked at me, waiting for me to go on. Wanting to make sure, I asked him, "So, I just want to check before I go on, do you think I'm crazy from what I've just told you? I mean, I don't want to get reported to the nurse or anything."

"No," he said, laughing a little, "Actually, from my point of view it's somewhat refreshing to hear someone talking about these kinds of things. But go on, I can talk more about that later; you said there was more?"

"Yeah, well, last night the Divine Hand himself showed up in my room." I stopped there to see how he would react.

"And?" he asked excitedly, "What happened?"

"Well, it started when my sword that my parents got me for my birthday fell in toward the middle of my room, which was totally impossible for it to do by itself. Then it rose up off the floor, out of its sheath, and flew across the room to right in front of me. A voice yelled at me out of the lion's head on it that said, "HE'S COMING!" and all of a sudden the whole room was filled with light like I've never seen before.

"I was more scared than I've ever been and felt like everything in me was completely naked, like I couldn't hide anything whether I wanted to or not. The Divine Hand talked to me out of that light and told me some things about why he's giving me these weird experiences and it was all really good.

"And then at the end, right before it was all over, my sword moved into the middle of the room again, still floating, and all the light went into and filled up my sword. It was amazing! And the Divine Hand had told me that my sword is like a picture of how he sees me, and I thought, 'Man, I want to be like my sword is now, not like it was before.' So I said, 'Can you fill me like you're filling my sword?' And he said, 'I will!' and this blast of light shot out of my sword and hit me square in the chest, knocking me onto my back and filling me with everything good you can imagine. I have never felt that way before and never even knew you could.

"When I woke up I still felt the same way and I started thinking, 'I am never going to be the same again. I don't want to ever be the way I was before, because it's like I'm alive for the first time.'

"And that's kind of my problem, because I don't know how to be different when what made me different is something so weird that none of my friends would believe me. It's like I'd almost rather be crazy and get help for it than to just be treated like I'm crazy when I'm really not."

"Hmmm," Mr. Gustafson said, leaning back in his desk, "so before I answer, let me clarify your question. You've been having these radical experiences and last night you had one that you say changed you forever and you don't want to go back to the way you were before. But now that you're different, you're afraid that people might reject you for being different and you're asking me what you're supposed to do, is that your question?"

"Yup, that's it," I answered. "And that's definitely what I'm afraid of, for sure."

"Alright," he said, "well, obviously, you care about the friends you have right now, so you don't want to have to get new friends, and you'd like to know how to keep the ones you have.

"I think you can look at it two ways. You can look at it like a salesperson, where you have to somehow sell your experiences to them and convince them that they're a good thing; or more to the point, that the change they've caused in you is a good thing. A benefit of going that way is that they might even want to have the same experiences, and if they actually get them then they might change in a similar way and you would all be different together.

"The first disclaimer to go with that is that your experiences have been strange by our standards, to say the least, which means that you take a risk right from the start of being rejected just for talking about what has been happening to you.

"Second, assuming that they believe you about your experiences, the convincing them that these things are good and the waiting for them to receive their own will both take time. And in reality, they will almost certainly not have the exact same kinds of experiences that you've been having. What they experience might be similar to what you did, or it might be much less dramatic or immediately life-changing. Either way, time is the issue and your friends would have to be willing to stick with you while they wait for their own encounters."

"I'm not sure I like either of those ideas," I said.

"Understandably," he replied, "So another way of looking at it is that you basically treat the relationships as if they're brand new, because you're brand new. If you look at it this way then you act toward your friends as though you had just moved to town and you're trying to make new friends. If you treat this as a new beginning to your relationships, then it may have a pull on your friends that helps them to accept the change.

"On the other hand, it might feel awkward to your friends because they'll still feel the transition and wonder why it's happening. Change is rarely comfortable if we like where we already are, and we tend to fight it if we don't have enough value for what's on the other side of it."

I sighed and said, "That option doesn't sound good either!"

"They both definitely have risks and potential payoffs," Mr. Gustafson said, "but do you want my real opinion?"

"Will it help me more than either of those options?" I asked glumly.

"It should," he answered.

"Sure, then, anything that can help," I said, starting to feel hopeless about keeping my friends.

"Michael, there are two things I will tell you that can help you a lot if you choose to use them, but it will be totally up to you," he started.

"The first of those things is that the real issue behind your fear is that you don't trust their commitment to you. The only reason you're afraid is because you think they might reject you.

"Now, I'm not saying that they won't, but I'm saying it's not a healthy place for relationships to be. If they would reject you simply because you changed without seeing what the new you is like, then chances are they are either afraid the new you will reject them or they were only friends with you for what you could give them. Do you see why this is an unhealthy way to have relationships?"

"Um, well, it sounds pretty selfish, I guess," I said.

"Exactly. When someone is just in a relationship for what they can get out of it then it's very selfish. To be fair, I don't think most people do that on purpose; they just do it because they don't know there's a better way out there."

"So what's the better way?" I asked.

Mr. Gustafson leaned closer to me and said, "The better way is to be in relationship with people for what we can give, not what we can get. You see, when we know for ourselves that we're valuable and that we have significant things to offer the people around us then we can be confident to give what we can to our friends, making their lives better. But when we don't know how valuable and significant we are then we tend to suck the good things out of the people around us, afraid that if we don't then we won't have anything for ourselves.

"That's when we get selfish and feel threatened when our relationships change, because we subconsciously question whether we will still be able to get what we need from that relationship. Sometimes, rather than waiting to see, we'll ditch the friendship out of fear. Does that make sense?"

"Yeah, that makes a lot of sense," I said, feeling like somehow those words were finding their way deeper in me than just mentally understanding the point of what he said.

The sound of clanging lockers filtered through the walls. The busses had arrived and our time was getting short. Mr. Gustafson continued, "Good, then quickly the second thing that might help you, let me ask you a question. Each of us has different strengths that no one else has, but that everyone else needs, right?

"Right," I said hesitantly, not sure I knew what I was saying.

"Well, if we act just like all the people around us then will we ever become who we're supposed to be and be able to give them the strengths they need?"

The gears in my head were really turning. "I don't think we would," I answered.

"Exactly, Michael; good job. So here's the point – In order to become who you were made to be then you have to allow yourself to be set apart from everyone else. If you truly are going to be you, then you can't try to be like everyone else.

"More than that, if I can bring the Divine Hand back into the conversation, I think he's trying to help you become who you really are. Somehow he knows who you're supposed to be and he wants you to become that person, but as long as you value what your friends think of you more than what he is teaching you then none of what he's teaching you will work."

"What do you mean?" I asked.

Mr. Gustafson pursed his lips and looked up toward the ceiling like he was thinking, popping the cap off his dry erase marker a few times absentmindedly. "Let me try saying it this way – This Divine Hand person is trying to do something in your life that will help you become who you're supposed to be. You have to choose whether to let him do that work in you and be okay with the impact that has on your current relationships, or to reject that work and pursue fitting in instead.

"Although, honestly, our whole conversation up to this point assumes that your friends would abandon you for being different or if they found out about your strange experiences. It could very well be that they would stick with you. Or, obviously, some might stay with you and some might leave; we don't know.

"But for the sake of our conversation, and for you to be able to wholeheartedly move forward, you have to decide whether or not you are okay with losing your friends. You don't have to like the idea of them leaving you, but you have to accept the risk of whatever actions you decide to take.

"Michael, you face a choice, and it won't be the only time in your life you'll face it – You can choose to stand out and be significant, maybe changing your life and your friends' lives forever, or you can choose to reject the experiences you've been having in order to be safe and fit in.

"I can't make that choice for you, and I'm going to say one more thing to make it a little harder for you," he said with a sly smile, shifting in the desk a little. "My advice to you going forward from here would be to ask the Divine Hand another question before you make your decision regarding which way to go.

"See, while losing friends is never easy or fun, I think the only reason you really are struggling with this choice is because you don't know if you can trust the Divine Hand to help you if your friends do leave you. You trust your friends to stick with you if you don't change, but you don't trust the Divine Hand to stick around if you do. When you resolve the question of trust then I think your decision about whether to embrace this change in your life will become a lot easier. What do you think?"

My mind felt like a track meet, I had so many things running through it. "I think that's a lot to think about, Mr. Gustafson, but I think you're right. Thanks."

"You're very welcome, Michael," Mr. Gustafson said as he got up from the desk he had been sitting on. "And good job, by the way, on the pop quiz I gave you yesterday."

"Um, thanks," I said, as he went to his desk and picked up a stack of papers. He rifled through them and found the one with my name on it, handing it to me.

I thought, *I don't think I'll keep up with school if I'm thinking so hard about this other stuff.*

Putting my quiz into my backpack, I reflected on how my day had started off in ecstasy, glowing in the wake of what had happened in the night, but now I was torn. How could I go back to the way I was before? I could not stand even thinking about it.

But I was afraid of losing my friends, or even worse, of word getting out to the rest of the school and getting a reputation as crazy, becoming someone with whom no one would want to be friends. I felt like I could lose everything that was important to me.

So that was it. Mr. Gustafson was right, I couldn't know what my friends would do, but I had to be willing to accept whatever happened because of my decisions. My choice was to either reject the Divine Hand and the new life he had given me, or to be willing to suffer rejection from all the people who were important to me and be hindered in making new friends by a bad reputation.

When I asked the Divine Hand to make me like my sword I hadn't thought about what I was doing. I was caught up in the moment, but now I understood, and I knew that my choice would cause a permanent change in my life from which I would never go back.

How could this big of a choice possibly be laid on a 13 year old? I thought to myself. *I am way not ready to decide something this big!*

But there was no one else, and there was no other way. I had to decide, and the weight of my decision hung on me with the weight of a tsunami.

Maybe that's why I did what I did during lunch; I'll probably never know for sure. All I can say is that what happened at lunch forced my change to be forever.

Chapter Ten
A Slice of Pie

I GATHERED WITH MY FRIENDS AS I ALWAYS DID. We sat in our same seats, at the same table, in the same spot of the lunchroom. The meal of the day was pizza that looked like it had sat in a microwave too long. It was soggy, small, and smelled like a third world street vendor might use higher quality ingredients than whoever made this poor excuse for Italian pie.

The sight of what was on each of my friends' trays made me love my mom and the fact that she made me lunch every day. I opened my bag to find a ham and turkey sandwich with mustard and cheddar cheese, a bag of tortilla chips, a little salsa, some baby carrots, and a slice of our homemade apple pie.

"Aw, yeah! My mom packed me some of the pie we made!" I exclaimed to my friends, not intentionally rubbing it in that they had to eat their floppy-pizza-on-cardboard-crust instead. I pulled out the fork and spoon my mom had included with my lunch and noticed that there was a sticky note on the pie container that said, "Check your bag's other pocket. Love, Mom."

I quickly zipped open the upper pouch of my two-pouch lunch bag and pulled aside the little ice pack to find a small dish of ice cream to go with my pie!

"Oh, man, my mom is the best!" I shouted as I showed off my discovery to my friends.

"Come on, Michael, just eat your food. You're only bragging that you don't have to eat this stuff," Austin said, tossing his head to the side to get his hair out of his face.

"Hey, Michael, I'll trade you my steamed vegetables for your pie," chimed Matt in a smooth salesman type voice.

"No way," I said, "I'm keeping all this stuff."

"How about just for your ice cream?" he persisted.

"No, I said I'm keeping *all* this stuff. You eat your own food," I replied.

They all unenthusiastically worked their way through their meals while I munched and crunched happily through mine. I was just putting my ice cream on my pie when Liz spoke up.

"Where do you suppose Nick is? He hasn't bugged us since last Thursday, and he never leaves us alone that long," she said.

"I don't know, but who cares?" replied Austin. "The longer he stays away the better. Besides, it's not like we're the only people in the whole lunch room for him to pick on. Maybe he's scoping out people who might be better victims than we are."

Dylan, my quiet friend with the short, nappy afro, turned to look over toward where Nick and his gang usually sit, but Matt snapped him back with a sharp, "Don't look! If he's going to leave us alone, then just leave him alone. We don't want to do anything to draw his attention!"

"I'll look," I said, "I'm already facing him so it won't be so obvious."

I craned my neck carefully around a few watermelon heads between me and the bully-table, trying not to be too conspicuous, and found them right where they always are. Nick was sitting in the middle of the group, quietly separate from the inane violence his lackeys were doing to one another –

stealing food and playing keep away, trading jabs and punches whenever someone dropped their guard, mocking faces leering at one another like they were competing to find the worst insults. It looked like a practice field for the school of How-To-Be-The-Most-Annoying-Person-In-The-Whole-World.

On most days, Nick would have been the president and chief professor of their private university of idiocy, but today for some reason he was not living up to the role he seemed to love so much.

I squinted for a moment, confused about what I saw, and noted that Nick didn't have any food in front of him, and saw no sign that he had eaten anything. Then, before I knew what I was doing, I grabbed my pie, stood up, and began walking toward Nick's table.

Leaving behind cries of, "What're you doing?" and, "Where are you going?" I wove through the tables and made my way to the row where Nick sat.

His table was in the least travelled corner of the cafeteria and the shortest route to it led me along a path where he and his crew would easily see me coming. I did not know exactly what I was doing or why I was doing it, but at this point it was too late to pretend I was just getting up to throw away garbage.

My throat closed so it was hard to swallow and my heart beat faster. I imagined that the whole room quieted as people stopped to see what was going to happen – usually people only walked up to Nick if they were crazy enough to pick a fight with him.

The thugs were still smacking each other around and making the cleverest sarcastic comments they could think of as I got close enough to hear what they were saying. All around their table the floor was covered in food from their game of keep away. I remember thinking, *I just hope this pack of ogres doesn't eat me.*

I drew a mixed response as I stepped up to their table – some of them looked at me with hostility and others with indifference, barely pausing in their bothering of one another to bother about me. I stood silently for a moment, waiting for Nick to look at me, but he just sat there, apparently lost in his own world or for some other reason not caring that someone stood at his table.

One of Nick's agitated henchmen, an overweight 7th grader I had seen in enough fights that I knew I did not want him messing with me, started shifting in his chair in a way that made me uneasy. I figured I had better speak up quick.

"Hey, Nick," I said, trying to sound as friendly as I could without sounding fake.

No response.

"Um, hey Nick, so, uh…my family picked some apples and made some apple pie this weekend, and, um, well, I just thought I'd give you some of it."

That got the attention of his whole crew. A dirty looking brunette girl who was in my science class dropped an ice cream sandwich on the floor she had been trying to keep from her dirty looking boyfriend, who wasn't too happy about losing the sandwich. Now they were all looking at me, all of them except for Nick.

I did not understand this. Usually it seemed like all we had to do to attract Nick's attention was think about him and before long he would come around our table to "clean up our scraps" or make our lives miserable in some other way.

What do I do with this? I thought. *I'm sure he wants this pie; I don't know why he won't talk to me, though.*

I felt the gaze of my friends burning in the back of my head and just put the pie and ice cream on the bare table in front of Nick, saying, "Well, here you go. It's really good stuff and I thought you'd like it."

And with that I walked away from their table, probably a little faster than I had walked to it, wanting to make my get away as fast as I could without running.

I knew that probably everyone in the lunch room had seen what I had done and news of it would spread through the whole school by the end of the day. I also knew what sort of questions waited for me when I got back to my friends, and I started asking them of myself before anyone else even had the chance.

Why did I just do that? What could I possibly be thinking? How am I going to explain this to my friends?

Austin welcomed me back by demanding, "What're you doing?" and I could tell from their body language that all my friends were wondering the same thing. So was I.

I sat back down, not looking at any of them, and quietly said, "I don't know."

"You don't know?" Austin said angrily. "That kid has beaten us up, stolen our food, and generally made our lives miserable since we got to this school and you just gave him your pie that you wouldn't share with any of us? That is not cool. You don't do that, man."

Great, I didn't even try to make my decision yet and I'm already losing my friends. Shaking my head, I looked back at Austin and said, "You heard what I said. I don't know why I just did that. I just looked over there and saw him and the way he was sitting. I saw that he didn't have any food and something just made me stand up and do something about it."

"Something just made you stand up and do something about it," Matt chimed incredulously. "Great. So now it's not good enough that he just takes our food, you have to go and give it to him before he even asks for it. That's real smart."

"Look," I said, "You're treating me like I'm the one who's been bullying you guys, but I'm not. I'm Michael, your friend. Why's it such a big deal to you anyway?"

"Because you're supposed to treat your friends better than your enemies, Michael, that's why," said Matt.

"Back off, guys," said Liz. "It was Michael's pie and he can do with it what he wants."

"You must have not heard what I just said," Matt retorted, "It's not about the pie. It's about how you treat your friends and not treating the people who beat on you better than them."

"Yeah, it seems that Michael's been forgetting how friends are supposed to treat each other a lot lately," Austin shot as the bell rang. He quickly grabbed his tray and bag and walked off, tossing a, "See ya, Dylan," over his shoulder as he went.

Matt followed Austin's example, leaving in a hurry and heading for his next class.

Liz and Dylan both looked at me, the aggravation at Matt and Austin's slighting of Liz and me showing on their faces.

Somehow I knew that I had a choice in that moment to say something that would diffuse the situation or enflame it, and that whatever I said, both Liz and Dylan would hold on to it and it would determine their side in the situation.

Not knowing what to say, I just opened my mouth and heard my voice say, "Let it go, guys. They're just afraid that what I did will make Nick come around more often. But you just watch, what I did will help make Nick come around for real, and Austin and Matt will thank me for it."

The countenance on Liz and Dylan's faces softened somewhat and Liz said, "Yeah, well, whatever. I gotta get to class. See ya, guys."

As she walked away through the near empty lunch room, Dylan grabbed his backpack and waited for me to quickly repack my lunch bag. We had our next class together and as we made our way through the halls he said, "Michael, I have to admit, I don't know what would make you give your pie to Nick and not to your friends, and I'm a bit scared that he will come around more often. He treats us badly enough already and I think just giving him something will only encourage him to take more."

I was silent for a moment before responding, "Dylan, I honestly don't know why I did what I did; I can't tell you for sure. I know that I've really had a lot of weird things happening to me lately ever since my birthday and maybe this is just part of that. I don't know.

"But when I looked at him, I just knew somehow that he was feeling really bad about something and for whatever impossible reason, I felt sorry for him. That's what made me do something for him; I just don't know where it came from. And I've just got to believe that if he really felt that bad then one little nice thing I did for him probably means a whole lot."

Dylan accepted my answer and it seemed to comfort his fears some, at least enough that he was willing to try stepping into my belief and see what would happen instead of just expecting the worst. Honestly, I could not even say where I came up with those answers. It felt like I was just opening my mouth and words came out almost all by themselves.

I was glad that Dylan accepted my answers about what happened, and I suppose that those answers were good enough for me, too. They were true, after all. But I still had to wrestle with why I had done it in the first place. Where did that compassion come from? What actually moved me to get out of my seat? What gave me the answers to my friends' questions, helping me to have just the right things to say?

When I had been in awkward situations before I had never known what to say to explain things, but this time I found the right words, at least for Liz and Dylan. Matt and Austin would come along, too, I was sure, when they saw Nick starting to be nice to us.

But there was another thing – how was I so sure that Nick would all of a sudden stop terrorizing us just because I gave him a piece of pie?

Dylan and I arrived at our next class, which was English, and found our seats. Proof that news of my deed was spreading through the school came right away, as an outgoing boy named Tim who was not in my lunch turned around in his seat and said, "Hey, Michael, I heard you gave some food to Nick today."

Technically, he did not ask me a question and I wanted to say as little as possible, so I casually shrugged my shoulders and replied, "Yeah, I gave him a little."

"What'dya give him?" Tim asked.

"Does it matter? Why do you need to know?" I asked back defensively.

Apparently, Tim either was not curious enough to press me further or did not think I could tell him anything juicy enough to make it worth hearing so he dropped it. I braced myself for more questions like that the rest of the day, and maybe the rest of the week.

Seriously, why did I do that? I asked myself, just trying to figure it out for myself and feeling a little angry. Just then, a little whisper of a thought flitted through my mind, something from what the Divine Hand had told me in the night. The thought was like a word on the tip of your tongue, and I struggled to capture what I knew was there.

What was it that the Divine Hand said last night? I thought with a sigh. *Something about his light shining from me, what was it?*

I felt the ticking of the clock and knew that class would start any second. I shook my head as I struggled to find the words that would express what I was trying to remember, but nothing came. My teacher walked into the room as the bell rang and immediately began his lecture as he always did. Once this teacher started talking, there was not room to think about anything else. He was demanding and the moment he caught you not paying attention he would ask you about what he had just said. As much as I wanted to solve my mystery, I did not need even more embarrassment and shoved thoughts of what happened at lunch aside.

The next class was pretty much the same, with not much time to think about other things because we went to the library to do research for a newly assigned project. Unfortunately, being in the library meant more ability for others to ask me about Nick.

"What happened?"

"Why'd you do it?"

"What were you thinking?"

Not even two hours after it had happened I heard at least three different versions of the story. According to one person, I gave my whole lunch to Nick after he beat me black and blue, though I am not sure why he bothered asking me to confirm his story when he could clearly see my face in one piece.

Another person said she had heard that Nick and I were secretly meeting outside of school and that I was trading test answers for drugs. She suggested that I had failed to get him the answers to a test and was trying to buy back his favor with food.

Still another person had heard that Nick was my half-brother who had been quietly raised by his mom to save my dad from the news getting out that he'd had an affair with his high school sweetheart, but now my dad had told me the truth and asked me to look out for him.

When I heard the last story I just couldn't believe that someone would bring my dad into it as though that was somehow even remotely true. I could not believe that someone would even think it was okay to make an accusation like that against him, and when I heard it I had to bite my tongue to keep from losing my temper.

Glaring at girl who told me the story, I said, "Is it so impossible for you to believe that someone would do something nice for Nick that it's actually more plausible to you that this story is true? Seriously. I gave him a piece of pie. That's the whole story. Please don't tell anymore lies about me or my family and anyone you hear doing it, please tell them to stop it. It's not cool. Don't do it."

My body was tense with anger and I quickly walked away from the research computer with my scribbled note of book titles and the numbers that told me where to find them.

*How can these people come up with this stuff? Do they just think of the most outlandish story they can conceive and tell everyone that it's true, that they heard it from me or one of my friends? What would make them think it's even okay for them to do this? Do they honestly think I'm the one on drugs when **they're** the ones coming up with this stuff? And really, my dad had an affair with Nick's mom? Come on. Agh, I can't stand it!*

My plan was to just keep moving so no one had time to corner me with any more questions. I hurried from bookshelf to bookshelf, avoiding anywhere students were already looking for books on their assigned topics. I risked getting close to one of my classmates only once, figuring that the person was normally so quiet that she would be safe and she actually ran away from me. She probably saw the oncoming thunderstorm in my face and decided it would be better to find some shelter.

With a sigh of relief, the bell rang just as I finished checking out my books. I practically ran through the door, hoping that if I just kept moving fast enough then no one would be able to talk to me.

My eyes kept scanning the crowd like radar, looking for any threat against my quick and safe arrival to a seat in my bus. I got to my locker without any problems and opened the lock as fast as I could, messing up the combination twice because of my hurry. I decided to leave my research books in my backpack to save time and threw in anything I might need for my homework, stuffing in my lunch bag on top of everything while trying to disappear in the bustle of students around me.

I quickly glanced around at the crowded halls before closing my locker and making my break for the busses. Groaning under the weight of my overloaded bag, I walked toward the door like I was seconds away from being late for a final.

Then, just ten steps into my escape I caught a flurry of movement at an intersection of hallways out of the corner of my eye. Without breaking stride, my eyes instinctively focused on this disturbance and I recognized Nick, already fifty feet down the hallway, running so fast he had already knocked two people to the ground, leaving a small traffic jam in his wake.

I was in too much of a hurry to think about it then. All I cared about was getting on my bus. *The sixth graders aren't at this school yet; maybe I can sit next to one of them. They wouldn't know or care anything about Nick and whether or not I gave him something at lunch.*

The busses were just pulling into the parking lot as I shot through the doors and made my way to the spot where my bus would pull up. Shifting from side to side to keep a lookout for anyone who might shout out a parting insult at me, I again noticed Nick, who had just hit some smaller kid in the face while they waited for their bus.

A couple of Nick's thugs rode the bus with him and they quickly stepped up to ensure that no one would go after Nick and try to avenge the kid. They did not need to. Everyone on that bus knew better than to mess with Nick, and besides, I knew enough about that kid to know that he tried to make up for his size by talking big and annoying everyone. No one liked him, so no one would defend him and he probably asked for what he got, not that I wanted to see him hurt or anything.

I wonder if Nick's getting the same junk I am, I thought to myself, and then quickly focused back on my bus, which had just opened its door. In the rush to get on, I noticed Brandon behind me in line trying to get my attention, so when I found an open seat I grabbed the spot by the window and pulled him down next to me.

This was a complete switch in strategy for me, going from I-hope-I-can-hide-in-a-corner-and-everyone-will-leave-me-alone, to maybe-I-can-look-involved-enough-with-a-friend-that-everyone-else-will-leave-me-alone. And I was reluctant for it because I knew it meant talking about what happened at lunch when I still did not know why I had given Nick my pie.

The good news was that Brandon seemed to be trying to protect me, letting me shrink off into my own world while he used his overweight size to sort of shield against everyone still looking for their seat. Of course there was still a comment or two, accusations like, "So Michael, are you Nick's newest whipping boy now?" followed by laughter all around as though the question had been the latest one liner from a viral YouTube video.

"Shut up!" Brandon demanded. "You just wish someone gave you homemade food so you didn't have to eat school food."

"Yeah, whatever, Brandon," sneered the most vocal boy on the bus. "Your buddy used to just be a mama's boy with those homemade lunches. Now he's Nick's boy, too!" He laughed as he sat down and got high fives from his friends.

I'd had enough. I knew I should just leave well enough alone, but I turned around in my seat and said, "Really? What happened here? All of you were my friends this morning, and now you're all laughing at me? Do you really hate Nick that much, that someone does one nice thing for him and you all of a sudden make it your purpose in life to make fun of him for it? Seriously, come on now."

I faced forward again and tuned out their jeers as best as I could. Brandon leaned over to me and said, "I heard about five different stories about what happened and Matt was so mad he'd only say you betrayed us all. What in the world did you do?"

"I just gave Nick the dessert my mom packed me for lunch!" I replied, exasperated with the whole thing. "That's all! I just gave him a piece of pie with a little bit of ice cream on top."

"That's all? What's the big deal then?" he asked.

"I don't know! By the way people are reacting you'd think I made some sort of blood pact with him and declared him my lifelong, eternal, best friend in the whole wide world forever in front of everyone. Geez!"

"That's crazy, Michael, but why did you give it to him? You had to know people would notice."

"I did know that," I said, "but I didn't know it would be like this! And I don't know why I did it. I just saw that he didn't have any food and that he looked pretty sad, and for some reason I can't explain I just felt sorry for him and walked over to him with my pie. I don't know, man. That's just what happened."

Brandon shook his head and asked, "Then why are Matt and Austin so mad at you?"

"I don't know," I answered. "They were talking about how you don't treat enemies better than you treat friends. I think they're either just jealous that I wouldn't give the pie to them or they're afraid that it'll make Nick steal even more of our food."

Brandon replied, "Well, to be honest, I have to say either of those is a fairly reasonable way to feel about it. If they'd asked for the pie and you wouldn't give it to them then they might be angry that you gave it to someone else, especially to Nick."

"Would you be mad about it?" I asked him.

"I don't know, Michael. I probably wouldn't, but I'm not them. You know them. They get angry more easily than I do."

"You're right," I sighed.

I felt stuck. Most of my friends either felt betrayed or were holding me at a distance now since the whole school seemed to turn against me. *Great,* I thought, *I do one nice thing and I've already lost my friends. Maybe it won't be so hard to stick with the Divine Hand after all.*

Thoughts of my morning conversation with Mr. Gustafson seemed years ago after the events from lunch and the afternoon, and my incredible night with the Divine Hand seemed even longer ago. Now that I sat on the bus quietly for a moment it all came rushing back to me.

My head was swimming and my heart was churning. I desperately wanted to get home so I could be alone, let my defenses down, and just think for a while.

Brandon wrested me back to reality with the question, "What are you going to do about Matt and Austin?"

I shook my head and rolled my eyes, replying, "I don't know, Brandon. Right now I have so many other things on my mind than them that I really haven't even thought about it. Honestly, if the whole school doesn't back off soon, then I'm not going to care what Matt or Austin do, unless they decide to actually stick with me instead of siding with everyone else."

Brandon was silent for a moment, apparently thinking to himself before saying, "Michael, I don't understand this whole thing. I've never seen the school turn on someone like this and I'm a bit worried about getting caught up in it, but I want you to know I'm with you. I don't know why people are doing this stuff to you, but I do know you've been an awesome friend to me and I still want to be your friend."

"Thanks, Brandon," I said, "That means a lot."

The high schoolers were on the bus now. Since they didn't know who Nick was or care much for middle schoolers, it made my antagonists settle down some, making the rest of the bus ride more peaceful.

Finally getting off at the stop that left the least walking distance to my house, I scurried home as fast as I could without looking like I was afraid, lest I earn even more teasing. Breathing a sigh of relief as I closed the door behind me, I jumped up the stairs, regretting that I had packed my bag so full.

Arriving in my room, I set my bag down at the foot of my bed and flopped onto my back, rolling over to stare blankly at the ceiling. I grabbed my head; somehow it made me feel better, as though I was laying hold of my swirling thoughts and commanding them to settle down.

I realized that I needed my thoughts to distill into distinct issues so that I could figure them all out one by one, so I just started to retrace my steps through the day.

Okay, I woke up and remembered my crazy night with the Divine Hand, still feeling beyond words awesome. I felt that way until I was in the shower and thought about what my friends might think about all this if I start changing a whole lot. That was the first problem: What is everyone going to think if my strange experiences start changing who I am, or what are they going to think if they find out about them?

What else is there? I went to school and talked to Mr. Gustafson about my first issue and he gave me another one; what was it?

I thought back to my conversation with Mr. Gustafson and what he had said about being in friendships for what we can give to our friends instead of what we can get from them. I guess when everything started happening at lunch I just forgot what he had said. It was probably good that I remembered it now, since I felt about ready to ditch Austin and Matt if they didn't come to their senses by the next time I saw them.

But that's also where Mr. Gustafson loaded me with a bigger issue to deal with than my first one – the issue of whether I trusted the Divine Hand or not, I thought. Would I choose to risk what might happen if I let the Divine Hand change me, or would I choose to reject what he was trying to do in order to stay safe, staying who I have always been?

Thinking back on it, I remembered how incredible I had felt that morning and recognized that all of those feelings were still happening in me, just not as much. When I felt those feelings again, I remembered what made me get out of my chair to give Nick my pie – those feelings!

I remembered all of a sudden how something stirred in me when I saw how dejected he looked and how he did not have any food. It was so brief when it happened that I barely caught it, but that is what it was, and that is what kept me moving toward him the whole time, and that is what made me stand up to my friends when I got back to the table. I had felt smaller versions of the same feelings I experienced when the Divine Hand filled me like he filled my sword! Strength. Boldness. Compassion. Love. Peace. Joy. Confidence. These were the things I felt last night and these were the same things that made me give Nick my pie.

So it was all because of the Divine Hand! I marveled at it all and said to myself, "That's what I was trying to figure out before science class! The Divine Hand said something about how when I'm filled with him and do things like he does things then his light will shine from me and the people around me will feel it. I was feeling his Presence like I did last night when I did what he would do!"

I sat up and shook my head slowly, thinking about it all, and a frightening revelation washed over me. "And that's what my life would be like if I let the Divine Hand keep doing what he wants to do with me."

It really came down to one question; I faced a fork in the road of life and I had to pick a direction – Do I choose what felt safer, to do life on my own without the Divine Hand and everything from last night that I said had changed me forever? Or, do I choose to do what I was afraid to do, life with the Divine Hand, letting him have his way in me and trying to live in such a way that I became a living version of what I had seen in my sword?

I want to go both ways! I thought, exasperated.

My sword was still lying next to my bed where I had tossed it in my hurry to get out the door in the morning. I picked it up, almost absentmindedly, thinking about how it had looked when the Divine Hand was in it, remembering what it felt like when all his Presence shot out of it and into me. I wondered whether all of that was still inside me somewhere, lost in the churning emotions and repressed by my indecision. I realized that I had felt him during the day, but what I felt at lunch or even sitting there in my bedroom was immeasurably small compared to last night.

Looking deeply into the lion's face, I asked with a sigh, "Where is everything that happened last night? How can I be so confused about something that seemed so good? Do you remember what it was like to have *him* inside you?"

At this last question a fire sprang up in the lion's red diamond eyes and the flicker caught my attention. I settled my gaze on the eyes and pulled the sword closer to my face so I could see better detail.

Light sparkled in the eyes of precious stone, but there was something else that I could see. I concentrated more, and recognized that I saw a picture in the eyes, moving and living, far more than just the usual dazzle that they held.

The more I looked, the more the picture grew and took on normal colors. Then suddenly, it swallowed me whole.

Chapter Eleven
Finding Perspective

Flickering light was all I could see, casting faint, dancing shadows upon a stone wall, and I strained to understand what I saw. The colors became clearer and I recognized the light to be tongues of fire.

Slowly my vision drew back and I saw that the light was just a modest fire in an open hearth. The entire room was built of similar stone to the hearth, and the drapes on the windows hung open to reveal a clear night sky. The room was about half the size of a tennis court, and the walls were lined with shelves covered in ancient looking scrolls and manuscripts of various kinds.

Between two shelves was a table, and at the table a man sat scratching away with a feather quill on vellum. I watched as my vision continued moving toward the man, coming alongside him and pausing for just a moment.

Vemrilun! I thought, but had no time to think about him any longer, for the vision moved again, focusing on the parchment that lay before the High King's seer.

The words he had written were the same script from that world I had seen before, and I could read it this time no more than I could the last time I had seen it, but the vision continued to draw closer still to the vellum until it was all I could see.

Vemrilun's hand entered my vision, dipping the quill in a bottle of ink and scratching a few more lines. As he wrote, I saw the letters move, coming together to take on the form of a ship with many men aboard.

"Hurry!" I heard one man shouting, though he still appeared as no more than a stick figure. "We must gain land before the barbarians do!"

My vision closed upon the moving letters and they began to look more like real people.

"Do not worry," another voice said, "When has the Divine Hand ever granted me a vision too late?" I recognized this voice as belonging to Vemrilun, but it strangely came from the letters on the vellum, not from the man sitting at the table.

I felt the sway of the ship as it crashed through the waves.

"It matters little whether we make land before the barbarians. We will trample them under our horses whether they run for the village or hide in some weak defense on the beach!" boasted a thunderous voice. It was Delthun, the enormous king and warrior who speared the boar that had chased me in the woods.

The letters and parchment faded away completely now, and the whole scene opened before me. A chill wind filled the sails and I saw several boats cutting through the waves.

The voices I heard came from the boat right beneath me as I somehow flew midair above and a little to the side of it. I saw Vemrilun rushing about, helping to bring horses on deck and instructing the men to arm themselves for battle in any spare moment they had.

Delthun stood already armed, towering against the horizon in the foremost part of the ship, leaning against the railing as though he could will the ship to move faster. His muscles twitched with readiness for action, waiting to be near enough to either land or enemy ship to spring upon them in his battle frenzy.

A man stood by the rudder, cloaked in fur, and I assumed he must be the captain. He shouted orders to the crew – adjustments to the sails to maximize their speed, eyes on the rails to watch the depth of the water, hands to help Vemrilun with the horses and keep them calm so they were not hurt in the chase. And I watched as men, half of them dressed for war and half for sailing, ran here and there, skillfully accomplishing the tasks before them while taking shifts preparing in the armory.

This ship led the way for others close by. They sailed together as a small fleet and I saw that similar preparations were being done on the other ships as well. All together, the ships and the voices of the men filled the sea air with a din that would shake the coastal hills beyond the shore.

As one they rounded a point and a cry went up as they all saw the quarry they hunted – Barbarian ships, a dozen of them at least, sailing about two miles ahead and turning straight toward a harbor.

Sailing with such great speed, the High King's navy quickly closed the gap, but by the time the distance was only half what it was before already at least fifty boats had been lowered from the barbarian ships and were making their way to land. There would soon be nearly a thousand barbarians armed and ready to welcome the knights on shore.

Each ship now was flying at full speed, warriors manning their positions in the ship with spear in hand and sword on their thigh, ready to jump on their horses as soon as the water was shallow enough.

With only three hundred yards to the beach, I could see the barbarians forming ranks on the rocky slopes surrounding the harbor, which were lightly dusted in snow. They had faced these horsemen before and chose ground that would provide the best shelter from the horses' speed and size.

At one hundred yards we began passing their ships anchored in the harbor, and the men raised their shields to defend against the hail of fiery arrows that rained down from the archers still aboard the barbarian ships. They formed a human wall around the horses and not one injury came from the deadly assault. Any fires that started were quickly put out.

I sought shelter myself, but didn't need any. The arrows passed right through me as though I was not there.

Twenty yards, and still the ships kept charging toward the beach, now out of range of the enemy archers' small crossbows. The men were on their horses, ready for the charge.

Ten yards, five yards, Delthun cried out in his fierce bellow, and the horses leapt forward as the ships settled into the sand, jumping over the rail one after the other.

All around us the other ships dug into the shore and anchors were thrown down to keep the boats from slipping back out with the tide.

Each warrior knew what to do and fell into rank behind their kings. I recognized some of the leaders as those who had sat at the High King's table and ridden with him in the hunt. These were kings whom King Fidelas trusted, some of his highest and mightiest followers. Each of them had men under them and together they formed a powerful army of two hundred horsemen.

Delthun led the charge, directing his horse at full speed straight toward the enemy ranks, then feinting to the right at the last moment and circling up the side of the heights. Vemrilun led a second column to the left to come around the other side of the barbarians.

This move caught the enemy by surprise. They were not prepared to fight two different forces. Their leader quickly grunted some orders and his ranks began to reorganize into two groups, each one of them five hundred strong against only one hundred horsemen.

I soared higher and higher above the battle and could see what Delthun was doing. Only the heights facing the beach were rocky, while the land beyond them was plain. He simply circled around and would soon drive the barbarians down the hill and crush them against the stronghold in which they had trusted. Those who survived the charge would be under fire from archers who had remained aboard the ships. This battle would not last long.

My stomach turned as I saw the horsemen close in on the barbarians. I remembered being in battle before and had no interest in seeing it again. It did not matter, however, because whatever was moving me through this vision pulled me away. I flew across the land to a town just a few miles from the shore.

It was a small town, yet large enough to have a rough wall of hewn timbers for protection. Crude farms dotted the countryside as far as I could see. I saw no men in the town, but women had armed themselves as best they could with leather shirts, wooden pitch forks, and a very few swords. They watched over the walls to see what would come.

Here and there women shepherded children into houses, directing them to hide in the food cellars. Conversations were few, as everyone kept silent, listening to the noise of battle. A nervous calm lay over the place. Whispers echoed in the hush.

"What's happening?"

"We saw the barbarian sails, but who were those other ships?"

"Is that terrible High King going to come destroy us and share the spoils with them?"

They asked one another these things, but no one had answers.

The sound of battle faded away and smoke rose on the horizon, provoking even more concern. "What sort of horrible war machine are they building against us? They're coming to burn our city to the ground!" some shrieked.

"Be quiet!" others said, "They must have destroyed each other on the beach and this is just the fire of their ruin."

Other theories abounded, but they had no choice except to wait and see what would come over the hill to meet them. Finally, they heard the sound of horses riding steadily down the road.

"Get ready, here they come!" shouted one woman stationed on the wall.

"Careful," said another, "That's not enough horses coming our way to do much; they must be trying to trick us!"

Eleven horses crested the hill and slowed as they approached the town. A rider bearing the High King's banner rode in the lead with Vemrilun and Delthun right behind him. Each rider bore a large parcel.

When they drew near enough to speak, Vemrilun broke from the column and called out, "Hail, brave townspeople, in the name of the High King Fidelas! Do not fear, we come to you in peace and have no ill will against you.

"We do not ask for your trust, as we are confident that enough lies have been told to you that this is not yet possible. However, we would have you know that this day one thousand barbarians came right to your doorstep and would have destroyed you had it not been for the goodness of the High King.

"While your king, under the leadership of King Borgas, leads your husbands and brothers into battle against the High King, forsaking the protection of his own land and family, High King Fidelas has ordered some of his army to patrol the waters and intercept all barbarian attacks so that no Cotherian may be destroyed.

"You may see proof of the High King's protection on the horizon, as smoke rises from the burning barbarian ships, or you may witness the ruin of war on the beach for yourselves after you have seen our sails leave your island.

"Either way, know that the good High King woos you for a time to hold faithfulness with him, and earnestly desires that all of you would turn from your rebellion, embracing his lordship and the blessings that come to all those who remain under him. He offers you this favor now until all bear witness to his goodness toward them, but have a care, for the High King will not endure division within his kingdom forever.

"As a token of this kindness, we present gifts to you of food, drink, tools, medicine, and treasure to ensure your safety through the winter months. We will leave these before your gate for you to take or to leave as you will, and we will leave a written record of what has been done for you this day signed by the great kings who have today been your salvation so that your lord may hear of it. We extend the blessing of the High King, but only you can choose whether or not you will receive it.

"We bid you good day, and hope that you will meditate on what you have heard and received today, thereby coming to understand the goodness of your High King and repenting of your rebellion. May these gifts keep you well!"

Concluding his message, Vemrilun dismounted, set his parcel on the ground, and then remounted. One by one, each rider did the same, leaving a large pile of goods for the townspeople. When the last one had remounted his horse, they quickly reformed their columns and rode away.

The women of the town looked at one another with astonishment and confusion on their faces. None of them had expected this and none of them had ever heard of anything like it.

Most were still skeptical, expecting there to be an ambush waiting for them as soon as they opened the gate or for the gifts of food to be poisoned. Some said they refused the gifts and thought they should be burned as soon as possible. Others were moved by Vemrilun's words and said they should do as he said and turn back to the High King. Still others wanted to investigate the battle first to see if what he said was true.

I did not see what happened there, or even what happened with those kings and warriors who fought the battle, for I was lifted away to an entirely different place. The scene I had been watching faded away into dancing letters on the vellum and I again heard the scratching of Vemrilun's quill.

He carefully set aside the page he had been writing and prepared a new one, pausing for a moment as though remembering something that caused a well of emotion to spring up within him. He sat back in his chair with his eyes clenched shut, brow furrowed with grief.

Slowly, his eyes opened, revealing an ocean of thought in his heart, unfathomable as the deepest trench, determined as the strongest tide. With a heavy sigh he leaned forward and began his scratching again, clean, deliberate strokes filling the page line after line.

There was a rhythm in his writing, an undulating flow, a pulse that I felt as his pen moved across the page. Again, the words began to disappear and scenes opened before my eyes, but unlike before, I did not settle into one event.

Rather, I watched many events as though I were outside of time. Years of history passed before my eyes and entered my memory as though I had lived it.

I saw many other sea battles like the one I had first witnessed, on seemingly every coast of every island throughout Cotheria. King Fidelas sent his army throughout his entire kingdom to chase down and destroy the barbarians, not only because that war did not end when the rebellion started, but because he fought to protect all those who rightfully belonged to him. He fulfilled the role the petty kings had abandoned and maintained his responsibility as High King to watch over all the land.

Vemrilun led the war against the barbarians, always knowing from a dream or a vision where they were going to attack next. Without fail he led the High King's men to intercept them before they had done any serious damage.

War raged on the island of Unitia, too, as the rebellious kings led their armies against High King Fidelas. Every spring I watched them lead their men from their diverse islands and join together to besiege the High King's stronghold where I had talked with Vemrilun upon the wall.

The fortress was well repaired and housed the kings, their men, and all their families. It withstood the attacks it suffered. Many times, the outer wall was claimed by Borgas and his fierce warriors, but they never discovered the secret tunnels and were never able to mount a significant offense against the inner wall. There simply was not enough room between the walls for them to use the siege weapons that helped them gain the first wall.

I watched the seasons change. War came with spring and summer, and fall ushered in the wintery seasons of recovery. But for those in the stronghold, recovery was a struggle. Even though Borgas only maintained the siege through the warmer months, it was enough to prevent the High King from planting fields, so his supplies grew fewer and fewer as the conflict endured.

The first three years were the most intense, as the zeal of the rebellious kings was fresh and hard. They despised King Fidelas and all who would side with him. They saw them as evil, foolish, a blemish in the land that needed removed.

After the third summer of war, High King Fidelas took account and saw that there were not enough supplies for winter even with sparse rations. Taking counsel together produced no new options, and all began to cry out to the Divine Hand to save them.

In the lands of the rebellious kings, however, things were vastly different. The kings would return to homes that were not burnt, crops that were ready to be gathered in, families who were safe and healthy, and reports that certain followers of the High King had diverted an attack by the barbarians that would have surely destroyed everything.

Often in those early days, the women burned the gifts they were given, suspicious of traps and aware that many of the High King's men had lost their families in that first summer of the rebellion before they all took shelter in the stronghold. They feared revenge.

But gradually they began to realize the kindness the High King was showing them by defending their homes and families while the men were away. It was not lost on them, either, that in doing this the High King put himself at greater risk by sending out his highest advisor and many of his greatest warriors, giving away precious food and supplies that were desperately needed within the stronghold.

They began to understand that every wound they inflicted was against a King who handicapped himself for their sakes to keep them from injury. They saw that they were starving a King who sacrificed to ensure their fields remained whole and their bellies well fed. And they knew it was not just the High King who chose to take this risk, but all the other kings who had remained faithful, who had families, who owned land, who raised crops, and had much to lose.

The weight of this revelation wore heavily on many of the rebellious kings, and in that dark hour when the noble kings faced destruction – not from a force of war, but from starvation and winter cold – the first of the rebellious kings returned to his due allegiance.

Fearing retaliation from King Borgas, he emptied his village and brought all his people with him to the stronghold, along with their entire harvest and all their livestock and flocks. The influx of supplies enabled them to last through the winter.

Many times in the years that followed the faithful who hid in the castle were threatened with starvation, for even though more and more rebellious kings returned, bringing fresh supplies with them, their increasing number also increased the demand for supplies.

Finally, enough kings had submitted again to High King Fidelas that the stronghold was full, so they took counsel and decided to appoint an army whose sole responsibility would be to raise and protect crops on one of the outlying islands. They chose one of the remotest islands, hoping to avoid detection by Borgas or the barbarians, and succeeded in bringing enough supplies that everyone in the stronghold was easily fed.

With this renewed strength, along with the added numbers and Borgas' depleted ranks, the end of the war was in sight and High King Fidelas spoke of how short the time was.

His voice echoed up from the swiftly moving vision, "I will not wait long. Soon the time will pass when they may choose me because of my goodness, and I will not allow them choose me because of my might again. We have given them warning, but those who do not return to us soon will be cast out from my kingdom by force."

Time began to slow and the vision became clearer. One character stood out from among the rest, one whom I had seen repeatedly through the years of war. He had been the High King's chief advisor in the place of Vemrilun while the seer was away leading the raids and had overseen the transition of the rebellious kings into the noble society.

He had also fought alongside Aerlic and the other mighty kings defending the fortress during the repeated attacks. This is where I first took real notice of him, for he carried my sword into battle. And now that the vision slowed and became clearer, I realized that he bore similar features to mine as well, but was much older, probably about twice my age.

I watched the last campaign of the rebellious kings rise and fall. They fought bravely, but without heart. I could see that they were driven more by their fear of Borgas than by a passion for their cause.

This fear was the only thing that held their camp together, for with one voice they would whisper to each other by their fires at night of their desire to serve the High King and of the goodness he had shown them over the twelve years of war. They spoke of how they hated the thought of dying in a battle against someone who had done so much to help and protect them, and to die for a man like Borgas, who had lied, threatened, intimidated, and manipulated from the beginning in order to keep his followers.

They knew the real Borgas by now, and they knew the real King Fidelas. They knew whom they wanted to serve as their king, but they were afraid. Borgas was crueler than ever, sensing the discontent among his men and knowing how many had already left him. He drove them ruthlessly, and began to even make the night time rest difficult for them so they could not conspire against him. He expected rebellion. It was all he knew.

But these men had learned something from their High King – Justice. And they knew that they had no right to Borgas' life, at least no right compared to what High King Fidelas had. They could not just quietly kill him and be done with it, hoping for the army to dissipate without its leader driving them.

No, they had to take a risk. Anyone who wanted to defect would have to publicly confront Borgas and hope enough people backed him that he would keep his life.

Finally, someone broke. One particular captain was struck with the thought that he would rather risk dying in opposition to Borgas than risk dying for him. When Borgas ordered him to lead his men in a charge, he refused.

Borgas ordered another captain to kill the insolent knight. He refused. Desperate, Borgas called for anyone to help him. No one moved.

Together, the two captains disarmed Borgas and led him out of their camp unhindered through what army remained. Taking a white flag of truce, they approached the stronghold's main gate.

"We ask to speak to the High King regarding terms of surrender," the first captain said.

King Fidelas stood near at hand and quickly appeared on the wall. The captains reported the condition of the rebel camp and told of how they apprehended Borgas, presenting their old king as proof of their sincerity.

Time sped in my vision again and soon I saw the High King upon his throne, dressed in his royal robes and surrounded by the lower kings with their queens, also clad in regal attire. Here and there a queen whose husband had died in the battles sat alone.

They were all gathered together in a great, long room with high vaulted ceilings. The walls were adorned with tapestries made by the women during the winter months, when there was more time and fewer wounded for whom to care. Royalty sat on thrones upon a dais, extending out from the high throne which was in the middle. The dais itself was raised seven steps above the main floor. Seats like bleachers had been placed along the walls to make room for the whole assembly to gather, as the entire army came as witnesses.

On King Fidelas' right hand stood Vemrilun in wine colored robes. On his left was the stranger I had seen with my sword wearing a blue tunic that shimmered like a star filled night, resembling the one I had been given the night of my coming of age feast.

The remnants of Borgas' army stood before the throne first, Borgas himself stood bound behind them, and everyone had stern looks on their faces.

High King Fidelas addressed Borgas' men:

"I thank the Divine Hand that you have returned your loyalty to me of your own free will. I have heard how you served King Borgas at first out of genuine hearts, but how in these latter days you have served him only because of fear. You have seen my goodness richly demonstrated to you over these past twelve years and my goodness toward you will not change. Therefore, I invite you now to examine your hearts and decide for yourself if you truly do renounce your loyalty to King Borgas and declare fealty unto me. Know this as you consider – I swear to you now that your lives will be spared, even if you choose to remain steadfast in your rebellion. If you wish to retain faithfulness to King Borgas, step forward now."

He paused for a moment to see if anyone would accept his offer. No one did.

"Very well, then," he continued, "The only law I impose on you is the law of my heart. When I made myself known in Cotheria I came with no army and made no attempt to conquer you. After that, when you saw the military of those kings who received me and unwillingly sided with them to make me your king, and later when you decided to rebel with Borgas, I did not hold you by force, but freely allowed you to leave. Through the entire war that has now ended, I never raised my hand against you to conquer you, but only defended those who willingly made themselves my own. As I have acted toward you from the beginning, so I will act toward you always.

"Now you have seen my heart in truth. In response to the kindness I have shown you even while you rebelled and brought destruction to my people, you are choosing this day with your own will to submit to me as your High King.

"This submission means that you agree to assist in my mission to exalt the lowly, ensure justice for the oppressed, father the orphans, and protect the kingdom from evil, until the kings among you are kings of kings and the lowest among us is mightier than the greatest champion elsewhere. This is my heart, and therefore this is my law. Do you so choose, and take on this mission as your own? If so, come forth and declare it to me with this congregation as witness."

One by one, all of Borgas' men ascended the steps of the High King's dais and took their oath, renouncing their rebellion, kissing his hand as they knelt before him, and offering their swords to him as symbols of their lives. Before each man rose, the High King placed his hand on their head and pardoned them for their offenses.

When the last of them had passed before him and taken his place among the witnesses, Borgas was brought before the throne. His face was filled with hatred. Bitterness writhed in his countenance. Rage overpowered him and caused him to shake in his bonds. He spat accusations at those who passed closest to him, "Weaklings! Has he deceived you now, too? Do you think he'll really let you live now, after you fought him this long? Fools!"

King Fidelas turned sad eyes upon him. He was silent for a moment, and I could see that he was examining Borgas in a way, as though he were remembering something about him that was lost long ago. Finally, he spoke.

"King Borgas, we are sorrowful to see you so brought before us. You were to be one of the greatest leaders and kings in the history of Cotheria. You have such strength, not only in the power of your arms, but in the might of your heart. That strength should have led countless others to be as great as and even greater than you. Your broad, strong shoulders should have had thousands standing upon them, with your arms lifting them up into the greatest they could be.

"How great would you have been then? Perhaps you could have been the greatest ever, a true king like us, with kings following you who have kings following them who have kings following them. You could have had this as your legacy.

"Indeed this was the dream in the Divine Hand's heart when he created you. This was his purpose for your life, and you will be measured not by your rebellion, but by the distance of how far you fell short of that dream.

"Until today, that purpose for your life was still open to you, but today that way is shut forever. Until today, you could have repented and I would have had mercy on you. You still could have become an exalted king in this kingdom, but no longer. Today you are brought before the judgment seat and you will receive your just condemnation.

"Observe for yourself the legacy you now leave! See the widows who sit with me whose husbands you killed in battle! See the maimed warriors who line the walls, those who bear horrible scars, false limbs, and patches on their eyes because of you! See the men whose families you destroyed in the first summer of your rebellion! See the sons and daughters who have no fathers! See the men whose brothers are dead!

"And now see many years from now, those children who will not be born because you destroyed their parents. See the legacies this world will never know because you cut them off. See the benefit, not only of your own life, but of countless others' lives that this world will never receive because of your selfishness, your rebellion, your hatred, and your pride. See the destruction you have caused!"

King Fidelas paused and I could hear his voice echo through the large chamber. Fire burned in his eyes as he said, "Now hear our judgment. For your attempt to raise yourself into the position of High King, your rebellion against we who are the rightful possessor of the throne, and your effort to lead your fellow Cotherians astray that led to untold death and destruction, you are hereby forever cast out of the Kingdom of Cotheria and all of its dominions, ordered to spend the rest of your days among those with whom you have demonstrated a common heart – the Barbarians. With them you will make your home and with them will be any future you have left to you. Your life alone is granted to you this day, but it is forfeit if ever again you place one foot within our dominion. Come forward and receive your sentence."

Borgas thrashed against the guards who dragged him forward, trying to bite them and butt them with his head – the last weapons he had left – but he was powerless in their grip. They brought him up the stairs and forced him to kneel before the High King.

Rising from his throne, King Fidelas placed his right hand on Borgas' head, rendering him motionless with a force beyond his natural strength, and declared, "Borgas, you are now cast forever from our presence and dominion.

Wherever our rule extends, you are forbidden to enter. You, who were to be glorious, will now be loathsome and deplorable.

"Your strength is taken from you. Your honor is stripped from you. All glory is bound from you eternally. Your name will forever be a symbol of destruction, not only because of what you inflicted, but because of what you suffer.

"Among the barbarians will you walk, and according to their ways will you live. We condemn you to be keenly aware of the height to which you were called in contrast to your total abasement. You will be tortured with ravenous pains because of this awareness and you will curse the day you were born.

"Even the barbarians will hate and despise you because of the corruption in your heart. They will reject you for your foolishness and scoff at you for your demise.

"You sought to gain everything, so you are condemned to have nothing. In the end you will be abandoned by all, alone, rejected, and destroyed in every way.

"We issue this sentence over you, Borgas, according to the justice due you, by the authority granted to us by the Divine Hand."

Concluding thus, the High King removed his hand from the treacherous former-king and commanded the guards, "Release him, but do not give him much distance."

They let him go and, raising his hand in the air, King Fidelas declared, "As you have demonstrated your heart to be, may you so appear before all men's eyes!"

Immediately, Borgas began to convulse as a transformation came upon him. His once strong back bent double like an old man. His hair broke out of its ties and grew matted, unkempt, and filthy. His arms and legs shriveled until his strength that used to best a thousand men in contests could not even hold up his own body. His face contorted into a gaunt, ugly mask with crooked and black teeth. His fingers bent and cracked, warping as with rheumatoid arthritis, and the nails upon them grew long and yellow, full of rotten disease. His skin, too, became spotted and wan, appearing in places to have painful open sores.

A shudder swept through the room and many turned away in horror at the wretched pile of a man lying upon the floor. He was so marred that he looked more beast than human and more dead than alive.

High King Fidelas looked upon his ruined enemy with sorrow in his eyes again and he sighed, "Carry him away to his new land."

He watched the guards take Borgas' withered form between them and soberly remove him from a hall. I looked at his face and saw him still seething in unrepentant, unbroken hatred and pride, and I was in awe that such a transformation had done nothing to soften his heart. But as the doors closed behind him, I realized his outward condition was now just the visible manifestation of what had always been his inward one. If he had not let anything else King Fidelas did over the years change his heart, then certainly this would not touch it.

Once Borgas was finally gone it was as though a shadow lifted off of the court, and, seeming to acknowledge the change, King Fidelas raised his hands before all the people gathered and exclaimed, "My good people of Cotheria, I declare this war finished!"

A great cheer rose up from all the people and many threw their hats in the air in celebration. Hands were clasped and friends embraced all over the room. Both men and women wept openly for joy at this moment that at times looked like it would never come.

Even though I was only watching it, unable to participate, I was moved with emotion as well, for I had seen the beginning of this war, and was overjoyed to also see its end.

King Fidelas gestured for silence and spoke again, "I cannot thank you all enough for what you have done to bring about this victory. However, I do now order that preparations be made for us all to feast for the next seven days!"

Again, cheers rose from the people and the High King allowed them their celebration before calling them to order again. "At the feast tonight," he continued, "I will present rewards to those who have served me and Cotheria during this war. I will call all of you to honor with me those whom I honor, and I know that you will.

"This celebration is but the beginning of the freedom I desire you to have. And, bless the Divine Hand, while fighting this war we have also won our war against the barbarians, and for the first time in any of your lifetimes our land is filled with peace!"

Great shouts rose up and filled the hall with resounding joy. It was true that no one alive, nor their parents, nor their grandparents for many generations, had known a Cotheria at peace. This was truly something worth celebrating!

The High King himself cheered along with his subjects, his eyes bright with laughter and a smile extending across his face. Finally, he called them to be quiet once more and said, "I will say one final thing before I release you to your full celebration, for there is one last matter to address before our council is done.

"All you who have today sworn loyalty to me, come forward, please."

A look of concern came over those who had remained faithful to Borgas until the end. They worried that perhaps they had been tricked and now they were going to be transformed into barbarians, too. Seeing their fear as they came together, King Fidelas said, "Do not worry! I am not calling you out for punishment, for your offense is already forgiven. I am bringing you forward to release you into your destinies."

With that, he turned to the man at his left whom I did not recognize and said, "Michael, would you please come forward and address these men?"

"Yes, Your Highness," the man said. And as he walked forward, I thought, *How can that be me? I'm here, wherever here is, watching this happening. I can't be watching and living the same thing at the same time, can I?*

The man whom the King called Michael looked at the men and said, "It has been a long time since any of you have seen me, except perhaps in battle. Indeed, it has been since that fateful night twelve years ago on which the good High King Fidelas gave me a coming of age feast. Yet I stand before you the very same Michael whom the High King honored that night.

"I prove this to you by showing you my sword, which you will all recognize as the treasure sword the High King gave to me," and he drew it out of its scabbard, holding it out for all of them to see. It definitely was my sword, being held by someone claiming to be me!

"The night you rebelled, I also disappeared back into my own world, but by the grace of the Divine Hand I have returned several times, finally coming to stay. In my time here the seer Vemrilun has trained me in my gifts and helped me to become a valuable counselor and servant to the High King.

"When those who were among you began to return to us, the High King gave me responsibility over their transition back into our company. As I assisted them with this process, so will I also assist you.

"There is one major reason for this that concerns you. It is because we recognize that there are certain mindsets that led you to rebel. We know that these mindsets are partially renewed because you have now repented from your rebellion, having experienced and come to trust the High King's goodness, and swearing to serve him in his mission. However, it is almost certain that there is still some of this mindset remaining in you that we desire to help you remove.

"We are not concerned that you would rebel again. We simply desire to help you live the fullest life you possibly can, and these mindsets will keep you from that. Moreover, you have sworn to uphold the High King's law, which is his heart, but a law of the heart is learned in a much different way than an ordinary law.

"So to accomplish this reformation of thinking, each of you will be placed for a time near others who have already grown in this area. As you interact with them and observe their way of life, your life will also be transformed.

"In addition to this, the High King asks you to join him three times a year for banquets, during which time the whole kingdom will meet together and encourage one another with stories of how life is flourishing and of accomplishments worthy of praise. Or, if there is some need, then those with strength can help those who are in need.

"When you have renewed your mindset to match that of the High King's, then you will be released to go wherever you desire, or to stay with those to whom we have entrusted you."

It was the oddest thing to watch what was apparently an older version of me speaking to these men as a leader, someone whom the High King trusted and kept as a close advisor.

I remembered how I felt standing before those men when King Fidelas gave me my sword – embarrassed, ashamed, and afraid to stand out, which was only compounded by Borgas leading his men in rebellion and saying the harsh things he said. Somehow this Michael standing before the same men had found confidence, for he clearly was not afraid of being known as who he is or of any negative reaction they might have at seeing him again. Rather, he proudly introduced himself and proved his identity, even displaying his sword that pushed the rebellion to fully manifest.

Seeing "myself" stand before those men again brought me back to the day I first saw them. I had fainted in battle only to recover in the company of many kings who were arguing over my fate. Of course the High King won the argument, which meant that I was to receive a feast to celebrate my 13th birthday.

King Fidelas presented me before all the men, treating me as though I were his own son and giving me a lavish gift. And as I watched my older self assign faithful leaders to this new round of returning warriors, the High King's words returned to me.

"Michael, I am confident, will be a great leader and warrior, strong in counsel and noble in character," he had said. I looked at the Michael before my eyes and I realized that he was everything King Fidelas said I would be.

Then something clicked for me. This Michael had said to the returning soldiers, "When you have renewed your mindset to match that of the High King's..." The High King's mindset about me was that I would become a great leader and warrior, strong in counsel and noble in character. The reason he could trust the older me to be a leader in his kingdom is because at some point during the twelve years of war, that Michael believed what the High King thought about him.

The older Michael had finished dividing the men up now and was giving more instructions. "I give you comfort again, good men of Cotheria, for your time under these leaders to whom I have assigned you will not be as you may suppose.

"You are not slaves to them, or even servants, but you are free men, and as such they will treat you. They will help you plow, plant, and harvest your fields. They will invite you to share with them of their table. They will celebrate with you the things that bring you joy and comfort you in time of mourning. By any means, they will ensure mutual interaction, so that you may observe their attitude and learn from them, asking them when you have questions and receiving their answers.

"Your instruction in the heart of your High King will not be formal, for he does not desire subjects who only *know* what is in his heart. He desires subjects who *share* his heart, and that can only come as you see it demonstrated. You must not simply hear about it, rather, you must experience it until it becomes a part of you as well, so that you may also demonstrate that same heart to others. This is how your High King governs his kingdom."

That Michael finished speaking and turned to face King Fidelas, bowed slightly to indicate that he was relinquishing the floor to him, and then returned to his place next to the High King. "Thank you, Michael," King Fidelas said from his throne before addressing the men still gathered before him.

"Gentlemen," he said, "I give one word to you before I dismiss you. As you have heard Michael address you, I warn you to guard your hearts. When you repented to me for your rebellion then you lost your right to be jealous of any whom I have honored. Let not offense poison you again as it did before lest you be caught in its grip and torn away from the wonderful life that now awaits you.

"You are new men! Consider all from your past to be as though another had done those things, for it is all forgiven and gone. Only a future as you have never imagined lies before you. Set your eyes upon it and enter it with full abandon! It is yours for the taking as we move forward together!"

High King Fidelas stood and addressed the entire congregation, "People of a united Cotheria, I rejoice with you! Let us now begin the celebration for which generations of our forefathers longed. Let us dream together of the glory that will shine from this nation as we continue to give of ourselves to one another. Let us give honor generously to all, let us remember those who have fallen along the journey to this moment, and let us heartily welcome our newest brothers with their families into our fellowship with the enthusiasm that befits the promise upon their lives!"

A deafening roar burst from the assembled host and they broke out in a race to welcome their old comrades reunited. I only heard the sounds of celebration for a moment, however, for my vision began to fade again and the scene before my eyes turned into dancing letters settling into their places among the lines of indecipherable script, penned in fluid motion by the hand of Vemrilun.

He finished the line, put down his quill, and leaned away from his work, sighing, "Ah, another chapter of our history is recorded. Soon the works of my generation will be done and it will be time for you to record the history that your generation has built upon our shoulders!"

The door had just opened and he turned to face whomever he had addressed. A voice replied to him, "Congratulations, my teacher! But I do not think I am ready to fill your shoes yet." The person to whom the voice belonged laid a hand on Vemrilun's shoulder and my vision followed it up the arm until I could see the face. It was the other me.

The old seer said, "Oh, you will more than fill my shoes, my son, for you have honored me and received of my gifts and of my wisdom, and so you will make my successes without making my failures, adding successes of your own upon them. And this you must do, for I have been as a father to you, and you as a son to me. You know these things well!"

"I do know these things, father," the older Michael replied respectfully, "I simply mean that your accomplishments are not yet complete. Though I am ready to continue your work without you, I prefer to work alongside you as I have done for many years."

"This is good, Michael," Vemrilun said, "Yet all the same, I charge you to raise a son of your own, for you must have eyes not only to receive from me, but to give to others so that what I have given you will not die, but continue to grow. This is how our nation will continue to increase in its glory. And more importantly, it is right to do!"

The two of them continued talking, but their voices began to fade. My vision no longer saw them, moving back to the fire where it began. The tongues of fire danced against the stone, glowing bright red, burning deeper and deeper until suddenly they were only the eyes in the lion's head on the hilt of my sword that rested in my hands.

I was back in my room, sitting exactly as I had been before as though nothing had changed...but something had changed. Something big.

Chapter Twelve
A Changed Man

Seeing myself in the future – or some other future, however that works – did something in me. When I picked up my sword and was drawn into the vision I was filled with uncertainty, worry, and doubt. Now I felt confident, strong, and at peace.

I thought through my vision to try to figure out when the shift had happened. Just being in a vision was distracting enough to make me mostly forget how I felt, and watching the battle certainly gave me something else to think about, but being distracted is not the same as being changed.

Nothing changed when I saw the two captains hand Borgas over to High King Fidelas, and nothing changed when Borgas was exiled from the Kingdom, transformed into his withered barbarian form. Even when I saw myself standing next to the High King and heard myself speak to the returning men, even then nothing changed.

It was when I realized that the older me was different because he believed what King Fidelas said about him, that is when I changed. When I realized it came down to what I believed, that is when seeing myself older and confident, doing amazing things that I never thought I could do changed me. It was as though the High King's words were proved true, so then I believed them and was changed in my world, not just in my vision.

But then another question popped into my head. If High King Fidelas is just someone that I saw in my visions and not a real person, then what does it matter what he said to me, no matter how real it felt?

I sat there for a moment trying to figure it out, and then it came to me. *Ah, it's because King Fidelas was never the one actually talking to me anyway. It was always the Divine Hand really talking to me because he's the one who has given me all these visions in the first place. He's the one saying all of it, just as much as it was him talking when he was in this room last night!*

So that was it! The only reason that it mattered what King Fidelas, or Vemrilun, or Perilan, or anyone else said about me in the visions is because it was not really them – it was the Divine Hand, and I had experienced him in my own world, not just in my vision and dream world.

He was the constant. He was the reality that connected everything. He was the one who had the power to give me these dreams and visions and make my sword from one world appear in the other. He was the one whose words mattered. I needed to know what *he* thought about me.

Right away I looked at my sword again because he said it was crafted to represent me. I looked all over the sword very quickly and excitedly, and then stopped and laughed to myself, "I'm glad that I'm like this sword, but I have no idea what that means!"

Lying down on the floor, I held the sword to myself and tried to think of everything anyone from my dream and visions had said about me.

I shut my eyes and said them out loud, "I am a gifted leader! I am great in counsel and noble in character! I am a seer! I will lead people into who they were made to be! I will help people see the gifts they have and teach them how powerful those gifts are!

"It's good that I'm unique, and me being who I am will help others become who they are! There is nothing wrong with me!"

It felt really good to say those things about myself, especially because I knew that it was true, because I didn't make it up myself. The Divine Hand said those things about me!

While I knew thinking this way might seem crazy to most people, I did not care anymore. If the Diving Hand really had given me the experiences I'd had, and if he really was so good that he said those things about me and wanted to see me fully become them, then why would I not believe in him and let him help me become who he said I am? He obviously was able to help me do that, and who he said I am is way better than who I was before, so of course I would follow him with whatever he wanted to do.

A huge wave of relief washed over me and I realized that I had been hoping all day to choose the Divine Hand, even when everything started going bad with my friends. What he did in me when I saw him in my room, I could never forget that and nothing was more important to me now than staying in his presence.

"Divine Hand," I said, "I'm sorry for my doubts today, but I do choose you right now. I want you. I want your presence. I want you to help me become everything that you say I am. Speak to me, give me dreams and visions, do whatever you want to do, but I want to be with you no matter what else I do in my life.

"Just like those rebellious kings gave themselves back to King Fidelas, I give myself to you. Your heart will be my law. You are my King and my sword is yours!" I held my sword in the air above me as though the Divine Hand was physically there to take it. My sword did not move, but I felt his peace and joy come over me as it had that night, like a wonderful hug that chases away all worry and makes you want to laugh from the deepest place in your heart.

I knew he was saying that he accepted my offer, and that he would lead me in life wherever I went and raise me up into the greatest Michael I could possibly be, in this world or any other world to which he wanted to take me.

The freedom that I felt was like nothing I had ever known. I had just seen myself as a high advisor to a king of kings – who could limit what I could become? I would also become a king of kings, maybe not with official position, but I would carry that heart and raise others up to be kingly just as I had seen High King Fidelas do.

We would all be kings and queens together, making more kings and queens wherever we went until the whole world became noble! And why not? Could anyone resist true nobility? Could anyone see that kindness, feel that calling to become great, hear that voice saying, "You can do it!" and somehow reject it all, choosing to stay base and lowly?

I certainly could not resist it. I was all in, sold out, jumping in with both feet. My life was determined – I would become all I was made to be and take as many people on the same journey as would come with me. The world could only be a better place for it, and there was no more certain way to enjoy a full life.

Excitement pumped through my veins and I struggled to know just what to do with myself. I felt like I had to let it out somehow, but I did not know how to explain what was going on yet. I forced myself to settle down enough to think.

"Alright, so the only people home right now are Mom, Stevie, and Amy, and I haven't really been talking to any of them about this stuff, especially Stevie and Amy. So I can go and talk to one of them and hope they'll understand, but they probably won't.

"Or I can wait and maybe talk to Dad about it tonight. I probably owe him another conversation after this morning anyway since that was the last time I talked to him and he doesn't know anything about what happened at school."

Deciding that this was the best way to go, I said, "I hope he comes home soon!" and I started unpacking my overstuffed backpack to find my homework for the night. Despite all the books I brought home, I actually did not have that much to do if I put off working on the couple of projects I had.

It did not take long to finish my work, so I headed downstairs to the computer to do some more research while I waited for Dad to come home.

My paper on Mother Theresa needed to be five pages long, and I needed to have ten sources, citing five of them in the paper. My ten sources needed to have three note cards each, with a different piece of information that I could use on each one. I managed to find three good sources, filling nine note cards before my dad got home.

He walked through the door happily, stopping in the entry way to breathe in deeply the wonderful smells of dinner. "Ah, it's good to be home!" he said.

Amy ran to him yelling, "Daddy!" and I heard his bag hit the ground as he dropped it to open his arms and catch her.

"Oh, Amy! I love you so much! I just can't get enough of your hugs! You make your Daddy feel so special!" He oozed affection all over her and planted a big kiss on her forehead as I came around the corner.

She skipped away, humming, and Steve was next in line. He was somewhere between me and my sister in terms of enthusiasm. I think in his heart he wanted to run up and give Dad a hug like Amy did, but he kind of wanted to look grown up, too. So he greeted Dad with a big hug and a kind of shy, "Hey, Dad."

"Thanks, Steve! I love you so much, son, and I'm so proud of you. Thanks for your wonderful hugs!" Dad said before letting him go.

After Steve left, I stepped in and gave my dad a hug. "Hey, Dad," I greeted him.

"Hey, son! How are you?" he asked with his usual excitement, pulling me close.

"I'm really good, Dad, and I'm looking forward to talking to you about it," I said. "Can I come up to your room in a couple minutes when you're done changing out of your work clothes?"

"Sure, Michael, of course you can," he said, smiling at me curiously. "I've got some things to share with you, too."

"Cool. Well, I'll come up in a minute, then. I just have to finish up some research really quick and put my stuff away."

"Sounds good, son," he said and started to walk away to greet Mom.

I quickly walked back to the computer, not wanting to waste any time that I could have talking to Dad. I knew he would be a couple of minutes, but I would rather wait for him then have him waiting for me.

Taking a last look at the website I had been researching, I closed it down and threw my note cards in my folder for Mr. Gustafson's class and stuffed all my things into my backpack.

Running up the steps two at a time, I hurried into my room to quickly deposit my backpack and make my way to my parents' room. I knocked on the door softly and my dad replied, "Just a minute," so I stood outside, waiting.

When my dad opened the door he said, "Come on in, Michael. Grab a seat and tell me what's on your mind."

I sat down in the big, overstuffed chair that my parents have always had in their room and began, "Well, it's kind of a long story, but there's a lot that's happened today.

"First, I woke up this morning, having had that experience with the Divine Hand in my room last night that I told you about. Then I went to school and talked to Mr. Gustafson about it.

"He said that my struggles with my experiences really came down to whether or not I wanted to become who I really was made to be, knowing that becoming that person means that I'll stand out from everyone else and people might not like that. I realized that I had to choose between the Divine Hand and my friends, because letting the Divine Hand change me might mean that I lose my friends.

"I kind of thought about all that until lunch time, but during lunch something else happened that made the rest of school just terrible.

"We were just eating and everything was normal, and I was just about to eat my pie when I realized that Nick, the bully who picks on us and steals our food, hadn't eaten any lunch, and he didn't have anything to eat.

"Something happened inside me and I just stood up and took my pie to Nick and gave it to him, with everyone in the whole lunchroom watching.

"When I got back, Austin and Matt started accusing me of betrayal because I treated Nick better than I treated them and they ran off to class before we could work things out. The rest of the day just got worse and worse and people were saying terrible things, making up stories and spreading lies about me, teasing me and making it horrible for me. I just wanted to come home and never go to school again. It was that bad.

"Finally, the last bell rang and I got on the bus and came home. I came upstairs to my room without even saying hi to Mom. I just wanted to think for a second, because it seemed like I was already losing my friends and I hadn't even tried to make a choice yet between them and the Divine Hand. So much had happened and I needed to try to sort it out."

I paused for a moment and took a deep breath, letting it out in a sigh. I looked at my dad and asked, "I know I'm not really giving any details, but I'm trying to make it short since dinner will be ready soon. Am I making sense?"

Dad looked at me from the edge of the bed where he sat, puzzled, and said, "Yeah, I think I understand what you're saying just fine. I'm sorry that your friends did that to you, and the whole school! My only question is about that, because it all sounds very terrible, but you seem to be doing okay. Are you okay?"

I shifted in my chair and replied, "Um, yeah, I am okay, because while I was thinking, trying to figure out what to do, I had another vision, and it really helped me. This time I watched a whole bunch of things happen in that other world, but I didn't do anything there. I saw a lot of things, but what's most important, and it's kind of weird, but I saw an older version of myself."

I glanced at my dad again to make sure he was following me, and I saw the gears turning, but he nodded to say he was with me, so I continued.

"I'm not saying that I'll be living in the world from my visions twelve years from now or anything – I don't know how that works. I think the whole thing isn't so much specifically about what I see, so much as it's about something the Divine Hand is trying to say to me, and that's just how he's trying to get his point across.

"Anyway, the older Michael said something that really stuck with me. He talked about thinking of ourselves the way the High King thinks about us, and how that's the way to fully become who we were made to be and find the freedom with him that we always wanted. I could see that the older Michael did believe what the High King said about him, and that this was the reason he was able to be the second highest advisor. It was the only reason the High King could trust him at all, because in the process of believing the High King's words, he also learned his heart. And when King Fidelas knew Michael had his heart, then he knew he could trust him."

Dad leaned back, eyes moving around the room in thought. I waited for him, nervous because of our morning conversation, but hoping that he would be happy about what I had just said.

Finally, he nodded his head slightly, as though he had come to some sort of conclusion about whatever he was thinking. He glanced over to me and asked, "So, this older version of you says these things and it sticks with you; then what?"

I swallowed hard, because I realized that now I was about to say pretty much the same thing that had made him unsure that morning: I wanted the Divine Hand to change me. Pulling together my courage, I fired off a quick, *Divine Hand, help me say this right!*

"Well, when I thought about the vision after it was done, that statement stuck out to me because when I heard it something changed in me. I sat in my room thinking about all of it, and I asked myself why it mattered if I believed what the High King says about me. He's just some guy that I've seen in my visions and, as real as they feel to me, I don't think they are real, which means he's not real – so why does what he says matter?

"Then I realized that it matters because the Divine Hand is the one who gave me the visions, which means he's really the one who's been talking to me in them. And I've seen him in our world, not just in the other one, so what he says is actually important.

"I knew that something had changed in me while I had this vision, something good. And I figured it out that the change came when I saw my older self, because then I believed what the Divine Hand has said about me through my dream and visions.

"He's said I'm a great leader, a seer, and a whole bunch of other things that make me feel so much more confident and important than I did before. But because of the war that I saw in my visions, I also realize that my gifts only do any good when I use them for other people, to help them understand who they are and what gifts they have, bringing them along the same journey I've been on.

"So, Dad, I know this is all really weird, and I don't know how things are going to be from here on out, but I really do want to let the Divine Hand do what he wants to do in me, and with me. I want to go back into my school and be the leader that I know I am now. I want to help my friends become noble, kingly people like the people I knew in my visions, and I want to see what would happen in our school if we do that.

"And," I concluded slowly, "I told the Divine Hand that I would." I looked at my dad to see if I could tell what he thought.

He was quiet for a few seconds, just looking at me with a little smile, and then he said, "All this definitely is strange, there's no question about that! But you sound like you're asking me for something, and I'm not exactly sure what."

I thought for a moment and answered, "You know, Dad, I wasn't nervous to talk with you about this until you got home and it was actually time to do it. Until then, I was just excited.

"I had such a bad day at school, I cannot tell you how bad it was because I don't even want to think about it. But, when I had that vision and saw myself strong and confident – I mean, in my vision I was talking to a whole bunch of warriors who had just agreed to be loyal to the High King again. He was talking to the same people who had walked out when King Fidelas gave him his sword, my sword! He was talking to people who hated and resented him, but he did it like he didn't even remember that ever happening. He talked to them like they were his friends.

"Seeing that just did something to me, so that I knew I could go back to school and talk to my friends, and to all the people who said horrible things to me. I knew that I could face the rumors, the rejection, the whatever came, and I could do the right thing and at the end of the day stand in front of them and help them be noble, too.

"That's what the older Michael did. He helped the people coming back from their rebellion become a part of the noble society the High King was working to create. And I know that I can do that, too."

I stopped to think some more, and my dad waited patiently. Speaking up again, I said, "I guess what I'm trying to say is that, even after the worst day ever, learning to remember and believe what the Divine Hand says about me made me ready to face the same people who treated me so badly today. Anything that can help me do that, I want as much of that in my life as I can possibly get!"

Dad looked at me and chuckled, "So, you're asking me for what? You didn't answer my question."

"I'm saying I want to change. I want the Divine Hand every day of my life, and as much of him as he'll give me. But this morning you didn't seem to like that very much. And while I'm okay facing my friends and having them disagree with me, I want to be able to come home and have everything be okay here."

Dad seemed surprised and looked sad. "I'm sorry, Michael, if the way I acted or the things I said this morning made you think that things wouldn't be okay at home. You're right that I was concerned about your experience last night when you told me about it, and you're right that I do what I can to protect my family if I believe they need it.

"However, I have been thinking a lot about what you said this morning, and about your visions in general, all day today. I've taken into consideration the timing of them and what I've seen them doing in you as you've been having them. And I've come to a conclusion:

"If I didn't have a problem with them even when you did, then I shouldn't feel threatened when you embrace them. If I had concerns about them the whole time then that would be a different thing, but from the very beginning they seemed to only be teaching you good things, things that your mom and I are trying to teach you ourselves.

"I don't know who the Divine Hand is, but he seems to be helping the things your mom and I are trying to do, not hindering or contradicting them. And though I'm definitely weirded out by the whole thing, and it stretches me quite a bit, I'm willing to be stretched if it's a good thing."

He never stopped looking at me the whole time he spoke, and, still holding that little smile, asked, "Does that help you feel better?"

"Yeah, it does help me feel a lot better," I replied, "But I still feel weird about the whole thing, too, like I'm not sure what to do now."

"I wouldn't worry too much about that," he said. "The Divine Hand and you seem to be doing a pretty good job of communicating with each other, so I don't think you'll have any problems."

"No, I don't mean that," I said. "I'm not worried about communication or how to go forward like that; I just talk and he talks back somehow. I mean, this is just a really big thing, you know? This morning I said that it felt as though I'd never been alive compared to how I feel now. That's a big change!"

"Yup," Dad said, "That'd be a pretty big change."

"Well, it's just, I don't know. It just feels like I'm still missing something. Where are the fireworks? Where's the soundtrack that says something important just happened? Where's the big parade, or celebration, or, I don't know – just something to acknowledge that a butterfly just came out of its cocoon or whatever. Like that big of a change shouldn't happen so easy or something."

"I think I know what you're saying, Michael," he said. "You feel like it's too big of a thing to go through and not do something to celebrate it or draw attention to it, something like we would do for anything else important that happens."

"Yeah, that's how I feel," I confirmed. "I mean, if it's the beginning of something so new and different, there ought to be something to kind of recognize the change. Someone needs to say, 'Go,' or the gun needs to go off to start the race, or whatever. I don't know, I just feel like something should happen to say, 'It's time to start; things are different now.'"

"I hear what you're saying, Michael, and I agree. Unfortunately, right now I hear the table being set, so I think it'll have to wait while we go eat dinner, but how about this – You and I will sit down together tonight and finish talking about this before you go to bed. You can tell me more about the visions you've been having and we can do a good job of recognizing and appreciating what the Divine Hand is telling you. It's not exactly a celebration, but would that help make it feel more official, do you think?" he asked.

Nodding my head, I answered, "Yeah, I think that sounds great, Dad. And maybe Mom can join us, too."

"I'm sure she'd love to," Dad said, standing up from the bed. "Let's go grab some dinner!"

"Yeah, I'm hungry!" I said, and raced him down the stairs.

We enjoyed a tasty dinner together as a family and talked about lots of different things. I found my mind wandering, though, as I looked around the table.

Nothing was different about tonight than any other night. Mom and Dad sat where they always do. Stevie, Amy, and I had all sat down wherever we wanted to sit, just like we always do. But as I looked at my family, I could not help but wonder who they were made to be.

Was Mom just made to be a mom? She was definitely good at it, at least I thought so, but was that all there was for her? I had always been pretty good at being a kid, too, I thought, and now I found out that I was a leader, made to help others find who they were made to be. Besides, one day all her kids would move out; then what would she do?

And Dad, was he just made to go to work every day and come home? Or was he just made to be a dad? And how did those two things fit together? What more is out there for him to become?

Stevie was one of the most interesting for me, because I had always just seen him as my tolerably pesky younger brother. We got along great, but I had never taken interest in who he was supposed to become – I just didn't like it when he tried to become me! Now I had something I could tell him that would help him become his own person, which would help both of us.

Amy was probably the hardest to think about this way because she was only half my age. I always sort of knew that the older we became, the more we would have in common, but at thirteen and seven, our interests did not often put us in the same place at the same time. I was not usually interested in talking about dolls and princesses, either, which was her entire world.

But now I wondered whether her interest in princesses said something about who she was made to be. If I wanted to be kingly, and she wanted to be a princess, then maybe those two things are related.

Eventually, we finished dinner and my parents served pie while the rest of us cleared off the table. It was nice to have the pie and ice cream that I had given up for lunch and think about what that might have meant to Nick. I wondered if I would ever know.

The rest of the evening was filled with normal family activities, which basically meant that each of us did what we wanted to do. I grabbed Steve and we went outside to throw around a football. Dad took care of some things and came out to join us, prompting Amy to come, too. Mom joined us as well and completed the party.

The football was a little big for Amy, so she mostly just chased down our bad throws and missed catches, but we all had fun out there together.

I really did feel like a different person, too. It was more natural to be nice to my siblings instead of seeing them as annoyances, especially as Amy tried playing a game that she really was not big enough for yet. Consequently, it seemed like we laughed more, and I could see the sparkle in Stevie's eyes as I was nice to him, giving him a chance to play with his big brother. It told him that he was important to me, and that meant a lot to him. And for the same reason it meant a lot to both of us for Dad to come play with us – we felt important to him.

It gets dark fairly early that time of year in our part of the country, though, and we headed inside. Soon it was time for bed and one by one, Amy, Steve, and I went off to our rooms. But before I went to sleep, Mom and

Dad joined me in my room, and we sat down together on my bed to talk about my dream and visions.

I told them in detail everything that I could remember, starting from the first moment of my dream that started it all – ducking under the deadly barbarian blade and being whisked off to safety by High King Fidelas – to the last flickering flames of my most recent vision.

They were astonished the whole way through, asking me questions and exclaiming their amazement at various points throughout the story, and as I finished, over two hours after I started, they sat there staring at me, smiling in their wonder at all that had happened.

My dad spoke up first, "Wow, Michael, you've been through a lot more than I think either of us realized over this past week. And can you believe it's not even been a week since this whole thing started? I mean, it's only Tuesday night and you had your dream last Thursday night!"

"I know, Dad. It's really been crazy. That's why I haven't known what to do with all of it and a lot of it was really hard for me," I said.

"I think you've been very brave to deal with all this as well as you have," said my mom, "And we're both proud of you for coming through it the way that you have."

"Yeah, we certainly are proud of you," Dad said. "I wish I'd known more of what was going on while it was happening, but I wonder if I'd have known what to do with it or whether I would have tried to somehow shut it all down. Though now I see that this has all helped you."

"It really has," I agreed. "I hated it on Saturday and just wanted to be normal, but now that I have a new life I realize that it'd be like dying if I had to be normal, because that would mean I couldn't be who I was made to be."

My parents chuckled and my dad said, "Well, Michael, that's some pretty extreme language, but I see what you're saying, and I think you're right. The life we're meant to have is one that we can only get by being who we were made to be, and we become that person by believing what the Divine Hand says about us. If we settle for any other life then it's almost like we're only partially alive, or not alive at all."

"I think this is all a lot like what you said to me while we were playing Risk," I said. "You told me that you wanted me to conquer the world, but not like we do in that game. You also said that in order to actually conquer the world, you had to change peoples' identities so that they were actually glad you conquered them.

"I think that's what the Divine Hand just did; he just conquered me, and I'm glad he did. I want to go teach other people what he taught me until everyone is like the noble kings in my visions. That's just the only thing that makes sense to me, and you know, it's not like a lot of major things change when you get conquered. You just have to start caring about other people and then do something about it.

"The biggest thing is you have to listen to the Divine Hand and let him help you so that you know how to help others. And I'm excited, because I know that as I listen to him he's going to teach me his nobility, and I'll become like the High King.

"You know, Dad, it's a lot like what you said you're trying to do at work, too, which must mean you're already doing a good job demonstrating the Divine Hand's nobility."

"Well, I don't know about how good of a job I'm doing," Dad said, "I maybe have to make some headway first, but my heart's there, at least. And you're right about the Risk thing, and about what I'm trying to do at work. This is exactly what I've been talking about to you.

"I thought of that earlier today when I was trying to figure out what I thought about all of this, and that's why I decided that these visions and the Divine Hand were a good thing."

"Maybe the Divine Hand can help you if you ask him," I suggested.

Mom smiled at Dad, who smiled back and then turned to me again.

"Michael," he said, "you are a leader, and I can see that a big change has happened in you already from all of this. When I talked to you on your birthday, I said your mom and I wanted to do a coming-of-age thing for you, and we gave you your sword. I told you two things about that.

"The first thing I told you was that I didn't know how to do a coming-of-age thing because I've never seen one. Well, I think the Divine Hand has helped me with that one.

"The second thing I told you was, 'Today you have become a man.' Now, I don't know if anything special really happened in the moment when I said that, but you know what Michael? I see the change, and you are a man."

He choked back some proud tears and struggled to finish what he said. Mom nodded in agreement, and they both reached out a hand and put them on my shoulders. My dad gave me a gentle shake and said, "You *are* a man," nodding his head as though to express how strongly he felt.

None of us really had anything else to say after that. My mom gave me a hug and said, "I love you, Michael. I'm proud of you." She stood up and walked to the door, waiting for my dad. My dad put his hand on the side of my face and pulled me close, giving me a kiss on the forehead and a strong hug, and he said, "I love you, son. I love you so much."

"I love you, too, Dad," I said, leaning hard into his hug and trying not to cry.

They left that night, a little different, I think. I certainly was a changed man.

A changed man. Hmm.

I was a changed man who felt ready for whatever might come the next day at school.

Chapter Thirteen
THE CONQUEST BEGINS

The morning came without any fireworks, no dreams or visions in the night, no special message waking me up in the morning. In fact, I was rather less than excited to hear my alarm going off because I had stayed up late talking to my parents.

Despite my groggy awakening, however, I was looking forward to my day. I did not know exactly what I was going to do, but I knew that today I had a chance to make a statement in my school that would get people's attention.

I knew that what I did today would set the tone for my relationships for a long time. It was a fresh start. A first impression, not just for me, but for the message I now carried – that everyone is way better than they think they are – and I had the secret to help them.

This was my new reality, my new life. I had seen myself in the future and I knew where I was going. I knew I had the ability to win over my enemies, to reconcile with those who had betrayed me, and to stand with confidence before those who mistreated me.

I was not sure exactly what I would say or how I would do it, but I was determined. And I was not alone.

Making my way to the bathroom, I turned the shower on, enjoying the peaceful sound of the falling water. I stepped into the tub and leaned my head back into the hot stream, letting it wash the nighttime weariness from me.

"Good morning, Divine Hand," I said. I could feel his presence. "I'm going to need your help today. I don't know what to say to everybody at school, but I need to say something that will keep me connected to them so that I can teach them how to be kings and queens. Will you help me?" I asked.

Yes, his voice said in my thoughts, *I will always be there to help you whenever you need it.*

"Thanks. I think today's going to be really fun," I said, and I felt his delight well up inside me.

I finished my shower and headed downstairs for breakfast. Mom and Dad were already there waiting for me, looking a little sleepy themselves.

"Morning, Michael," Dad said, "How's you sleep?"

"Like a rock, but it was a little short of a night," I replied.

"Us, too. Would you like more pie in your lunch today?" my mom asked.

I thought for a second and answered, "Yeah, I would, but do you think I could have two pieces?"

Dad laughed and asked, "What, are you planning to give another piece away today?"

"I think so, but I'm not sure who I'll give it to yet. But at least then I have the option and can still have some for myself, too," I said with a smile.

"Smart boy – man, I mean – smart man," Dad said.

"That's okay, Dad, I know what you mean," I said.

"I'll put some extra pie and ice cream in your lunch bag for you. If you end up not using it, you can obviously bring it home, too," Mom said.

"Thanks, Mom; we'll see what happens," I said as I grabbed some cereal. Dad picked out a bowl from the cupboard and sat down by me.

"I'm feeling good about today for both of us," he said.

"Yeah? I'm excited for my day. You're excited, too?" I asked.

"Well, I took your suggestion last night and your mom and I asked the Divine Hand to help me at work. Nothing happened right away, though we weren't really expecting that, but both of us had really similar dreams last night. They weren't anything like the dream you had, but it's unusual for us to both have dreams on the same night that are pretty much the same dream. Plus, those dreams for some reason just gave both of us a sense of hope and expectation.

"So we'll just see what happens. We can come back tonight and share stories with each other about how our days went."

"What are you guys talking about?" It was Steve, and he had walked up behind us while my dad was talking.

"Oh, good morning, Stevie! We both just have some special stuff going on today, so we said we'd come back tonight and talk about it together," Dad said.

"No, not that. You said something about a hand and some dreams?" Steve trailed off with a look of confusion on his face.

"Ah," Dad said, "Well, that's a little longer answer to really explain, but it all has to do with those strange things your brother's been experiencing lately."

Steve's face turned from confusion to concern, not knowing what to do with more news of weird things happening, especially with his parents.

Reading his face, Mom quickly said, "It's okay, honey. It's a long answer to your question, but we'll tell you all about it soon, maybe tonight even."

"Yeah," I added, "I was just telling Mom and Dad all about it last night, so maybe I can tell you tonight."

Steve still was not completely sold on the idea, but he went along with it, sort of. "Um, okay," he said, and went after some cereal for himself.

I was done with mine and it was time for me to go, so I cleaned up my stuff, put my lunch in my already full backpack, and hugged my parents.

"We'll see you, Michael. You'll do great today, and we love you. We're proud of you, son," my dad said.

"Love you, Michael. We'll see you when you get home," Mom said.

"Love you guys, too. You'll do great, too, Dad, and we'll see you later," I said, and saying goodbye to Steve, I walked out the door.

Other students were already lining up at the bus stop, and I took a deep breath before I started toward them, letting another, "Help me!" escape as I took my first step.

One of them saw me coming and quickly pointed me out to the rest. I felt the struggle rise up in me between my old habits and my new life, but I reminded myself that I was a new person and that the Divine Hand would help me say kingly things instead of my old defensive reactions.

"Here comes Nick's little helper!" the vocal boy called out. "Hey, are you Big Nick's little elf helper? Too bad Nick needs you to make presents for him! Ha ha!"

Wow, I thought, *who'd have ever thought someone would compare Nick to Santa?*

"Oh, shut up," I heard a voice say. "You're not funny." It was Brandon.

I walked up to him and softly said, "Hey, Brandon, how's it going?"

"You're almost as funny as everyone else here," he replied. "I can't believe you even came. If I were you, I'd stay home today."

"No way," I said, "Today's going to be a great day."

"Are you smoking something, or do you just like being the joke of the school and having everyone make fun of you?" he asked.

"Well, obviously I wouldn't choose those things if I had a choice, and no I'm not smoking anything. I just – I don't know, it's kind of hard to explain – but after school yesterday something happened that made me think about everything differently."

"Oh yeah? Must have been something pretty big to make you actually enjoy this stuff," he said, gesturing at the others who were still talking about me quietly to each other, occasionally glancing back at the two of us. I felt badly, because I was sure that Brandon was probably being woven into the stories, too, now that he had chosen to stick with me.

The bus pulled up and we all got on. Brandon and I sat next to each other, this time with me taking the aisle seat.

"It *was* something pretty big," I said.

"Well, what was it?" he asked.

I thought for a second, and answered, "You know, what it was isn't as important right now as how it changed my thinking. It showed me something about myself so that I know who I am, and while I obviously don't like people doing this kind of stuff to me, it doesn't shake me anymore. More than that, I know that I'm able to lead people into something better."

Brandon looked at me curiously, like a ray of light had just broken through the clouds gathering more thickly over his circumstances, but he wasn't sure whether to believe it.

"I don't know, Michael, but I think you might be crazy," he said.

"I'm not crazy. In fact, I've never been more sane in my life. You just watch today and see what happens. Everything's going to be different from now on."

"I'm sure it will be," he said with a shrug, and I could tell he meant that things would be different for the worse.

I understood where he was coming from. After all, just the day before I thought I had lost almost everything that had been important to me. I thought my life was going to be miserable, maybe not forever, but for long enough that I could not see a change coming any time soon.

All of that did change, though, when I saw myself in the vision and believed what the Divine Hand said about me. *How do I help Brandon see that he's going to make it? And what does the Divine Hand say about him?* I thought.

We sat together quietly for a few minutes, neither one with anything to say. The bus stopped to pick up some more students and a boy getting on slammed his backpack against me as he walked past us to his seat, drawing some laughter from his buddies.

"See, that's what I'm talking about," Brandon said.

"What? What's what you're talking about?" I asked.

"That! People who've never had a problem with you before doing things that hurt and make your life, just, not good anymore!" he replied.

"Ah, who cares if they do that kind of stuff?" I said.

"I do! I don't want people to do that to me. Ever!" he answered.

I sighed. Things were not going quite as well as I thought they would. "Brandon," I said softly, "I don't want that kind of stuff either. But you know what? It's not going to change who I am, no matter what they do."

"You're just being weird," he said.

"Yeah, maybe I am," I admitted. "But if being weird means being secure, confident, and unshaken even when everyone acts like they hate you, then I'd sure rather be weird than normal."

A quick thought flitted into my head and I felt like I had caught a glimpse of what Brandon was thinking. I took a gamble and jumped on it.

"I understand why you're saying those things, because that's where I was yesterday. You're only talking to me like this because it's easier to stay hidden away, expecting the worst, because then if the worst happens then you feel like it won't hurt as much.

"And I get that; I'm just saying there's a better way out there."

"Like what?" he asked sharply.

We were pulling into the school so I knew my answer had to be quick. "Brandon, I've been through a lot in the past week since my birthday. It's done a lot in me that's brought me to where I am today. Maybe I'll tell you the whole story sometime if you want to hear it, but for right now I'm just saying that something happens in us when we see to the other side of a bad situation and realize that we're going to be okay. It helps us not worry so much while we're going through a bad time, and, for me, gives me confidence to look for and be a solution to the problem however I can.

"You don't have to trust me, and you don't have to stick with me. I'd really like it if you did, but that's up to you, because I know it'd be a lot easier just to lay low for a while. But for me, I'm moving forward and doing what I can as best as I know how."

Brandon looked over at me and said, "Michael, I'm with you. I don't know what that means, but I told you yesterday that I still want to be your friend and I meant it. You're just being weird today, though, and I don't know what I think about it yet."

I smiled at him and said, "That's okay."

Any other thought I had was cut short by the bus door opening, so I just said to him as we made our way out of the bus and to the building, "Don't worry, everything's going to be fine."

"I hope you're right," he said.

I nodded to him and said, "We'll both find out. I'll see you later."

With that we parted ways and headed in different directions toward our lockers. I caught a few people pointing and staring, but mostly people just wanted to get to their lockers and go find their friends. I expected that once they were in groups was when any trouble might happen.

There was no sign of Nick yet, though his locker was in a different part of the building from mine. I never found out if he had been treated worse than normal because of what I did, so I had no idea whether he might skip school.

I was glad to get to my locker and unload my backpack. *Seriously, I thought, why didn't I take some time to think about my homework and not stuff my bag so full?* I laughed at myself and reloaded my bag with what I needed for the first couple hours of classes, then shut my locker and headed to the lunch room to find my friends.

We always gathered there at the start of the day before we had to go to class. Sometimes we would play card games. Sometimes we would just talk.

Today it looked like we were going to have an argument; at least, that is what was happening before I walked up.

"He's our friend!" I heard Liz say loudly enough that I understood it from fifty feet away over all the hallway noise.

"He *was* our friend," Matt retorted, "I'm telling you, friends don't do stuff like that."

"Do stuff like what?" Liz shot back.

"Like give stuff to your worst enemy!" Matt answered hotly.

"And why is what he did so bad?" Brandon asked, having walked up shortly before me.

Austin answered, "Look, we never asked Nick to mess with us, but he did. He's the one who chose to be the bad guy. You know that phrase, 'The enemy of your enemy is your friend?' Well, the friend of your enemy is your enemy. Michael is not our friend anymore!"

As though on cue, they noticed me coming and greeted me with a mixture of looks that said, "Oh great, here comes the plague," and, "Oh good, maybe you can set these morons straight!"

"Hi guys!" I said cheerily, catching them all off guard.

Matt and Austin immediately glared at me and looked the other way. Liz said, "Would you say something to these two to make them stop being so stupid?"

"Do they want to listen?" I replied.

No one answered; they just looked at me.

I looked back at them and smiled a little. "I never forced them to be my friends. I would love to stay friends with them if they want to, but I won't try to force them to stay." I felt like King Fidelas telling his faithful kings to not hinder Borgas and his kings from leaving. That is when I realized that what I had seen in my visions might actually help me in knowing how to deal with what was going on at school.

Focusing on Matt and Austin, I said, "You guys are my friends, and you've always been good friends. I care about you guys a lot; you're important to me. But what you think about me isn't going to change who I am or what I do.

"I know who I am, and part of that means I'm going to be nice to everyone, not just to my friends. I'm going to do everything I can to help as many people as I can become everything they were made to be. That includes you, especially if you're my friends, but it also includes Nick."

Several voices started yelling all at once. I quickly held up my hand to stop their reactions, and continued, "If you're not able to be okay with that and stay friends with me, then you don't have to. But if you choose to not be my friends anymore, just know that you are the one choosing to leave – I am not making you leave – and you can choose to come back anytime you want. The choice is up to you."

No one knew what to do. I had walked into the middle of a tornado, competing winds blasting each other from opposite directions. Yet here I stood, an unshakable rock, confident in the midst of the storm, and it confused them.

Austin was the first to come to. He shook his head and said, "Whatever, man, you've lost it. You're just blowing us off. I know plenty of people who'll be better friends than that."

He chewed on his cheek, shook his hair out of his face to look around at the others, and asked, "You guys gonna stick with him or are you gonna come with me? Realize that if you stick with him then you'll have the whole school against you; just ask Brandon."

Brandon didn't like being made the focal point of this conversation and glared at Austin. Liz was too angry to speak.

Dylan spoke up, "I don't want to have to pick sides, and I don't know why I have to lose either of you as a friend. Is what Michael did yesterday really that bad?"

"Look around you, Dylan!" Austin spat. "The whole school is watching us right now to see what we're going to do. If we stick with Michael then everyone is going to turn on us. It would be horrible to come to school here."

Brandon said, "So it's better to just leave Michael to face all of that by himself? Yeah, 'cause *that's* what it means to be a good friend!"

"Guys!" I interrupted, "Nothing that you decide right now is permanent, so there's no need to be so serious about it. It's not like if you choose to not be friends that you can't say you're sorry later if you want to come back. Let's just not argue over it and make things worse than they are. Do what you need to do to make up your own minds and I'll be at our usual table at lunch, ready to hang with anyone who's willing – or if none of you are then I'll grab my own table, but you can tell me then, okay?"

Clearly few in the group, if any, were willing to take directions from me at this point, and I knew the argument was going to go on, so I just grabbed my bag and headed to Mr. Gustafson's classroom.

The five minute warning bell rang as I walked through the door and soon other students came and sat at their desks. Mr. Gustafson sat at his desk in the front of the room, finishing up some quizzes he needed to grade for another class.

The last students lunged through the door as the bell finished ringing and Mr. Gustafson took attendance. He started class by reminding us that our project due date was coming soon and gave us an idea of where we should be in the research process by now.

"I want to talk to you a bit about those projects," he said. "I know I've said a lot about them already, but I really believe that this project will be one of the most important projects you ever do. I realize that's saying a lot, so let me tell you why I believe that.

"This project is called the Heroes in History project. Each of you picked a hero from history and is writing about what made them a hero. There are two reasons that I am having you do this. The first is to help you think like a hero.

"But more than that, I'm having you do it because we don't just study history in order to know what's already happened in the world. You know, there are a lot of people who say we study history so we can learn from others' mistakes and not repeat them. That's true, but if we stop at just avoiding mistakes from the past, that leaves all of us stumbling into a future hoping that we get it right, hoping that we do more than just survive, hoping we do something that actually makes history.

"History isn't made haphazardly; it isn't made on accident. History is made on purpose when people like you and me decide that we can do something worth remembering.

"That's why we study history. It's not so that we can see how people messed up or so that we can memorize a bunch of names, dates, and events. That might be part of it, but the real reason we study history is to be inspired by those who made history.

"We study heroes in history so that we have heroes whom we aspire to be like, heroes who once sat in classrooms just like this, who had families just like yours, who had friends the same as you have. We study heroes who were just normal people like you and me until they saw a problem and decided to do something about it.

"And when these normal people fought and overcame the problem in front of them, they weren't just normal people anymore. They were heroes who had made history.

"History doesn't just embrace people who do something great; people who do something great create history. Every one of you is able to do this, and I'll tell you how –

"Find something you would be willing to die for, and then live for it. If there is something so important to you that you would give your life *for* it, then give your life *to* it, and keep at it until you've won. If you do this, then you will make history."

Mr. Gustafson moved on in his lecture to his actual subject for the day, but his words kept running through my mind. They encouraged me a great deal and made me think of how I had said my new life was something I could not give up. If I went back to my old life it would be like dying, which I guess was like what Mr. Gustafson said.

If going back to my old life would be like dying, then I would give myself fully to my new life, and keep at it until I overcame anything that tried to make me embrace life without the Divine Hand again.

I also reflected on my brief conversation with my friends that morning, which had not gone as well as I had hoped. I was pretty sure that Liz and

Dylan would join me at the lunch table, but I really did not think Matt or Austin would.

At the beginning of the day, I had kind of imagined that I would come in and be able to say just a few words and everything would be okay again, but when I thought about King Fidelas then I realized it might be a process that took some time.

I was open to anything good that might happen, and certainly would like it better if my friends would just come to me like the kings did when King Fidelas first appeared in Cotheria – quick and without effort. But if they did not, if I had to fight a sort of war to convert them from thinking like barbarians, then I would do it, and I would believe that they would come back just like all those rebellious kings and warriors came back.

They would eventually see the kings and queens walking around the school and want to be one, too. I was confident of that, because I really did believe one thing – No one could resist true nobility; it just makes too much sense and feels too good.

The day progressed without incident. People still got quiet and whispered to each other when I walked past, and here and there I caught parts of new stories that were making their circulation around the school. But the blatant mockery and insults happened less often, or at least it felt that way.

None of it bothered me today nearly like it did yesterday, which was an unspeakable improvement. Obviously, I enjoyed not feeling hurt from what people were saying, but maybe even better than that was the reason it did not hurt so much.

When anyone said anything bad to me, it was a strange experience, because it was as though that person had not actually said those words. I looked right past the words to see their hearts, and I realized that there were only two reasons they said such terrible things.

The first is that no one ever told them that was not how you talked to people. In fact, that was the main kind of communication they had seen demonstrated. It was normal for them to be insulted, and consequently they were hurt. They somehow believed that making others hurt would make them feel better, or at least give them company with which to commiserate.

Either that or they were insecure. They did not know who they were and did not want anyone looking at their problems, so they gladly highlighted me so that everyone looked at me instead of them.

Those people actually became fun, because when I saw their heart, I would catch glimpses of their deepest dreams, things they were too afraid to tell anyone about because they could not afford to have them crushed. I would see these dreams and the Divine Hand would help me gently talk about them, encouraging these people and telling them they could do it, telling them it would make it through their hard time, telling them that they were awesome.

Some people got angry when I did that, and most who did just tried to deny their dreams. But most people lit up with excitement, saying, "How did you know about that? I've never told anyone! Do you really think I can do that? Do you really think that about me?" I would just say, "Yeah, of course you can; it's written all over you. That's totally what you were made for!"

Almost every time, those people then apologized for being so mean to me, and of course I forgave them. When I would do this, I noticed something starting to happen.

The people that I encouraged would completely forget about what I did for Nick and started spreading word about what I had done for them. A couple of times, classmates even came up to me before a class started and asked me if I could do the same thing for them that they heard I had done for someone else.

It must have just been something I could do because of the Divine Hand, but everyone who came up to me, either insulting me or asking for encouragement, I could see their heart and speak to their dreams, leaving most of them surprised, excited, and often crying good tears.

I do not want to make it sound like I did this for a whole bunch of people that day, because I did not. Really, it was only about half a dozen, but I was sure that the ripple effects would start working against the rumor mill. People would start to understand what I was trying to do.

Finally, it was time for lunch, and while I had seen a couple of my friends in the hallway or in classes, I had just kept my distance and they seemed fine with that. But now they had to decide whether to risk sitting with me and showing loyalty or whether to shun me and show they were part of the crowd.

I took my lunch bag to the table and was first there, as usual, since I did not have to go through the line. Looking around at the other chairs, I saw Dylan's bag, so I knew he was coming. Brandon would not be here because he ate in another lunch. And Liz had not dropped her bag at the table, but that was normal for her, so I would not know about her until she was through the line.

Nick had come, too. He did not have lunch again, but he was stealing some from one of his lackeys. He seemed to be avoiding looking in my direction.

My heart beat fast, hoping that my friends would come. When it came right down to it, I was okay if I had to live without my friends for a while until either they came back or I made new ones, but I did not want to. I did not want to have to rebuild.

As I opened my bag, I saw Austin come out of the line with his tray. He glared at me and made sure I was looking as he sat down at another table. The people around him at that table also looked over at me and sneered.

It hurt, badly. I had tried to get through to him and thought I had said the right things, but now he had made his choice and I did feel very betrayed. After being best friends for years and with everything I wanted to do to help him get through the difficult time his family was going through, he completely rejected me. I started to think, *Go ahead, Austin, sit over there. And all you people can have him! Some friend anyway, who ditches you over a piece of pie. Seriously.*

But then I caught myself and thought of all the people who had insulted me all morning, how I had seen each of their hearts and was able to look past the hurt and find something amazing hidden inside each one of them.

No, there has to be something amazing inside Austin's heart, too, I thought. *I just have to find it.* As I chose to let it go, I felt the Divine Hand's presence well up inside me, confirming to me that I was doing the right thing and helping to comfort me.

Just then Liz slammed down her tray, clearly still angry about everything that was happening.

"Hi," I said.

"Hi. I see Dylan still has a brain in his head. I wish I could say the same for Austin," she replied, nodding in Austin's direction just in case I had not noticed.

I took a bite of my sandwich and said, "A little upset, I see."

She erupted, "Of course I am! Aren't you?! Austin's sitting over there with all those smug idiots who think they're somehow better than us. He's talking all big about you betraying us and being a terrible friend and then he does this! How could I not be upset? How are *you* not upset?!"

Her wild gestures threw taco ingredients across the table. She took a bite as though she did not notice, attacking the tortilla like she was biting off Austin's head.

Dylan put his tray down across from me and brushed some beef and lettuce off his chair before sitting down.

"Hey, Dylan," I said.

"Hey, Michael. Hey, Liz," he answered. "Any sign of Matt or Austin?"

Liz grunted her disgust and ripped off another bite of taco. "No sign of Matt yet. Austin's over there," I said, pointing with my eyes so hopefully only Dylan would notice. Dylan twisted around to look anyway. Austin noticed and quickly turned to talk to the person on the other side of him.

Looking up, I noticed Matt finally coming out of the lunch line and I watched quietly to see where he would sit. He walked toward Austin and slowed down to look at him as he walked past, but he kept walking and joined us at our table.

"Well, you did come after all!" Liz exclaimed sarcastically. "I didn't think you would when I saw traitor Austin sit over there with his new friends."

"C'mon Liz, let it go," I said, "If Matt's sitting here then it means he wants to be friends, not enemies, so let's treat him like one.

"Hey Matt, thanks for sticking with us. It means a lot to me," I offered.

"Yeah," he replied halfheartedly. It looked like he was about to say more, but he held it back. I could see in his face that he was not sure he made the right choice.

We sat there in awkward silence for a while, everyone either too angry or too afraid to talk about what was on all of our minds and not interested in talking about anything else.

I crunched away on my carrots and remembered that I had an extra piece of pie in my bag. I knew what I wanted to do with it, but looking around the table I figured it would cost me all my friends to do it, maybe even Liz and Dylan. They might forgive me for being weird once, but if I did it twice then they might be gone.

My heart started racing again, feeling the tug of what I knew was right to do but being afraid to do it. I could feel my face getting flushed and I had to work harder to swallow my food. Lunch time would not last forever and then I would lose my chance for today.

For today. It was a slightly comforting thought. *Maybe I can just wait until tomorrow, or next week, or something. Sometime after things have settled down again.*

But, no. I knew that if I wanted to make a change in my school then there was no going back. I could not retreat to my old life to stay comfortable and visit my new one only when I felt like it. I had to do something today.

I just don't want my friends to get angry with me again, I argued with myself. *I don't want all these emotional ups and downs that I've had yesterday and today. And I don't want to lose my friends, especially after they've just shown they'll still be my friends!*

Maybe there's another way. Maybe I can somehow say something to them right now that would help them to understand.

I fought to remember anything good that might help me. Right away, I thought of lying on my bedroom floor after my vision, clutching my sword to my chest, and saying over myself everything that I had heard in my visions. Forcing these things into my mind, I repeated them to myself until I started feeling better.

I am a seer! I am a gifted leader! I am great in counsel! I am noble in character! I will lead people into who they were made to be! I will help people see the treasure inside of them!

Over and over again, I said those things to myself, and then finally, I had one last thought – *You know, I don't think I've asked the Divine Hand for help yet and seen him not do it.*

Trying not to look too conspicuous, I just said under my breath, "Divine Hand, wherever you are, please give me something to say right now. Thanks."

My heart was still thumping, but I looked at each of my friends sitting with me and said, "You know, I know that not much has been fun for any of you guys since lunch yesterday, and I'm sorry for anything bad that's happened to you because of what I did, but I should let you know something – I'm planning to do more weird things like what I did yesterday."

There was a palpable incredulity among them as Matt groaned, Liz rolled her eyes, and Dylan slumped forward. That was not what they wanted to hear.

"Are you crazy?" Liz asked. "Why would you do more stuff like what you did yesterday when you've already seen what it did?" Matt and Dylan looked at me, their faces telling me that they wanted to know the same thing.

There was no way to say it but to just say it. "It's hard to explain, and I can tell all of you the whole story sometime if you want to hear it, but I have had some really big things happening since my birthday that have completely changed a lot for me. It's changed the way I think. It's changed the way I look at people. And maybe most importantly, it's changed me.

"I feel like a whole different person. I am a whole different person! And so I'm just saying that you shouldn't be surprised if I don't act like I used to, because I'm not like that anymore.

"That's part of the reason I told you guys this morning that it was okay if you chose not to be friends with me anymore, because I'm not the same guy you became friends with." I trailed off, sad to hear what I was saying and hoping that they did not take it as me asking them to leave.

They all looked to be in various stages of shock or rage, having too many things to say to pick which one to say first. I took advantage of the silence and kept talking.

"Let me try to explain some, because it's not nearly so bad as you seem to think it is.

"Yes, I'm different. Is that a bad thing? No, and here's why. It's not a bad thing because the way I've changed means that I care more about other people now than I ever have. It means that I see something inside people and recognize it as who they were born to be, and I have this driving passion to help them see it for themselves and become that person.

"One of the worst things I can think of now is for someone to not become what they were made to be, because I've seen a glimpse of what that really means. I'm not okay with just living life anymore. I have to do more. I have to help people. I have to *do* something!"

I could feel something come over me when I started to talk about the change inside of me. It was like a fire that would consume me if I kept it in, and I could see that as I spoke, some of the fire got on my friends, as well.

It was not much, but there was just a little spark in their eyes, most of all in Dylan's, and it gave me the encouragement to keep going.

"That's why I had to give my pie to Nick yesterday. It might not have been the best idea of something I could do for him, but it was something, and it probably worked better than trying to start a conversation with him. And if one little thing I do can help him become somebody great, then that was the best thing that I could have ever done with that pie."

I felt like I was getting through to them and was trying to think of what to say next when Matt said, "I still don't understand why you couldn't have given the pie to one of your friends."

Earlier in the day he looked angry, but now he looked sad. I realized the pie was only an issue because he felt rejected when I gave it to someone else, especially to Nick.

Smiling at him compassionately, I said, "Matt, if the pie is that big of an issue then just have some. Here, I had my mom pack an extra slice today." I reached into my bag and pulled out one of the slices and ice creams and slid them over to him.

"And if the pie is that big of a deal to either of you guys," I said to Liz and Dylan, "then just come over to my place after school and we'll all eat some together. Really, there's plenty!

"But to answer your question, Matt, think about this. If I give my pie to my friends, then how does that make me different from anyone else in this school? Pretty much anyone here is willing to share with their friends. But if I want to make a difference, then I've got to be different! No one gives anything to Nick, at least not willingly. And that's why I had to give him my pie, because it was something different enough that people would notice it, and if they notice it, then maybe they'll change."

Liz asked, "What's wrong with the way people are?"

"Well, maybe nothing really," I answered, "Except that they could be way better if they just knew for real who they were. Look, all day today people have been coming up to me and insulting me, saying terrible things, but somehow I've been able to ignore what they were saying and see their hearts. And when I'd see their hearts, I'd see something special they hadn't told anyone about and then I'd tell them about it.

"Do you know what happened every time? They forgot about insulting me and started telling everybody about this awesome thing I did for them.

"And do you know why I could do that awesome thing for them? Because I know who I am and because something's changed in my life that helps me to see people differently.

"All I'm doing for these people is helping them to see the treasure hidden inside of them instead of the junk everybody else tells them about. And when they believe that the treasure is truer than the junk, then they'll become the treasure where otherwise they'd at best stay somewhere in between.

All of them were silent. They were starting to get my point.

"Take Nick for example. Does anyone ever remember anyone who ever liked him? I mean, most of us have gone to school with him for years now and I've never seen anyone treat him nice even once. Even at events where our parents come to school, have you seen his family? He's had more guys claiming to be his dad than I can keep track of, and none of them have exactly looked nice. Who knows what his home life is like?

"Now, I know that he's never treated anyone else nice, but there's gotta be a reason for that. I'm just saying that maybe if someone starts to be nice to him, then maybe he'll change. If you think about it, his whole life is at stake, because right now he's a bully reject who gets terrible grades, and if that's the way he is in middle school then it's probably not going to get any better in high school, college, or the rest of his life. Someone needs to help him, and I'm willing to take the chance.

"After that, it's up to him whether he wants to change or not, but who would argue that some change wouldn't be good for Nick?"

No one said anything, so I said, "Right, no one would. Nick could use some change. But, honestly, if you think about how badly so many people reacted to what I did, they aren't showing themselves to be much better and could maybe use some change, too, because everyone here is better than they're showing themselves to be.

"Austin is better than what he is doing right now. He's better than a traitor. In fact, he is a good friend; he's just lost sight of that right now.

"I know that if all of us start doing for each other and for everybody else what I've been doing today, just encouraging people and telling them how amazing some of the stuff inside them is, then people are going to notice and they're going to change, for the better.

"Yeah, it might not happen overnight, and us being different until then might mean people make fun of us at first. But when you think of what this would do to our school if it actually worked and how it would change peoples' lives forever – Man, I just have to try."

They had all stopped eating, forgetting their food in listening to me, but they were not quite with me completely.

Dylan asked, "What are you talking about, Michael? If what worked? What would change people's lives forever?"

I was thinking hard, trying to come up with an answer beyond what I had already said. *What made the difference for me?* I thought. It was believing what the Divine Hand said about me, that much I knew, but it came to me that there was more to it than that.

I had to hear what the Divine Hand thought about me first. The thought hit me like a ton of bricks, because I quickly realized that either I would have to change the whole school by myself, or I would have to help people to hear the Divine Hand for themselves. I could hear what he thought about other people and tell them, but if they were going to then do the same for other people, then they would need to hear him for themselves. And that meant I would need to tell people about him.

My internal clock was telling me that I didn't have much time left, so I made my move quickly.

"Look, I can't explain it all to you right now, but there's so much more to what I'm telling you. Will you come over to my place tonight and we'll finish talking about it?" I asked.

Each of them nodded and said they would.

Breathing a sigh of relief, I said, "Awesome. For now, let me tell you one thing I know.

"I know that each of us is a leader. All of us have the ability to make someone's life better and teach them to do the same, and if enough of us do that then everyone's life changes and everybody gets better. If you do this with me then you are helping to start something that really can change the world. At the very least it will change our school.

"You guys really are important, I can't tell you how much. And I'm so excited to do what I can to help you guys see the dreams of your hearts become reality."

I paused and looked at them. There was hope in their eyes and anticipation about what was going to come.

"Something really did happen to you, didn't it?" said Matt.

"Yeah," I said, "Something really did happen to me. I'll tell you all about it tonight. For now, I've got one more crazy thing to do before lunch is over."

I opened my bag, grabbed the pie, and stood up. A ripple went through the room and I heard, "Hey, look," whispered from all directions.

Most conversations kept going, but everyone gave at least passive attention as I again walked my pie to Nick. This time he looked at me as I approached his table. There was a hint of internal struggle on his face over just how he wanted to greet me. He decided on indifference and just stared at me as I walked up.

I set the pie on the table, opened the ice cream, and put the two together. Sticking a fork in the Gladware container, I slid it in front of him, standing there for a moment, waiting for him to respond.

He did nothing, so I chose to shoot for it all. "I can't do this every day," I said, "I just don't have that much pie. But I want you to know that you are worth someone doing something nice for you, and for everyone who's ever been a jerk to you, who's treated you in a way you really don't deserve – I'm sorry, please forgive us. Please forgive me."

All the indifference melted away and he fought to keep control. Tears welled up in his eyes and his lip quivered. Unable to hold it together, he collapsed on the table as great heaves shook his giant body. Great sobs convulsed out of him as tears poured out on the floor.

No passive observers now. Everyone was looking.

I stepped closer to him and put a hand on his shoulder, giving it a slight squeeze. He cried harder.

"It's okay," I said, trying to comfort him. "It's okay."

The bell rang, but no one moved.

He kept crying, unable to stop. I tried to think of some way to help him, or even just to get him somewhere that he would not have everyone watching him. The only thing I could come up with was what had already worked for me with others.

"It's okay," I told him again, this time leaning in close to speak softly in his ear, "you're more amazing than you think." I gave his shoulder a little harder squeeze and began to walk away.

He grabbed for my arm and looked at me with desperate eyes. I held his gaze and said, smiling, "Don't worry. Everything's different now. I'll be here to help you. As long as you'll let me, I'll help you become everything you dreamed you could be."

I cannot describe the look on his face. Somewhere hidden under the tears and the snot I saw the look of freedom. Nick had never thought this day would come, but now someone stood before him and told him the things he had always needed someone to say.

It was not hard. Well, I mean that when you think about it I did not even say all that much. But just that little bit started something in Nick's life from which he would never go back. He was changed. He *would* become who he was made to be.

As I walked back to my chair to get my bag and head for my next class, I looked across the lunchroom. All eyes were on either Nick or me, completely silent except for Nick's sobbing, and I smiled.

Today is the beginning of something new, I thought to myself. *Everyone has seen a life change today, and soon they'll want it to be theirs.*

I stepped up to my table and repacked my bag. My friends looked at me with bewilderment and awe. "What just happened?" Liz whispered.

"A life was changed," I replied. "I'm telling you, I'm a changed man, and what I have I will give to whoever will take it. It will change lives, and if you want, you can be a part of it, too."

Throwing my bag over my shoulder, I started making my way through the confused mix of students, some quietly heading to class not knowing what they had seen and some pausing as they rushed to get the best position in the lunch line not knowing what had happened.

I could not help but smile as I heard one student in line suggest, "Maybe somebody finally beat him up."

They have it mostly right, I said to myself, *because I did beat him up in a way – I conquered him. I just didn't conquer him like that.*

EPILOGUE

No one knew how to react after Nick broke down at lunch. Apparently it is easy to make fun of a person who does something nice for someone everyone hates. It is a whole lot different when the thing that someone did made that person become a new man.

What happened in lunch that day was only the beginning of Nick's transformation. The next day at lunch he came to our table and asked if he could sit with us. My friends were all nervous, as was I, but we said he could. He did not say anything. He just listened to our conversation.

The day after that he found me before school and started asking me questions. Why did I do it? Why did I pick him? What was that all about? I shared some of my story and told him that he could have a story like mine, too. He wanted that, so I invited him over to my house to talk about the Divine Hand.

Soon he was having encounters of his own, different from mine, but just what he needed. He and I kept meeting to talk about our experiences and what the Divine Hand was teaching us. He became a core part of our group and helped lead the way in showing people how to be kings and queens.

The rest of my friends came along, too, though it took some convincing. I am really glad that the Divine Hand gave me my sword as something concrete I could show people, because otherwise I am not sure they would have believed me.

Brandon was actually the most skeptical of them all. He thought I just made up the whole thing after I got my sword, but he stuck around with us anyway because he liked the part about becoming a man. After a few months of seeing the continued change in all of our lives, he decided to be all in.

It became normal for me to see one of them – especially Liz and Matt, who were the most outspoken – boldly telling people about the awesome things happening in their lives and lifting up the others around them. Even Dylan started to be less shy, though it looked different for him. Most of the time he was still quiet, but now he had the confidence to know when he had something worth saying and he would say it. He gave us new perspectives on just about everything, stuff we had never thought of before, and it helped all of us become better.

I tried to reach out to Austin, but he resented what was happening. He was bitter and jealous because he felt like Nick had taken his spot in our group, and he chose an, I'll-show-you-I-can-do-it-on-my-own attitude that isolated him from everything that could have done him good.

That lasted for a season, until he passed into another stage of grief, becoming sad and lonely. Though he still hung out with his new friends, he had pushed them away in his bitterness. They saw that we were doing good things and did not entertain his anger toward us, so it left him isolated. He stayed like that for several months until the loneliness was simply too much for him.

In that place he realized that he wanted his old friends more than his new ones, and started making small efforts to reach out to us. He started with Dylan because he felt the safest, and Dylan helped him a lot toward eventually talking to me.

EPILOGUE

I talked to him much like King Fidelas talked to the returning kings and warriors, basically saying, "You're always free to come or go, but as long as you're here, why don't you let us help you become kingly? It really is wonderful and you'd love it."

He said, "You know, that's the dumbest thing about all this. I saw what was happening with you guys and wanted it so badly, but wouldn't come ask for it because I was just too mad." I assured him that it was not too late and told him about the Divine Hand. He said he was all for it, and we forgave each other. He soon became a leader in our circle of friends again.

The aftershock of Nick's breakdown that day shook some things in our school. On Tuesday, I had been the joke of the whole school. On Wednesday, I became a sort of phenomenon.

No one could explain what had happened except me, but most were afraid to come close enough to ask. People looked at me as though I had some sort of super power and they were afraid that something might happen to them, too, if they talked to me.

A few were brave enough to ask me, "What did you do to Nick?" I gave them the only answer I had, "I was nice to him." Probably no one believed me that day, but over time the whole school got the story straight from Nick's mouth, and they started coming around us all the time.

Especially when someone was going through a hard time, they would linger around us or get one or the other of our group in conversation. They just wanted to hear something kind, something different than they heard anywhere else.

The biggest thing, I think, is that the nice things we said were never just fluff. Everyone had heard before that they were special, but no one had ever said exactly *how* they were special.

We looked into their hearts, found their secret dreams, and told them they were made for something great. We showed them that the passions of their hearts were the blueprints for their destinies. And without a single exception, everyone felt more significant after talking to us than they had before.

Change did come to my school. It happened one person at a time, but I watched my friends learn who they were and become true kings and a true queen who raised others up to be the same. I saw rank after rank after rank of lowly boys and girls become noble kings and queens.

The transformation was so radical that new students in our school always talked about how they had never seen or felt anything like it. It never took long for someone to tell them the secret, and usually within a week they were well on their way to becoming a king or queen themselves.

Mr. Gustafson joined in the change, too, as did many teachers, though he was the first. I had the pleasure of telling him about everything that had happened and he believed the whole thing right on the spot. The testimony of change was all he needed to be convinced.

"I've taught social studies for twenty years, Michael, trying to teach people how to make history and not just study it," he said, "and I've never seen anything happen like this. If you've found the secret to actually making it happen, then I'm all in."

The change did not just happen at my school. After talking to my parents, my dad was freshly encouraged to keep the fight going at his work. He kept after his boss and fellow department heads, pointing out the dreams in their hearts just like we were doing at school.

Things happened more slowly there. People had reputations on the line and were more invested in their philosophies. One by one they came to him wanting to know more, quietly, at first, so as to keep it from the others. When the boss accepted what Dad was doing, all of them willingly came onboard to present a united front to the heads of the company.

Right away, Dad was busy helping to write seminars to train all the management staff, even working with some of the other departments to hype the change. The transition to Dad's management philosophy was a huge success. While not everyone came along, people at all levels embraced the new idea, making the switch much easier.

Dad credited the whole thing to the Divine Hand. He said, "I didn't really change what I was doing at work all that much, certainly not enough to explain the different result I got from my efforts. It had to be just because I asked for help and then tried whatever I felt like he was telling me to do."

The company-wide transformation caught the attention of other similarly sized corporations, and soon word got out about what they had done. True to the noble heart they had embraced, they saw that greatness was calling my dad to something new. True to their business sense, they invested in him and partnered with him to start a new business, releasing him to go teach the same principles in other places. He became a consultant and coach to large companies while still essentially under his old company, implementing this new "management philosophy" everywhere he went. As a result, the more his company worked to help other companies, the greater they became.

As for me, my life has moved on. I am out of school now and have a family of my own. I still have lots of encounters with the Divine Hand. In fact, I try to not let a day go by without one, but they are almost never like those ones that started it all. They are usually much less dramatic now; maybe because I know how to listen for him better, I do not know. But he still shouts once in a while, so to speak, when he really has something to say to me.

Now all these years later, something Vemrilun said to me returns to memory:

"Ah, another chapter of our history is recorded. Soon the works of my generation will be done and it will be time for you to record the history that your generation has built upon our shoulders!"

And so it is. The works of my generation are far from done, or even those of the generation before me, but this chapter in history is finished and so I have recorded it. Let the generations to come build upon our shoulders!

Additional copies of this book and other resources are available at:

www.megaphonepublications.com

Helping to Make Your Voice Heard